Books should be returned on or before the
last date stamped below

Lizbie Brown, mother of a grown-up son and daughter, was brought up in Cornwall and now lives with her husband near Bath.

CAT'S CRADLE

An actress dies with shocking suddenness while preparing to tread the boards at the famous Theatre Royal in Bath. Her ex-lover insists that she was murdered. And perhaps he was right. Bitchy and manipulative, Flora Messel had enemies . . . Widow Elizabeth Blair runs a patchwork quilt shop, but has a second job as a partner in the detective agency run by her lively young colleague, Max Shepard. When the Shepard Agency is hired to investigate La Messel's death, events conspire to get them entangled in a cat's cradle of mutual disloyalties with undercurrents of malice and distrust . . .

LIZBIE BROWN

CAT'S CRADLE

Complete and Unabridged

ULVERSCROFT
Leicester

First published in Great Britain in 2001 by
Hodder and Stoughton, London

First Large Print Edition
published 2002
by arrangement with
Hodder and Stoughton
a division of Hodder Headline, London

British Library CIP Data

Brown, Lizbie
   Cat's cradle.—Large print ed.—
   Ulverscroft large print series: mystery
   1. Blair, Elizabeth (Fictitious character)—Fiction
   2. Private investigators—England—Bath—Fiction
   3. Detective and mystery stories
   4. Large type books
   I. Title
   823.9'14 [F]

   ISBN 0–7089–4733–6

mys LP
1429631

Published by
F. A. Thorpe (Publishing)
Anstey, Leicestershire

Set by Words & Graphics Ltd.
Anstey, Leicestershire
Printed and bound in Great Britain by
T. J. International Ltd., Padstow, Cornwall

This book is printed on acid-free paper

For Olive and Stella with love

1

'Hello, darling, I'm on the train.'

Elizabeth Blair groaned inwardly. Here we go, she thought. Damned mobiles.

'We've just left Paddington.' The caller sat opposite. A woman in her early forties. Extraordinarily elegant in a skinny dark grey top and magnificently tailored jacket. 'How am I? Half dead, darling. The hotel? It was OK, I suppose.'

Elizabeth felt in her bag for the book she wanted to finish.

'Listen, Foxy, can you do something for me?' The woman's voice was haughty and designed to penetrate. 'I've lost my credit cards. Where? Sweetie, if I knew that . . . '

Sweetie? Yuk.

'What? I can't call them myself, I don't have the number. Anyway, you're better at that kind of thing.'

She obviously thought herself the only person in the carriage. In the universe. Elizabeth gave her a hard glare. Thought about a hard kick. It would be easy to pretend it had happened by accident. There was barely room for four sets of legs under one small table.

1

'*Pardon*.' This new voice was light and worried and the girl it belonged to was very young and very pretty. French, Elizabeth thought. Couldn't be anything else. That olive skin and a certain something. 'Can you tell me — this is the train for Bath?'

'Certainly is. Going there myself,' Elizabeth smiled at the girl reassuringly across the table.

'Thank you. I didn't understand the announcement at the station.'

'That's OK,' Elizabeth said. 'No one else can either. It's the stop after Chippenham.'

'Excuse me?'

'Don't worry about it. I'll tell you when we get there.'

'Thank you.'

'Pleasure.'

For all of five minutes, quiet woods flashed by the windows; blue-grey skies and rolling downs; trees and flowers alive again after the winter and blowing in the wind.

Bleep, bleep, blee-eep. Her Haughtiness reached out, hit a button on her mobile, said, 'Hello?' She listened for a moment, then said abruptly, 'No. No, I can't.' A pause. 'What do you mean . . . I have to?' She was looking distinctly bored.

Elizabeth tried to focus on her book.

'No, I'm not being bolshy. I don't care to

2

be dictated to, that's all.' She spoke with more force. 'Listen — the world moves on. It's time you did too.'

The train rattled and picked up speed, shaking itself into a new rhythm. Piping hot coffee slopped out of a polystyrene cup. 'Sorry.' The woman in the aisle seat produced a paper napkin and mopped up. Then she lifted her book — a fat tome entitled *Through Many Doors. A Practical Study of Regression* — and proceeded to dab away at it for all she was worth.

Across the way, the mobile was in action again. 'Hi. It's me. I'm on the train. My day? Don't ask.'

Bloody hell! Elizabeth thought. I've had enough. 'Excuse me,' she said, 'but would you mind keeping your voice down? Only I'm trying to read.'

There was a short silence while a pair of powerfully blue eyes met her own. Something almost childlike about the gaze, something faintly exotic that you didn't come across every day. She was rather beautiful, in a chilly sort of way.

'Couldn't you move?' the woman suggested, with breathtaking arrogance.

'I happen to have reserved this seat. So give me one good reason why I should.'

No reply. She simply went on talking into

the phone. There was only one thing for it. If you can't beat them, join them. Elizabeth hauled her own phone out of her bag and dialled a number.

'Shepard Detective Agency,' a voice said.

'Max, it's me,' she said. 'I'm on the train.'

'Is that why you're shouting?'

'Shouting? Am I? Well, I guess it's catching.' An experimental glance across the way revealed that the other woman had put away her phone and was looking huffy. Where *have* I seen her before? Elizabeth wondered. That thick, chestnut hair? Natural? Hard to say. The undeniable presence. The strength about the mouth.

'I'm glad you called,' Max was saying.

'Oh?'

'Yeah. Caroline had to go home.'

'So who's minding the shop?'

'Ginger's down there. It's pretty quiet here and she'd done the essentials.'

'So why did Caroline go home?'

'She was sick.'

'But Caroline's never sick.'

'No, I mean sick-sick. She threw up.'

'She didn't?'

'Yeah. All over one of your best quilts. The one you unpacked last week. The one you were raving about. Can't remember its name. Something to do with cats — '

4

'The Cat's Cradle? You're kidding?'

'Yes, I'm kidding. She managed to get to the lavatory in time.'

He was winding her up. He was extremely good at it. Well, he'd had plenty of practice. In the five years — or was it six? — since she'd opened her patchwork quilt shop underneath his office in Pierrepont Mews, he'd caught her out on countless occasions. Playing his little games. One day she would get her own back; one fine day when she was good and ready . . .

Max said now, 'So where are you exactly?'

'Do you really want to know?'

'No. Not really. But it's what people say on trains. I thought you might want to indulge yourself.'

'OK, I'm somewhere between Reading and Didcot. Listen, I can't get back to the shop before closing time.'

'No problem. Stop worrying. Ginger will lock up for you.'

★　★　★

Elizabeth signalled to the little French girl as they drew into Bath Spa. The other two women were also preparing to alight. Odd, Elizabeth thought idly, that we should all be getting off at the same place.

5

'Need any help with that?' she asked, as the girl heaved an enormous rucksack from the luggage rack.

'I can manage. Thank you,' the girl said.

The train came to a halt. Doors banged open, people got off. Elizabeth made for the steps, noticed the girl ahead of her peering at a piece of paper with what looked like an address written on it, and knew she couldn't just walk on by.

'Can I help?' she asked.

'Do you know where I can find Le Jardin des Plantes?'

'The restaurant?'

'Yes.'

'Well, you go straight up Manvers Street, past the police station — that's on your right — '

'I'm sorry. More slowly, please.' She had good manners and a devastating smile.

Elizabeth started again. 'You go straight out of the station — Oh, hang it, I'll show you.' She had intended going straight home and putting her feet up — London didn't get any easier on the legs — but another half-hour wouldn't make much difference. 'Come along. Give me your smaller bag.'

'Oh, no — it's not necessary.'

'I think it is. You're struggling.' She grabbed the bag and led the way down the

6

stairs and out of the station. They crossed the road, dodging the rush-hour traffic. Clouds were blowing up over Dorchester Street, murky weather coming in behind. 'Is this your first time in Bath?' Elizabeth asked.

'No. I come as a student. With my school. You know?'

'So how long ago was that?'

She had to think hard for the numbers. 'One year. No — thirteen months.'

'So you're coming back to stay with a friend?'

'No. I come to work. I shall be a waitress at the restaurant.'

'At the Jardin des Plantes?'

'Yes. Is a good place?'

'Very good. I sometimes lunch there. Excellent food. French cuisine. You'll be at home.'

'No.' The girl looked puzzled.

'No. You won't be at home. What I mean is, you'll fit in there. You'll be happy.'

'I hope so.' There was some sort of discomfort in her expression. She looked worried and a little vulnerable. Elizabeth, remembering how scared her own daughter had been on her first trip overseas, tried to sound reassuring. 'I was new here once. I'm American. I came over from Virginia. The locals are quite friendly, you know. So where

7

will you be living while you're in Bath?'

'*Pardon?*' She said it in the French way. A slight alarm in her eyes?

'You have somewhere to stay? An apartment?'

'Oh — yes.' She didn't elaborate.

'Bath's a great place,' Elizabeth told her. 'You'll have a ball.'

'Excuse me?'

'You'll enjoy yourself.'

'I hope so.' Something ignited in the girl's face. A warm glow, a momentary flash of life, as if she were remembering past joys.

'Look — I run . . . I have a shop called Martha Washington. A shop that sells patchwork quilts and such. It's in Pierrepont Mews. A good French name, you see. I've been there — let's see now — six years, so I know my way around the place. Any time you're on your own or you want a chat, pop by and see me. I make good coffee. You can tell me how you're getting along.'

'Thank you.'

'I'm Elizabeth Blair, by the way. I don't know your name.'

'Mireille. Mireille Bucolin.'

'OK, then, Mireille. Come see me some time. Don't forget now.'

2

'If you ask me, she's pregnant,' Max said to Ginger two days later.

'Caroline?' Ginger's grey eyes regarded him from behind little granny frames. 'You think so?'

'Why else would she be throwing up?'

'Stomach bug? Something she ate?'

'She's pregnant. You mark my words.'

Who said men don't gossip? Ginger thought. A pungent smell of coffee filled the first-floor office in Pierrepont Mews. Sun shone on creaky pitch pine boards. It was a bare, longish room that contained two large desks, a very old filing cabinet and, in the corner, an upright piano that had refused to go down the stairs when the previous tenant moved out. The long window-sill was littered with Mars-bar wrappers and pot plants. Outside, a warm west wind surged through the alley, sending the shop awnings flapping and rattling at the rickety windows.

Jane Dickinson — known to all and sundry as Ginger — sat tweaking and tidying the rough edges of a report Max had given her to look over. Very rough, some of them.

9

Spelling? What did that matter? Paragraphs? Who cared as long as all the facts got stuffed in somewhere? Max was never satisfied with one thought at a time. Sign of an agile mind, he always told her.

Ginger sighed. Free association. That's what I'd call it.

It wasn't easy trying to make sense of the odd arrangements that passed for business practice at the Shepard Agency, but Ginger got a lot of fun out of trying. From the first day, she had liked the intimate, happy-families atmosphere of the office. Unhappy-families occasionally, when Max was feeling stroppy and Elizabeth on her high horse. War work, it could be called. But it was never boring.

Ginger reached absently for the mug on her desk and cursed as hot coffee slopped over the sage-green top that set off her startlingly red hair.

'You OK?' Max enquired. 'I'm starving. Got any biscuits?'

'You're always starving.' Ginger scrubbed at her top with a tissue from the box.

'You know what they say . . . '

'No. What do they say?'

'A hungry man is a loving man.' He smiled at her with lazy blue eyes.

'You made that up.'

'Did I?' Max leaned over to kiss the back of her neck.

'Not now,' she said. 'We're working ... remember?' She rarely got flustered, wasn't the type, but if he only knew how hard it was to force herself to reach for the fire extinguisher ... But one of them had to. It was what they'd agreed upon. Well, what she had suggested and he had more or less gone along with. In the first intensity of a relationship that was only a few months old, Ginger felt obliged to put up barriers.

It wasn't always convenient to be so hooked on him. Not when there was work to do. She checked a longing to reach up and touch his face. Pathetic, really.

Max said, 'So how's it going with the new flatmate?'

She wished he hadn't asked that question.

'What's her name? Something Irish.'

'Oonagh. Oonagh Connor.'

'Bloody hell! And she's a shrink?'

'A therapist,' Ginger corrected.

'So where did you find her?'

'She replied to the ad in the paper.' Ginger sat running a finger moodily along the edge of the desk. Then opened the top drawer and fetched out a packet of chocolate digestives.

'And what's she like?'

'OK.'

'Only OK?'

'She talks a lot.'

'You didn't find out that when you interviewed her?'

'I didn't interview her. She interviewed me.'

'So why choose her if you didn't like her?'

'I do like her. She's really nice.'

'But?'

'But I didn't realise how much I would enjoy being on my own. And I thought she'd calm down a bit once we got to know each other. You know . . . be a bit less hyper.'

'So I suppose she'll be there tonight?' Max asked gloomily.

'No. She's away at a conference.'

Max tried to imagine a hotel packed with therapists, all droning on about Freud and failed marriages and delving back into their childhood traumas. He had a thought. 'You don't ever talk to her about us?'

'Only in the general way of things.'

'Good. Therapy's a waste of time,' he said. 'They don't really give a toss.'

'Can't agree with you there.' She tossed the biscuits in his direction. 'Oonagh's very dedicated.'

'And she gets well paid for it.'

* * *

Downstairs in her dolls' house of a shop called Martha Washington, Elizabeth had read the mail and was settling herself down in the beautifully decrepit rocking-chair to sort a box of calico scraps. The place was peaceful for five minutes, the pink Strippy Sawtooth quilt and the cherry-coloured Cat's Cradle draped in bright folds across the bow window that cut her off from the world outside. The cedar quilt chest filled with antique toys gave a mood of permanence; the wing chair in rose damask in front of the open fireplace an added tranquillity. The fireplace hadn't been used for months, but it lent a folksy charm to the room and in winter it was good to see a fire, albeit an artificial job with mock logs and an everlasting flame. People seemed to like it and when they were happy, they spent more. It put them into a good buying frame of mind.

Checks and plaids; early nineteenth-century rainbow prints; honeycombs and triangles; a graceful peony flower appliquéd on to nut-brown calico. Elizabeth was in her element, dropping into desultory piles the fabrics from the camel-back trunk that her son, Jim Junior, had recently unearthed — along with a dozen or so quilts — in a homestead in Oak Ridge, Tennessee. 1840s dress fabrics, worn-out silks, Confederate

swatches, degenerate-looking crazy squares
. . . Packed away on the top floor in an attic
room for nigh on a hundred years, they now
looked as if they were wincing at being
exposed to the light.

Some would go into stock. But there was
no reason at all why the most luscious bits
shouldn't go home with her. Can't bear to let
the pink silk go, she thought. Or the peony
flower. You'll never be a millionaire. Too fond
of squirrelling away the prettiest bits for
yourself. Oh, who cares? A thing of beauty is
a joy for ever.

★ ★ ★

'Working hard, I see?' said Max's voice from
the doorway.

'Absolutely.' Elizabeth sat back in the
battered old chair and brazened it out. 'I'm
stock-taking,' she said.

Literally.

'You're just knackered after your trip to
London.' He picked up the afternoon edition
of the *Bath Chronicle*, which had just flopped
through the door, and said, 'So how did it
go?'

'OK. Except for the journey back.' She told
him about it. 'Damned mobiles,' she said.

'You use one.'

14

'Only when I have to. And not on a crowded train unless in dire emergency.'

The door opened again and Ginger popped her head in.

'You're supposed to be minding the office,' Max told her.

'It's my coffee break. I needed to stretch my legs.' The rest of Ginger came through the door. She wasn't conventionally pretty, but there was something about her; something upfront and lively. 'Anyway, I can see if anyone goes up the — ' She stopped as her attention was caught by the cherry-red quilt. 'Wow! That's new. Great colour!'

'The Cat's Cradle? Beautiful, isn't it?' She had got to the bottom of the chest, so she closed the lid. 'There's an interesting old tradition about cats.'

Max rolled his eyes.

'You needn't look like that.' She started over. 'There's an interesting tradition of throwing the cat on the finished quilt.'

'Folksy nonsense,' Max muttered.

'It's not nonsense. It's fact. Ginger will be interested.'

'Quite right.' Ginger propped her slender bottom on the quilt pile.

'In the old days — '

'The good old days,' Max said.

She ignored him. 'In the old days, after you

15

finished a quilt and you were ready to take it out of the frame, you'd bring the children in. Generally two boys and two girls. And they'd catch the cat and when they took the last thread out of the lacing, the kids would each get hold of each corner of the quilt and they'd throw the cat in there and when the cat jumped out, the one closest to where he jumped out would be the one to marry first.'

'Bollocks,' Max said. 'You made it up.'

'I did not! It was fun. I've shaken many a cat in my time.'

'Explains a lot.'

'How old is it?' Ginger asked.

'The Cat's Cradle? Late 1900s.'

'It looks new. How do you get it so clean?'

'Well, you know how they'd do it in the old days.' She ignored the face Max was pulling. 'Put them in a big tub of water with plenty of home-made soap and rub and scrub. After that, you laid them out on a bench and hit them with a paddling stick. Whacked them just as hard as you could and everywhere you hit it, there'll be a clean place.'

'Hard work,' Ginger said.

'Life was hard back then. But laziness kills more people than hard work, isn't that so, Max?' Elizabeth waited for him to rise to the bait and was disappointed when he didn't. She enjoyed pulling his leg, had been at it

16

ever since he had talked her into becoming a partner in his detective agency.

'Max?'

He wasn't listening. He was deep in the sports page.

'I could set fire to him,' Elizabeth said, 'and he wouldn't notice.'

'You reckon?' Ginger said.

'I'd try it, but there'd be — ' She stopped. Got up from the chair to peer at something on the front page. 'Good God!' she said.

'What is it?'

'The woman on the train. The one I wanted to murder.' She reached out and grabbed the paper from Max.'

'Hey — '

'Her name is Flora Messel,' she said. 'She's an actress. Did a lot of arty French films.'

'*Danse des Femmes*,' Ginger said.

'That's it. That's where I'd seen her face.'

'You OK?' Ginger asked. 'You look as if you've had a shock.'

'You're not kidding. Flora Messel died yesterday afternoon.' She held the paper steady as she read:

Ms Messel died after suffering a seizure triggered by a peanut allergy. Minutes after biting into a chicken sandwich at her hotel in Pulteney Gardens, while taking a break

17

from rehearsals at the Theatre Royal, she was rushed to the Royal United Hospital in Bath, where she was quickly diagnosed as suffering from a severe allergic reaction and given an adrenaline injection. But she never regained consciousness and died in the intensive care unit at two p.m.

3

The matter might have ended there, with the strange, unsettling feeling that comes when, by sheer coincidence, call it fate or what you will, you come almost close enough to shake hands with the Grim Reaper. But Elizabeth had reckoned without Max's tendency to gossip over a pint in the local with his mate, Andy.

'By the way,' he said, popping his head round the door the following morning, 'Andy wondered if you could drop into Manvers Street when you have a moment?'

'Manvers Street?' Elizabeth's eyebrows rose a little. 'Andy wants me to report to the police station?'

'I was just telling him that you sat next to Flora Messel on the train. And his boss wants to see you.'

'What the hell for?'

He shrugged. 'Search me.'

DC Andy Cooper had helped them out on a good many cases. Andy was Max's oldest friend here in Bath: the first friend he had made, over a jar in the rugby club, after moving down from Manchester — seven years ago now — to set up his own detective agency. Andy was a nice guy, but Elizabeth wasn't altogether delighted to be hauled summarily down to the police station to talk about a woman she had scarcely met.

* * *

'I understand you were sitting next to Flora Messel on the train?' Andy's boss, Superintendent Denis Gleeson, was a deliberate-looking man. Deep brown eyes, forty-something, the pensive type.

'That's right.'

He leaned back in his chair. 'So how did she seem that day?'

What a question. 'Hard to say.'

'Well, could you make a stab at it?'

'I can try.' Elizabeth thought for a moment. 'I'd say she was quite spoilt.'

'Spoilt?'

'She was sublimely indifferent to anyone else in that compartment. Continually on her mobile phone. I asked her to keep her voice down and she was quite rude to me.'

He made a note of it on the report sheet in front of him. 'But in herself, how did she seem?'

'She wasn't full of the joys of spring, if that's what you mean. Not a happy lady.'

'So she seemed stressed?'

'Aloof, I'd say. In some other world inside her head.'

'These phone calls that she made while on the train. Could you tell me about them?'

'She'd lost her credit cards. The first was to ask someone called Foxy to report the fact for her and to cancel them.'

'Foxy?'

'You got it.'

'Christian or surname?'

'You tell me. And then someone called her — none too friendly — and asked her to do lunch, but she refused. She got accused of being bolshy. And she responded in kind. Told whoever it was to get lost.'

'I see. Male or female?'

'No way of telling.'

He looked at her across the desk. Picked up a peppermint from the bowl on the desk and popped it into his mouth. 'So was that it?'

'As far as I can remember.'

He pushed the peppermints in Elizabeth's direction. 'Feel free.'

'Thanks.' Elizabeth helped herself.

Glesson brushed a hand over the patch on his crown where his hair should have been. After a moment, he said, 'Did she talk to anyone else on the train?'

'Not that I'm aware of.'

'Anyone with her? Travelling with her, I mean?'

'No. The little French girl next to her was — '

'French girl?' The absent-minded look left his face. 'Can you describe her?'

Elizabeth did so. 'Nice little thing. A bit jumpy.'

'But they weren't travelling together?'

'No.'

'You're sure of that?'

'Positive.'

'No conversation between them?'

'Not a word. Why?'

'I just wondered.'

It was more than just plain wondering, if his expression was anything to go by. She thought again. Shook her head. 'I'm positive they didn't know each other. If they had, she wouldn't have asked me the way to the restaurant.'

'Miss Messel?'

'The French girl. She'd got herself a job waitressing here in Bath.'

'At a restaurant?'

'That's it.'

'And the name of the restaurant?'

'Le Jardin des Plantes.'

'Could you spell that for me?'

She did so. Twice. A knowledge of French

22

was obviously not in the police manual. 'It means 'The Plant Garden,' she explained. 'And it's in Holland Terrace.'

'Thank you. That might be very useful.'

Elizabeth couldn't see why or how. She said, 'I'm sorry, but I can't see — Miss Messel ate a sandwich that killed her. Why do you need to chase up this child?'

He ignored the question. 'So there were no untoward incidents on the journey as far as you can recall?'

'Not unless you count the regression woman spilling her coffee.'

'The regression woman?'

'Do you want me to spell it?'

He seemed to sense that she was being facetious, but said solidly, 'No. Just explain.'

'There was a lady sitting next to me who was reading a fat book about regression. You know about regression? No? Well, I knew someone once who believed in it. Once a fortnight or so, he would be put to sleep under hypnosis or something and this guy would take him back into a former life. Or lives. He said it used to help him go down pathways and open doors.'

The superintendent seemed baffled. A plain man, he was not about to pitch himself into anything so obviously irrational as the drama of a previous life.

Elizabeth said, 'Apparently he was a Roman senator in the time of Julius Caesar.'

'Your friend?'

'Uh-huh. I suppose it's a bit like having a strong dream. The first time, he said it felt as if his feet weren't quite touching the ground. He was in the Roman Senate House and several people came past, but none of them looked at him. It was as if they couldn't see him. He felt so relaxed. He was that other person. Even his voice had changed. That was the oddest thing.'

'Your friend?' he asked. 'Bit of an eccentric, is he?'

'Not usually. No. And there are more things in heaven and earth, Horatio . . . '

The superintendent's brown, gloomy gaze regarded her intently. 'This woman. This regression freak — '

'I didn't say that. She was merely reading a book on the subject.'

'And she spilled her coffee? Over Miss Messel?'

'No. Over her book and the table.'

'Can you describe her to me?'

'Plump. Short red hair. That dark, mulberry colour so popular with young people these days. She wore a pink jacket and dark trousers. I'm sorry. That's about all I remember.'

He put down his pen. 'Well, if anything should come back to you . . . '

'I'll let you know.'

'You didn't notice anyone else watching her or following Miss Messel?'

'No.' Abruptly she said, 'Can I ask a question?'

'Fire away.'

'What's this all about? I mean, the woman ate a sandwich and died. That's tragic, but I can't see why the police are so interested.'

'Just general enquiries,' he said.

Oh, yes? Elizabeth thought. There's something going on here that is making my nose twitch.

He rose from his seat. The interview was over. 'Righty-ho, Mrs Blair. Thanks for coming down to talk to us. Thanks for your help.'

Help? What use had she been to him? And why, if it came to that, did he need help? Why were the police bothering to investigate what was obviously a peanut-allergy incident? Elizabeth escaped into the pale blue of the afternoon. In Virginia the cherry blossom would be breaking. Here it was daffodils in window-boxes; forget-me-nots and pink tulips behind the deck-chairs in the Parade Gardens. I'll call Andy, she thought, and find out what's going on.

4

'So why are you so het up about the French girl?' Max asked.

'Because if the police descend on her, I shall feel responsible.' Elizabeth fixed him with a sharp, green glint over her gold granny glasses.

'You and your bloody conscience.'

She gazed out of the open window at the tourists ambling in the mews below. Pigeons on the rooftops. Faint Handel emitting from the Music Box next door. 'It's just that I feel I dropped her into it. She's a young girl away from home. What if a damned great cop turns up to grill her?'

'Grill her?' Max said, 'We're talking about Andy's mob. Grilling is something they do to a burger at the summer barbecue.'

'Even so,' Elizabeth told him, 'I'm going to pop round and warn her.'

'When?'

'Now. This morning.'

'You were going to look at the case of the missing tractor.'

'Boy, that sounds exciting!'

'Riveting. You were going to give me the

benefit of your female intuition.'

'I can do that later.'

'If I say that, you give me a mouthful.'

'Yes, well, I really will do it later.' Elizabeth swivelled round in her chair. 'So where's Ginger this morning?'

'Ginger? Oh, she overslept. She'll be in later. I said it would be OK.'

'You did, did you?' She sat there studying him. He looked a touch crimson around the ears.

'She had a late night. I mean a heavy night. Happens to us all.'

'So Ginger can take time out and I can't? I remember a time when you'd have bawled her out for not being able to get up in the morning.'

'Yeah, well. Times change.'

'They certainly do.' She made a show of looking him up and down. 'You look as if you had a hard night, too. And I do believe you're wearing the same clothes as yesterday.' Which meant that the heavy night had been spent at Ginger's flat and in Ginger's bed. 'Washing-machine packed up again?'

'No.'

'Only you're usually so fussy about your attire.'

'Pack it in, Betsey,' he said, heading for the storage-room-cum-kitchen to make coffee.

27

'So when are you two going to move in together and regularise your domestic arrangements?' Elizabeth called after him.

'When are you going to bug off and mind your own business?'

★ ★ ★

Le Jardin des Plantes occupied the ground floor of a late-eighteenth-century building in Holland Terrace. One window held a mock bay tree and the other a stack of ancient herbals and a pastoral-looking jug of yellow flag irises. Today's lunch menu was propped against the jug. It looked pretty damned good.

Cocotte de porc a l'ananas
Morue au Cantal
Gaufres à l'ancienne
Emincés de poire sur canapés

Inside, the place was as charming and unostentatious as ever. Scattered tables, green gingham cloths, two huge stone fireplaces, a pleasant assortment of unmatched chairs. The proprietress, a young woman with dark curly hair, was standing behind the reception desk. 'I'm sorry,' she said. 'We're fully booked for lunch.'

'It's OK,' Elizabeth replied. 'I don't need a table. I just wondered if Mireille was on the premises. If I might have a very quick word with her?'

'Mireille?'

'Yes. Your new waitress.'

'I think you're in luck. She just clocked on.' The woman had a comfortable — and surprising — trace of the west country in her voice.

'You're not French?' Elizabeth said.

'No, that's my husband. Luc. He's the one who does the cooking.' She sounded relieved at the thought. 'All I do is boiled eggs. Hold on a sec. I'll give Mireille a shout. Who shall I say wants her?'

'I'm Mrs Blair. Elizabeth Blair. We met on a — '

But her companion had vanished through a swing door into the kitchen. Elizabeth stood waiting. It was a good place to hang around and sniff. There was an aromatic *mélange* of garlic and — what was it now? — basil? Coriander? Deep Provence, she thought dreamily. Sun-drenched lavender fields, deep blue skies, giant cypresses.

The swing doors opened again and the little French girl came through them. 'You wanted to — ' She stopped when she saw Elizabeth. 'Oh. It's you.'

29

'Yes. It's me.' Elizabeth picked up a menu from the pile on the desk and began to fan herself. 'Warm day, isn't it? So, how are you getting on in your new job?'

'It's good,' Mireille said. 'Madare Valéry — Jill — has been very kind.' This morning she looked workmanlike in black trousers and a bottle green T-shirt. Her light brown hair was fixed back with two tortoiseshell combs. Intelligent grey eyes, Elizabeth thought. Something deep hidden behind them? Or am I imagining things?

'I told you it would be OK.' Elizabeth waited a moment, then charged ahead. 'This isn't just a courtesy call. I came because . . . ' How best to explain it? 'Well, you may have seen that tragic story in the paper about the actress, Flora Messel. The lady you were sitting next to on the train.'

'She died. Yes. I saw this. It is very sad.' She sounded quite calm about it. Composed.

'Well, I got hauled in to tell the police about the journey and — '

'I know this. They came here too.'

'That's because I told them about you. I came here to apologise for that and to say that I'm sure there's nothing to worry about.'

'Oh, no. There's no problem.' Mireille's cheeks did have a rosy tinge, but she remained quite dignified.

Elizabeth said, 'They seemed . . . well, very interested in you. I couldn't figure out why. You didn't know Miss Messel? You weren't travelling with her?'

'Oh, no.'

'I thought not. I suppose they were just covering all possible witnesses.'

Mireille didn't seem to follow. There was something very remote, preoccupied about her. There might even have been a hint of anxiety. Bright sunlight flooded through the window into the restaurant. Elizabeth spoke quickly and lightly, diving into easy pleasantries so as to bring the conversation to a skilful end.

'I'm so glad that you're settling down nicely. There are so many youngsters milling around Bath. Tourists, language students, local kids all out for a good time. You won't be lonely. But if you're ever at a loose end, remember what I said. Drop by my little shop and have coffee.'

'It's . . . a bit difficult at the moment. I don't know which days are free.'

'Well, when it suits you.'

'Thank you.' She sounded brisk. Elizabeth wondered what had happened to that shy little thing from the train. The girl in front of her was exceptionally sure of herself, cool, self-contained. A sharp little bird, waiting for her caller to leave.

31

'So . . . have a good day. *A bientôt*. I'd better pop off and let you get on with your work.'

★ ★ ★

It was about an hour after this talk that Elizabeth dialled the Manvers Street number and asked to speak to Andy. There was a pause, then the usual question. 'Who shall I say wants him, madam?'

'An old broad from Virginia. He'll know me.'

'Elizabeth — ' He came on the line sounding cautious but jovial.

'Hi. I just love being hauled down to the police station for a chat. Why the hell didn't you call me if you wanted to talk?'

'Sorry. I just happened to drop it out that you were on the train.'

'You don't say. So what's this all about? Why drag in witnesses about a tragic accident when we didn't actually see anything?'

'I'm sorry. I can't tell you at the moment.'

'What can't you tell me?'

No answer. He was playing it safe. Other ears listening.

'OK. So call me back when you're off-duty. And don't leave it too long or I'll come down there and raise merry hell.'

'Don't do that.' He obviously believed her.

32

5

Upstairs in the office Max was sitting with his feet on the desk, sipping at a mug of instant coffee. 'Ginger's got a new flat mate. A shrink by the name of Tallulah.'

'Oonagh,' Ginger corrected him.

'Whatever.'

'I'll remember that.' Elizabeth told him. 'A shrink might come in useful.'

'You reckon?'

'Next time you're driving me up the wall. So what about this missing tractor? Bet you didn't get those in Manchester.'

Max said, 'This is no ordinary common or garden tractor, I'll have you know.'

'No?'

'No.'

'So enlighten me.'

'This is a customised, two-engined, push-me-pull-you vintage model worth a hell of a lot of money.'

'And?'

'And the owner — a chap by the name of Willie Youlegreave — took it up to London to sell it.'

'As you do. Bond Street or the Burlington Arcade?'

'You may scoff, but apparently there's a fortune to be made these days in vintage tractors.'

'We're in the wrong business,' Ginger said.

'Anyway, Youlegreave did a deal on the phone with a guy who was keen to buy. And he fixed to park the tractor at the back of a disused cement factory in Catford.'

'You are joking?'

'No. They promised to exchange the tractor for dosh, but the buyer didn't turn up. Youlegreave gave him a buzz on his mobile and the guy spun him some yarn about getting held up in a traffic accident, and as by this time it was ten o'clock at night, he asked if our Willie would leave the tractor parked in the street and they'd complete the deal in the morning. Reluctantly, he agreed. Parked the tractor and spent the night in some dump of a hotel — '

'And when he came back next morning, the tractor was gone?'

'How did you guess? Anyway, Youlegreave's doing his nut. Wants us to watch the Channel ports.'

'Oh, come on! This is a wind-up.'

'No. He says it'll sell for even more in

Europe. There are secret collectors who'll pay any price.'

Elizabeth sat there shaking her head. Ginger was trying not to laugh.

'So,' Max said, 'fancy a spot of tractor trailing?'

Do I hell? Elizabeth was profoundly unmoved by the idea. She said, 'We'll talk about it tomorrow. I'm a bit tied up with the shop at the moment. Caroline's still sick and my part-time girl gets in a panic because she doesn't know where anything is.'

It was a good story. She got out before he could start to pick at it.

*   *   *

She spent the evening diving into her e-mails and finding out what her grown-up kids were up to. Jim Junior's neighbour had been brought home legless drunk in a taxi. Kate's life in Manhattan was on fast forward at the moment (when wasn't it?). Ed had had a collision with a set of traffic lights and Beth, his twin, was knitting a four-foot-long Aran sweater.

That was about it in a nutshell. A few titbits. Bits of their lives. Scraps they would never have bothered to put into a letter. She patted the machine as she switched it off.

Keeps us in touch, she thought. Odd that it's so much easier than a letter. Instant. Spontaneous. Tomorrow I'll tap a few messages back.

★ ★ ★

But something happened in the morning that put all thought of e-mails out of her head.

At ten minutes to nine, Dottie came running in from next door. Elizabeth had been lingering over a strong coffee as she stood looking down over the field to the distant terraces of Bath. Ought to be going, she kept telling herself. Don't suppose Caroline will be there to open up. It's Thursday. She's sick, so my guess is she'll take the rest of the week off.

A school bus was climbing the first long, zigzagging bend from the church to the Manor. A dog barked wildly. The sky was blue, mist still trailed along the valley like smoke and a scent of herbs came drifting in through the half-open door.

A delicate morning.

Really, I could just stay here and stitch.

Won't bring the pennies in. Better get going, damn it.

'Yoo-hoo! Are you there, dear?' Dottie called out.

Serves you right for hanging about, Elizabeth told herself. She drank the rest of her coffee in one gulp and turned to grab her bag. If she met the old buzzard on the doorstep, it would save ten minutes.

'I know you're in a hurry, but I had to show you this.' Dottie was Elizabeth's next-door neighbour, a stout old party with thin white hair and a pre-war accent. A bit of a plague at times, but on occasion you had to do the decent thing and be sociable. 'You know you were on the train with that poor woman who swallowed the peanuts? The actress. What's-her-name.'

'Flora Messel?'

'That's the one.' Dottie was all of a twitter. 'Did I ever tell you? I was wild about the theatre in my younger days. Fay Compton. She was my favourite. Of course, things were very different back then. More gracious. Less sex-ridden.'

Elizabeth closed the back door behind her and turned the key in the lock. This could take all day and she hadn't got all day. She put a parting smile on her face and said, 'Can it wait until tonight? Only — '

From behind her back, Dottie suddenly whipped out a rumpled tabloid. The *Daily Mail*. It looked as if it had been savaged by a mad dog and put back haphazardly in the wrong order. How did she get it into that state when it had only been delivered half an hour since?

Dottie must have noticed the frown. 'I know you don't like the rag, but I've taken it for years and it's the best one for cleaning the small panes on the upstairs windows.'

Elizabeth smiled courteously and attempted to make sideways tracks towards her car that was parked out in the lane. 'I really do have to go,' she said.

'I know, dear. But I just thought you ought to know. That friend of your actress — What's-his-name — Lovejoy — '

'Lovett?'

'That's the one. He runs the hotel by the same name.' Dottie paused dramatically.

'What about him?' Elizabeth pressed.

'Well, dear, this friend of hers — this Lovejoy thinks she was murdered.'

6

Elizabeth was waiting for Andy at his house when he got in that evening. Lounging on the sofa with her feet up, engrossed in a *Clangers* video, watching spellbound as melancholy little pink knitted creatures dined on blue pudding string and whistled to each other across lunar rocks.

'Hi,' she said. 'This is brilliant. Much better than the garbage they put on nightly for adult viewing.'

Andy sighed. 'Elizabeth. Is this a social call or — '

'Definitely or.'

On screen, a tin machine made for aliens landed on the little creatures' smoke-blue world. 'Across the vast, endless stretches of lunar space,' a voice murmured, 'we can imagine stars, stranger stars by far than ever shone in our night sky, and stranger people, too.'

'You don't let go, do you?' Andy shed his jacket and dropped it on the table. In his shirt-sleeves, he looked shaggy-haired and scruffy, like an off-duty bricklayer.

'I guess I'm like a dog with a bone. Once I

get hold of it, I kind of like the taste.'

'Max said I wouldn't get rid of you that easily.'

'Max was right.'

'So how did you know what time I'd be home?'

'I didn't. I just dropped by on the off-chance and Lyn said I was to wait.'

'Did she now?' He looked not very fondly in the direction of the stairs.

'That's two gorgeous kids you have there.'

'Yeah. Where are they?'

'Can't you hear? It's bathtime.' From the shrieking and splashing around coming from upstairs, there would soon be water coming through the ceiling. 'How old's the baby now?'

'Rosa? Six months.'

'Great age.'

'Hard work,' Andy said. 'Especially on the days Rollo takes against her. Sometimes it's a hell-house.'

'You don't say.' She cast her eyes around the room, noting the scattered books, the felt-tip scribbling on the cupboard doors, the tent stuffed with toys that took up the whole window bay. 'Just enjoy it, while they're here. Before you know it, they'll be grown-up and gone.'

'Can't wait.'

'Liar,' she said. Then, 'Tell me something. Flora Messel — are the police worried in some way about her death? I don't want to put you on a spot and I know you're not supposed to blab state secrets, but it's really bugging me.'

Andy said, 'I suppose you'll keep on at me until I tell you?'

'No. But I'd be grateful if you'd just humour an old woman with a long nose that's kind of twitching.'

'I'll give you the bare facts as we know them. Flora Messel was friendly with one James Lovett.'

'The guy who runs the hotel?'

'Right. He's an old friend of hers from drama school.'

'Who, according to yesterday's *Mail*, says she was murdered.'

'Yes, well. You know the press. They made a beeline for the hotel and he made a few unguarded remarks that got blown up out of all proportion.'

'So there are no grounds for suspicion of murder?'

'Not that I know of,' Andy said. 'He was in an emotional state and he came to us with his suspicions and we had to check, that's all. Miss Messel was staying at Lovett's Hotel. She was due to start rehearsals for the play

41

she was in the following morning. She went to rehearsal, seemed in fine form — a bit abstracted, perhaps. Anyway, instead of joining the others for lunch in the café in the theatre vaults, she did her usual thing. She went back to the hotel and had them make up a sandwich for her. She had this peanut allergy, so she was always very careful about buying stuff from cafés in town.'

'I can imagine that.'

'And she's a creature of habit. Chef said if she had a sandwich, it was always chicken or prawn mayo. No butter, nothing added, no dressings of any sort because of the peanut allergy. So Chef made the sandwich just as she wanted it — we have witnesses who watched him do it — but it seems that the one she ate wasn't the one that was delivered to the summerhouse.'

'Summerhouse?'

'There's one in the hotel garden. If she's in a play here, it's her favourite place for learning her lines.'

'I see. So her friend Lovett thinks someone doctored the sandwich between the kitchen and the summerhouse?'

'That's about it. The man was hysterical. Apparently he's always had a crush on her. Flora Messel. She would always have a laugh and a joke with him when she stayed at the hotel. As she nearly always did when she was working here. She has a house ten miles from Bath.'

'A house? So why didn't she go there?'

A shrug. 'Lovett says she liked to be close to the theatre when she was working.'

'So would you pay for a hotel room when all the comforts of home are a short drive away?'

'She didn't pay for the room. Lovett said she was a guest of the family. He never charged her.' Andy helped himself to a chocolate bean from a scattered pile on the coffee table.

'Stealing your kids' sweets. Can't get lower than that,' Elizabeth said. 'So who took the sandwich out to the summerhouse?'

'One of the waitresses. She's pretty shaken up. She swears the tray never left her hands on the way out.'

'So you have no idea how the peanuts got in the sandwich?'

'None at all.' He popped another Smartie in his mouth. 'There was one odd thing. One of the waiters clearing the tables on the garden terrace — we're not sure, but we think it was after the waitress delivered the sandwich — thought he heard Miss Messel talking to somebody in the summerhouse.'

'Heard?'

'Yeah. You can't see in there from the garden. It's a bit like a bandstand with trelliswork all round it. But the waiter thought he heard Flora Messel's voice — it's quite distinctive.'

Throaty and actressy, Elizabeth thought. 'She may have been practising her lines out loud.'

'True. Anyway, he thought she sounded angry.'

That wouldn't be hard to imagine. Elizabeth sat there thinking. 'Did you go through her house?'

'Yup. Fantastic old manor house. Didn't feel very lived in. Piles of unopened bills and business mail.'

'Anything that helped?'

He shook his head. There was a lot of bumping on the stairs, then Andy's family burst into the room. His wife, Lyn, shooing their two-year-old, Rollo, in front of her and carrying the baby — apple-cheeked and bandy-legged, on her hip. Lyn sat the baby on the floor against a nest of cushions and she beamed at Elizabeth.

'Hello,' Elizabeth said. 'Aren't you gorgeous?'

The baby gave her a single, clear-blue stare, then blew a raspberry.

'That's my girl,' Andy said.

'Like father, like daughter,' said Lyn, and told him to pull his finger out and put the kettle on.

★ ★ ★

By mid-evening Elizabeth was on her way home with a pile of information about Flora Messel under her belt. Lyn had seen to that. Lyn read *Hello!* while feeding Rosa and, boy, did she know her celebrities! I have never, thought Elizabeth, easing her Citroën through narrow Somerset lanes, heard such a breathless catalogue of biographical detail in one short half-hour. And she said she never had time to read.

Hello! doesn't count as reading. It's a comic for grown-ups.

Lyn had taken them on a quick spin through the unfortunate Flora Messel's life. Born the younger daughter of a doctor, she had started out as a dancer but, growing too tall, had turned herself instead into a brilliant, instinctive actress. 'She was a real wild child when younger,' Lyn had said enthusiastically. 'Done for carrying marijuana through Customs. For shop lifting. For drunk driving. But some Indian guru got her back on the straight and narrow. Except for sex.'

And off she had gone again into a

45

breathless account of the actress's sex life. She pulled men like nobody's business. Had gone through two husbands, the first a French actor, Paul Fournier, the second the English stage director, Martin Trevelyan. Both marriages had ended in acrimonious divorce. No children. All this alongside flirtations galore with whoever she happened to be filming with at the moment. And until Christmas she had been seen at all the best parties with Sean Donahue.

'The pop star?' Elizabeth had asked.

'The musician and lyricist,' Lyn had insisted.

'The one who trashes hotel rooms and broke somebody's nose in a fight?'

'That's him.'

'She has — had — homes in Chelsea and Rome and Wiltshire,' Lyn had recited, her eyes wide with envy. Pause for breath. Then she was off again delivering her lines in the voice of a showbiz PR girl soaring into her big speech. 'Her screen persona combined brooding sexuality with a child-like spontaneity. She played the lead in a string of art-house French movies throughout the eighties. But her first love was always the stage. What else can I tell you about her? She had a reputation for being difficult with journalists. She was a tiger when it came to guarding privacy. She often sat through interviews in a silent sulk.'

'You said she had a sister,' Elizabeth said.

'An older half-sister, but they haven't spoken since their father died. There was bitter animosity because the old man — he was in his eighties when he died — left Flora the house in his will. The half-sister threatened to fight it, because the house — '

'The one near Bath?'

'That's it. The house originally came from her mother's family.'

'So presumably it will go back to her now that the actress is dead?'

'I should think so, wouldn't you?'

Elizabeth changed down a gear, eased the car into the narrow lane that led to her cottage, her hands relaxing on the steering-wheel. It was an evening of utter serenity, the rich green of the fields touched by the calmest, almost uncanny gold light. So beautiful, she thought. It's a shame to go in. 'Maybe I'll sit in the garden for a while,' she said. What's that phrase Max was always using? Chill out. She parked the car outside the cottage, climbed out and locked the doors. It was as she was hunting for her house keys that she remembered something she had meant to ask Andy. May as well do it now, she thought, or it'll fall straight into a black hole.

She found her mobile and dialled his number.

'Hello?' It sounded as if there was a war going on in the background.

'Hi. It's me again. There was one other thing I meant to ask you.'

'Fire away.' His voice was resigned.

'Your Superintendent Gleeson. He jumped a mile when I mentioned the little French girl. Mireille.'

'Gleeson jump? He's not capable of it.'

'You know what I mean. He reacted.'

'You don't miss much, do you?'

'Not a lot. So what is it with little Mireille?'

Andy took a swig of something. 'A French girl called at Lovett's asking for Miss Messel just before noon on the day she died.'

'So what did she want?'

'Said she'd accidentally picked up something that belonged to Miss Messel on the train. A book. She wanted to return it.'

So she must have recognised Flora Messel, Elizabeth thought. There had been no sign of it all that time she was sitting next to her. 'How did she know where to find her?'

'She says she went to the theatre and asked.'

'So why didn't she just leave the book at the box office?' Elizabeth asked.

7

'Let's have lunch there,' Elizabeth said.

'At Lovett's?'

'Why not? It's open to non-residents. I checked. My treat.'

Max had almost told her she was out of her head, obsessed with the Messel woman, but he knew a good offer when he saw one. And if he'd refused, she'd only have taken herself off there alone, and where was the sense in that, when he had to eat anyway? No sense in missing a slap-up meal. He was assuming that Lovett's would be that kind of a place. From the sound of her, he couldn't imagine Flora Messel pigging it. Or eating an indigestible lunch.

Unfortunate thought, that, under the circumstances . . .

Lovett's Hotel took up the middle two of a row of trim Georgian houses just off Laura Place. It had been a bright day, but change was in the air, and by the time they got to Laura Street, the blue morning had dissolved into a fine grey gauze and people were hurrying for shelter as a light drizzle began to fall.

In the entrance hall, the receptionist gave them a vague smile, smoothing a hand over thin, fairish hair. 'A table?' he said. 'You might just be lucky. We're very busy this morning.' He flicked a wrist up to glance at his watch. 'At least, I suppose it's afternoon by now. Just the two of you? Yes, I think we might just fit you in somewhere.'

Business was obviously booming. One unfortunate death triggered by a peanut allergy hadn't killed commerce. The receptionist tucked two maroon menus under his arm and led them through an arched doorway into the crowded dining room. An eager sort of a bloke, Max thought, but harassed. All of a quiet fluster.

He stopped at a table in the far corner. 'Can I get you a drink?' he asked.

Max said, 'Gin and tonic, lots of ice. And a Campari and soda.'

'And no peanuts,' Elizabeth said, under her breath.

But not sufficiently *sotto voce*. The receptionist flicked her a look. It said, if there's one thing I can't stand it's bloody bad-taste jokes. He dropped the menus on the table.

'Sorry,' Elizabeth said. 'I shouldn't have said that. Can't think what came over me.'

I can, Max thought. You're fishing.

Throwing out a line and hoping he'll start gabbing.

Which he did. 'If you'd known her, you wouldn't joke about it.'

'You're quite right,' Elizabeth said. 'So you knew Miss Messel?'

'We were very old friends. We were at drama school together.'

'Then you must be James Lovett. You own this establishment?'

'That's right.' He looked at her in surprise. 'How did you know that?'

'I read the papers. Also . . . ' She appeared to hesitate for a moment, then said, 'Actually I'm a private detective.'

'Detectives?'

'It's OK. This isn't a working trip. We just dropped by for lunch. What I meant was that in this job you sort of read things and store them up. You never switch off. Sometimes it's a damned nuisance.' She flung him such a cheery smile that Lovett seemed charmed in spite of himself. Ridiculous, Max thought, how she gets away with it. Bloody Americans. More brass than a monkey.

'I'll get your drinks,' Lovett said, taking himself off.

'So what was that all about?' Max asked. As if he didn't know.

'Nothing.'

'Oh, yes?'

'I think I'll have the soup. And then perhaps something fishy.'

'Elizabeth, after we've had lunch, you're going to forget all about Flora bloody Messel. Understand? There's work piling up in the office.'

'The disappearing tractor. Yes, I know. I had a look at it last night over a beer in the garden. Seems to me we should be looking at the Channel ports.'

★ ★ ★

'That was wonderful,' sighed Elizabeth, as she laid down her knife and fork. 'Haven't had John Dory in ages. Pity the service is so slow.'

'What service?' Max asked.

'They're short-staffed.'

'You're not kidding,' Max said. There was a flap on over by the door, one waitress whispering frantically to the other. Shoving plates at her. Lovett had his eye on them and raised an eyebrow. The skinny waitress scurried back to the kitchen; the solid girl flushed and delivered the plates to the table by the window.

'Well, it's hardly a normal day,' said Elizabeth, picking up the wine bottle. 'They'll be all of a tizzy.'

Max held out his glass. 'They'll still charge the earth.'

'So what's it to you? I'm paying. God, you're a fidget. Relax, for God's sake. What do you think of the décor?'

'It's OK.' He hadn't really noticed, to tell the truth. But even now that he was concentrating, all that registered was the standard Bath hotel. A couple of glinting chandeliers, a row of long Georgian windows, swagged in pale green silk. Subtle quality. That was about all you could say.

'I expected something more dramatic,' Elizabeth said.

'Any particular reason?'

'Not sure. Because he went to drama school, I suppose. Lovett.'

'It's probably all down to his wife. Women buy curtains and such.'

'You think he's married?'

'Bound to be. He looks stressed out.'

She could see what he meant. Lovett was now pacing up and down between tables. Hands behind his back, something slightly camp about him. Pausing now and again to speak to the odd customer, but at the same time preoccupied with his own thoughts.

'I imagine he's in shock. Losing an old friend like that and in his own hotel. He'd feel responsible. That's why he wants to put the blame on someone else.'

'You reckon? Where's that bloody waitress? I want a dessert.'

'I'll stick to the cheese.' Elizabeth wasn't exactly on a diet. She didn't believe in them. But there were times when she had to draw the line because she could feel the bulges bursting out.

'Raspberry coffee meringue,' Max said. He had decided earlier.

'You won't be able to move.' So what's new? she wondered, not unkindly. Max sat with his feet on the desk and his sleeves rolled up most afternoons. Not quite taking a nap, but as near as damn-it.

In the far corner of the restaurant, an old cove sitting by himself was already dozing over a folded copy of *The Times*. Head slumped on chest; long, octogenarian legs stretched out underneath the table.

'He's coming over,' Max said. 'About bloody time.'

All of a dither with apologies, James Lovett stood beside their table. Deftly he cleared their plates, nodded to the girl to take them away. 'I must apologise for the delay. We're a member of staff missing and it's thrown us all out. Would you care for a dessert? Maisie will bring you a menu.' His hands brushed a crumb from the cloth, then rearranged themselves. There was something else, a desperation in his manner that suddenly erupted into a flurry of words. 'You said you were a private detective. I hope you don't mind — ' A glance over to the door and back again. 'I wasn't sure if — well, I was wondering, are you in a position to take on more work?'

'You want to hire us?' Elizabeth asked.

'If that's possible.'

'What's the problem?'

'It's impossible to talk here. I have an office upstairs. First floor, first door on the right. Could you join me there when you've finished your lunch?'

'Surely.'

'I'd be most grateful.'

★   ★   ★

The office was not as Elizabeth had imagined it. She had expected, well, more of the elegant-but-dead décor exhibited in the dining room. But here it was different. The room wasn't large, but it was stuffed with a jumble of nice old furniture, which had the appearance of being dumped there after a sale. There was a heavy Victorian desk, a mahogany bookcase, a couple of green velvet armchairs, a Chinese lacquered screen, bits of china, piles of books; even a card table in the corner.

Elizabeth thought, It feels like a stage set.

'Do sit down,' Lovett said. He smiled nervously. Moved a pile of books from one end of the desk to the other. There was perspiration on his forehead. He had once been a handsome man. The blue eyes were still quite striking, but the rest of his face had sagged, become flabby, almost feminine in its softness.

'So, what can we do for you?' Elizabeth asked, dropping into one of the armchairs.

'I'd like to know what kind of work you undertake.'

'Anything and everything,' Elizabeth told him. 'Well, within reason.'

'And you have a good reputation?'

'We're a well-established agency. Our office is in Pierrepont Mews. I think you'll find our work is of the highest calibre.'

'And your terms? What do you charge?'

From an inner pocket, Max produced a Shepard Agency brochure. He handed it to Lovett, who gave it a perfunctory once-over and seemed satisfied. 'Very well,' he said, with a nod. 'I imagine there will be forms and such to sign, but I'd very much like you to investigate Flora's death.'

Elizabeth looked across the desk at him. 'I

56

read in the *Mail* that you think she was murdered.'

He answered hesitatingly: 'It's a possibility. Yes.'

'But you're not sure?'

'I can't *prove* it. I regret talking about it now to that damned reporter, but he caught me at a desperate moment. People just seemed to accept that we were responsible for her death. No one would believe that we knew about her allergy, that we always take immense care with her meals. I'm — I was her friend, for God's sake!'

He seemed on the point of tears. He pulled a handkerchief out of his pocket and blew his nose. 'We would never have taken risks with her food and neither would Flora. She had a bad attack a couple of years ago and since then — well, she was fanatically careful about what she ate and drank.'

Elizabeth waited for him to compose himself, then said, 'She certainly didn't touch a thing on the train.'

'Sorry?'

'I should have told you before.' She explained about the train journey and its consequences. 'So, you see, I've already spoken to the police about Miss Messel's death.'

'And you actually met Flora?'

'Let's just say we had words. I objected to her use of the mobile phone and she gave as good as she got.'

Looking back, she thought, it could have been worse. Mostly you find yourself listening to pompous business discussions. Or puffed-up salesmen. At least Flora Messel's conversations were entertaining.

Lovett got up and went to the window. Stood there, hands in pockets, staring out. 'Flora wasn't always tactful. In fact, she could be difficult. There's no point in denying it. But she was the most wonderful friend you could ask for.'

'You had known each other a long time?'

'Almost twenty years. We met at drama school in Bristol, back when we were all young and had starry eyes.' He turned from the window and Elizabeth could see that he was all stirred up. 'I asked her to marry me when we were kids. She refused, of course.'

'Why 'of course'?'

He shrugged. 'Flora could have had anybody. Why would she settle for a half-baked fool with a schoolboy crush on her? As it happens, I'm glad she didn't accept. It would have been a total disaster. Friendship lasts longer.'

'Doesn't burn itself out so quickly,' said Elizabeth.

Max stretched himself in the other chair. The pudding was catching up with him. 'So she always stayed here when she was working in Bath? Is that right?'

'Yes. It gave her a base in town. And she didn't like to drive after a performance when she was dog-tired.'

'Why didn't she take a taxi? She could afford it.'

'Yes, of course.' Lovett looked a trifle irritated. 'But it had got to be a tradition. I liked to see her. We caught up with each other, had a good gossip.'

'And you didn't charge her for the room?'

'Of course not.' He looked shocked. 'She was a friend.'

'OK,' Max said. 'So what exactly do you want us to investigate, Mr Lovett?'

'I want you to find out who substituted the sandwich we sent up from the kitchen.'

'Substituted?'

'Yes. There was absolutely nothing that contained peanuts in any shape or form in the one Chef sent out to her. I actually stood and watched him make the thing. Bread, chicken and salad. Nothing else. I can swear it.'

'And the sandwich was taken out to the summerhouse?'

'Yes. I'd have done it myself — God, I wish I had. I was on my way with it, but I got

59

called to the phone. My accountant had a query, so I gave it to Sandra with strict instructions to take it straight up there and deliver it personally.'

'Sandra who?' Max had his notebook out.

'Sandra Shaddock.'

'And you trusted her?'

'Implicitly. She's worked here for over ten years. A very steady girl. I'd trust her with my life. She's most upset by the whole thing. I told her to take some time off. That's why service was so slow today. I couldn't get a replacement at short notice.'

Elizabeth said, 'We'll need to talk to Miss Shaddock.'

'Mrs. She got married last year. I'll give you her address and phone number, but all I got when I rang her this morning was the answerphone.'

Elizabeth pulled a loose thread from her skirt and rolled it between her fingers. 'I'm curious,' she said. 'Why not just let the police deal with the matter? They're very capable.'

He passed a hand over his eyes. 'I feel as if they don't believe me. I feel as if my reputation — the reputation of this hotel — is on the line.'

'You want to prove that you don't set out to kill your customers?'

'To put it crudely, I suppose. But it's more

than that.' When he spoke, it was seemingly heartfelt. His face was flushed, his eyes bright. 'It's Flora. She was my friend and I feel as if it's my fault that she's dead. Meeting you today — it was as if I could do something. I don't have to hang around helplessly waiting.'

There were brisk footsteps outside the door. It opened and a woman's voice said, 'James, we need to talk about —' She stopped. The newcomer was a huffy-looking woman in a dark suit. Green eyes staring at you like a cat from a safe distance. A plumpish face, well made-up. Bright lipstick on blotchy skin. 'I'm sorry. I didn't realise you had visitors.'

Lovett said, rather awkwardly, Elizabeth thought, 'This is my wife. Rosemary.'

Elizabeth got to her feet and held out her hand. 'Elizabeth Blair. And this is my partner, Max Shepard. We're private detectives.'

'Detectives?' Mrs Lovett was a short woman with blonde-to-greying hair, worn in a frizzy bob, and sharp blue eyes. Her white blouse was tucked into a severe dark skirt and the general effect was workmanlike but officious.

'We were having a very pleasant lunch downstairs when your husband decided to employ us.'

'Employ you? James, what on earth is going on?'

He explained. She wasn't pleased. 'Oh, for God's sake. You're not serious?'

'Why not?'

'Why not? Well, I know one shouldn't speak ill of the dead, but your *friend* Flora Messel has cost us already. It's throwing good money after bad.'

'I don't care about the money.'

'No. You never did. But some of us have to.'

'I just thought — '

'Thinking's not your forte, James. Give it up. You'll be much happier.'

Elizabeth felt the pulse of anger and resentment that crossed the room from husband to wife.

'I don't have to take that,' he said.

Rosemary Lovett turned to Elizabeth. 'I do hope you enjoyed your lunch, but we really won't be needing your services.'

'I rather think we do,' her husband insisted. 'Flora died on these premises and I have to find out why.'

'Then it'll be with your own money,' she said.

'Fine by me.'

'Right,' she said. 'Just don't come to me next time the bank manager's on your back.'

'Do I gather,' Elizabeth asked with seeming

innocence, 'that you didn't care for Flora Messel?'

'What?' Rosemary Lovett seemed taken aback at the directness of the question.

'You weren't a fan? It's just the feeling that's coming over.'

'My husband was the fan, as you may have gathered.' There was spite in her voice and a certain grimness. 'I don't know what the hell it has to do with you but, for the record, I couldn't stand the woman. I used to say that her face was like some of the furniture in this room. Tastefully distressed.'

Ouch, thought Elizabeth. It's getting uncomfortable in here. Quite interesting, though, this nasty little battle. I hope he wins. I hope we get the case.

* * *

'Bloody hell,' said Max, as they walked away from the hotel. 'Tastefully distressed! She doesn't pull her punches.'

'Mmn,' Elizabeth said. 'She thinks old James was having an affair with Ms Messel.'

'So Mrs Lovett could have bumped her off?'

'In her own summerhouse? Hardly the best place, would you say? And yet imagine knowing your husband had always been sweet

63

on another woman. The bitterness might soon start to creep in. Fear might make you attack.'

Max said, 'So will we get the job? I'd say not. She obviously rules the roost.'

'I'm not so sure.' Elizabeth sounded thoughtful. Things didn't always look the way they were. There had been a touch of steel — or arsenic — about the lady, and yet . . . 'He's tougher than he looks.'

'What makes you say that?'

'He made sure that Flora Messel stayed at the hotel even though his wife hated her. And for free.'

'Suppose you're right.'

'If we get the case, I'm going back there for a good nose around.'

'Sometimes,' Max said, 'I think that's why you're in this business.'

'Know what? You may be right.'

8

Caroline was in the shop when Elizabeth got back. Had she changed her make-up or was she paler than usual? Almost chalky. Elizabeth told her off for coming in. She looked like a small dark bird that had been pushed out of the nest too early. Not half so bandbox perfect as usual. 'You're still not well.'

'I'm fine, really.' Caroline's dark eyes looked away. She was dusting out the middle shelf with a delicate air.

Elizabeth didn't believe her. The girl looked as if something was dragging her down. Not that the aristocratic Caroline had ever been lively.

'It's just a virus,' Caroline said, sitting a patchwork cat back in its corner. 'Rupe had a touch of it last week.'

Rupe. Elizabeth said, 'And is he on the mend?'

'He was a bit hot last night.' Caroline pointed the feather duster at another shelf. She wouldn't know a *double-entendre* if it came bounding up to shake hands with her.

★ ★ ★

'Good thing you weren't there,' Elizabeth told Max later. He had unwrapped a bar of chocolate and was trying to decide which end to bite. 'You're not eating again?'

'It helps me think,' he said.

'It'll help you put on weight, too.'

'That's just it,' Ginger said. 'He doesn't. It's not fair.'

The phone rang. Elizabeth picked it up. 'Shepard agency.'

'Mrs Blair?'

'Speaking?'

'It's James Lovett.' His voice sounded a bit flurried. 'I — I just wanted to say that — well, in case you should be in any doubt about the matter, I would still very much like you to investigate Flora's death.'

'Fine.' Elizabeth gave Max the thumbs-up sign. 'I'd need to take a look round the hotel and chat to your staff.'

'When would you like to come?'

'Let's see now — tomorrow morning?'

'What time?'

'Say ten thirty?'

'No problem.'

'There's just one thing.'

'What that?'

'Your wife. She didn't seem too keen on the idea.'

'Don't worry about that,' he said hurriedly.

'My wife won't be a problem.'

No? Elizabeth wasn't sure she agreed with him. A bit of a dragon, she thought, unless I'm much mistaken. Oh, well, you know where you are with dragons. It's them or you. No beating around the bush. I quite like that. It's the other sort I can't stand. The ones who say one thing and mean another.

'Lovett?' Max asked, as soon as she had put the phone down.

'Yup. We're in business. Who says going out for lunch doesn't pay?'

* * *

'Zillion,' said Elizabeth triumphantly.

'Is that a word, dear?' Dottie Marchant asked.

'Definitely.' Elizabeth arranged the Scrabble letters on the board in front of her.

'But is it English?'

'It's in the dictionary.'

'You're quite sure?'

'Look it up if you like.'

'No, no. I trust you. Well, that's me done.' Dottie's fingers crept round the board gathering up the plastic tiles. 'What time is it, dear? I can't quite see on your clock. The electricity's not as good as it used to be, especially at this time of the evening.'

'It's nine thirty,' Elizabeth said.

'Time for bed.'

'What a shame.' Elizabeth wondered if the old dear would notice the falseness of her voice, but Dottie was so keen to go on gossiping that she noticed nothing.

'I had the vicar call on me this afternoon. I'd promised him some old coins to use in his sermon at the family service. 'Oh, hello, Vicar,' I said. 'The coins? I think they're in the tureen.' That's my blue Spode that Mother used to call Abraham's Bosom.'

'Abraham's Bosom?'

'Everything finished up there. Anyway, the Vicar's going to talk to the children about Jesus saying he didn't want to be the head on the coin. Which will lead very nicely into prayers for our dear Queen.'

'Right.' There were times when Dottie's conversation seemed to float into free-fall. But it was a kind of art form. It drove you mad, but it also fascinated.

'I don't care for the family service myself,' Dottie said. 'Dreadful business. Squalls of children racketing round the church — I know I'm just an old maid, but, honestly, dear, sometimes I'm glad of it. So, how's your investigation coming along? The hotel man and the actress?'

'Oh . . . you know . . . ' At the tail-end of

the day, the last thing Elizabeth wanted was to talk shop.

'I believe *la* Messel had a tendency towards little romantic adventures.'

Not romantic, Elizabeth thought. Now, sexual I might agree with.

'Ah, well.' Dottie heaved a sigh. 'She's done with all that now. I expect her funeral will be quite something. No cut-price coffins there.' The tiles went into the box and the lid was jammed on. 'I'm not sure I'd like to be an actress, dear. All that preening and posing for the cameras. I'm too fond of slopping around in my dressing-gown in the morning. Also, the telephone would be ringing all day long. I couldn't stand that, could you?'

'Ah, but some people feel naked without their phone,' said Elizabeth. 'That's why mobiles were invented. Miss Messel's was practically welded to her hand.'

And thinking about that, it suddenly struck her. We should check the calls she made on the train.

* * *

After Dottie had gone tootling off, Elizabeth read for a while and then suddenly felt so hungry that she went into the kitchen and cooked herself an omelette. Ham and cheese with half a tomato thrown in for good measure. She added a generous helping of home-made apple pie to the supper tray and told herself she would worry about the calories at a later date. As she carried the tray through to the sitting room, she glanced at the clock. Ten twenty. Good. There would be time after her illicit feast for a spot of sewing.

Might even have a guilty half-hour going through my fabric stash. Hi. My name's Elizabeth and I'm a quiltaholic.

She settled herself into a corner of the sofa, arranged the tray on her lap, cut a fat wedge from one corner of the omelette and was about to pop it into her mouth, when the telephone rang.

Damn and blast, thought Elizabeth, how do they know? Ignore it. Pretend you're not here. Wait just half a minute and they'll go away, whoever they are.

They didn't. The phone went on ringing. She swore and picked it up.

'Mrs Blair?'

'Yes,' she said shortly.

'James Lovett. I'm sorry to bother you at home at this hour.'

So am I, she thought.

'I'll be very brief. It's just someone called me this evening — a woman — wanting to speak to me about Flora. It was the wrong moment. We were terribly busy. And quite frankly, she seemed to me a bit unhinged. She kept babbling on about the article in the *Mail*. Seemed terribly upset about Flora's death.'

'Did she know Miss Messel?'

'I can't honestly tell you. She wasn't making much sense. She kept going on about being on the train with Flora.'

'On the train?'

'Yes. And then she started to ramble on about this girl called Maria who, as far as I can gather, used to work in our kitchens. I don't remember any Maria and it might not have any relevance, but I took her number and said I'd call her back. Then I thought perhaps I'd leave the matter in your hands. Have you got a pen handy? I'll give you her name and number.'

9

'Could I speak to Elizabeth Adams?'

'Speaking.' The voice was animated, cheerful, much more normal than Elizabeth had expected.

'My name is Elizabeth Blair. I'm a private detective.'

'Good heavens!'

'It's possible that you may be able to help us.' Elizabeth explained that she was employed by James Lovett and embarked on a very brief résumé of the case. 'I understand from Mr Lovett that you travelled down to Bath on the same train as Flora Messel?'

'At the same table, actually. That's where it all started, you see. That's how I knew — '

A Welsh lilt. Elizabeth's eyes widened. It couldn't be. Surely? 'You wouldn't be the lady who spilled the coffee?'

'I did spill my coffee. Yes.'

Well, stone the crows, thought Elizabeth. Aloud she said, 'I think we'd better have a little talk.'

★ ★ ★

Ten minutes later when she told Max about the call, she still felt immensely puzzled, no, bemused by this latest turn of events. 'She's a physiotherapist.'

'Who's a physiotherapist?' He was peering at something on the screen.

'Elizabeth Adams. The woman I sat next to on the train. The one who called James Lovett. I've arranged to go round to her flat.'

'Right.'

'Tomorrow. OK?'

'OK.'

'I'm also going to chase up Mireille. The little French girl.'

'Right.'

He said, 'You think she had something to do with the murder?'

'Possible murder. We still don't know what happened exactly. But I'd like to know what she was doing at the hotel. She didn't say anything about returning a book.'

'Perhaps she didn't understand. How good's her English?'

'Well, I'd have said at one time that it was pretty ropy. But now I'm not sure.' She had a feeling that little Mademoiselle Bucolin wasn't quite as innocent as she made herself out to be. For the first time she wondered why exactly the girl had returned to Bath. To work, she had said. Or had she? Come to think of it, she hadn't given away much on either of the occasions when Elizabeth had spoken to her. She seemed uncomfortable, Elizabeth thought. At the time, I interpreted it as shyness, but now I'm not so sure. She was uneasy when I asked too many questions. I wonder why. We'll have to find out, won't we?

'Did you like her?' Ginger asked.

'Like her? I thought I did.' But now, again, doubts were creeping in. 'She was sort of hard to be friendly to.'

'That's the French for you,' Max said.

Frogs, he would have said if Ginger hadn't been around to challenge him about his attitudes.

'I've been wondering,' Elizabeth said, 'if Flora Messel ever lived over there.'

'In France?' Max looked less than interested.

'It's a distinct possibility. She starred in a lot of French films. And if she ever happened to live near little Mireille's home town . . . '

'Bingo.'

'Well, let's just say it might be interesting.' A pause. 'No, they couldn't have known each other.'

'Why not?'

'They didn't say a word to each other on the train. And neither did Ms Adams. I'd swear it — no matter what she told James Lovett.' Elizabeth bent to pick up her bag. 'OK. So that's sorted. I'll see to the Adams woman and Mireille. You take care of the hotel staff and Nethershute.'

'Nethershute?'

'Ms Messel's country seat. Somebody ought to take a look around up there and find out what the locals thought of her.'

'As if I haven't got enough to do,' Max said.

Elizabeth ignored the remark. 'So how's the tractor hunt going?'

'It's not.'

'You've notified the ports?'

'Yes.'

'And?'

'And they wanted to know if we'd lost Daisy the cow as well.'

* * *

Sandra Shaddock hadn't been warned that Max was coming to talk to her. Which meant that she couldn't keep the expression of alarm from showing on her face. Not a particularly intelligent face, it had to be said. A tight little mouth, the remote eyes of a mechanical doll, a plastic moonface under a frizz of flaxen hair.

'What do you want to know?' she asked. 'I took the sandwich out to the summerhouse. That's all I can tell you.'

'And you're quite sure no one else touched it?' Max asked.

A faint flush of the cheeks. 'I said so, didn't I?'

'Yes. Look — I'm not trying to make you sound like a liar. It's just my job. Picking at what you say. Acting suspicious. Firing questions until I get something back that interests me.'

'Well, I still didn't let anyone else touch it,' the girl said sullenly.

'OK. Let's leave the sandwich for a moment. Tell me what you can about Miss Messel. What she looked like when you put the sandwich in front of her. How she sounded. What she said to you.'

'She said I'd taken a long time.'

'And had you?'

'No,' the girl said. 'It's just that she always wanted things done yesterday. Nothing was ever right. That's how she was.'

'She was difficult that day?'

'She was always difficult.'

'But that day worse than most?'

'Like the bloody Queen of Sheba. She'd already had a go at Craig for sending that girl up to her room.'

'That girl?'

'The French girl. I don't know her name.'

'Mireille? Mireille Bucolin?'

'No idea. All I know is that Craig got a flea in his ear.'

'So what did she say to Craig exactly?'

'Like how dare he tell a complete stranger her room number. She was a real bitch. I'm glad she's dead. And I'm glad Mrs Lovett gave her a piece of her mind.'

'When was this?' Max asked.

For a moment, the girl looked discomfited. 'Don't tell her I told you.'

'Mrs Lovett had a row with Flora Messel?'

She frowned and refused to answer.

'You may as well tell me now that we've got this far.'

'I'll get into trouble.'

'I won't let on. Promise.'

'You say that now.' The frown got deeper.

'Cross my heart and hope to die.'

But it was no good. She refused to say any more, just stared into the distance with an exasperating blankness.

★ ★ ★

The hotel was quiet, almost deserted. Craig Royle was in the lounge wiping over the low tables. He was a tall, dark young man with an indolent air. He wore the charcoal grey waistcoat and red bow-tie of an exquisitely dressed flunkey.

Max dived straight in and asked if he had directed Mireille Bucolin to Flora Messel's room on the day she died. His face took on a comic, resigned expression as though he had been caught red-handed committing some clandestine operation.

'How was I to know she wasn't to be disturbed?' he asked.

'Miss Messel?'

'I saw her go upstairs.'

'What time was this?'

'When she got back from the theatre. About twelvish. I knew she was up there. I thought the girl had something to do with the theatre. That she'd come with a message or something.'

'What made you think she was from the theatre?'

'Well, she was foreign and she was carrying a book in her hand.'

Max didn't quite follow his logic, but he didn't bother asking him to explain. 'What kind of a book?'

'A paperback. Pale blue.'

'I gather you weren't flavour of the month with Miss Messel?'

'She came down and tore me off a strip.'

'What time was this?'

'Half past twelve or thereabouts. We'd just started serving lunch.'

'And how did Miss Messel seem to you at that stage? Apart from spitting fire, I mean.'

He shrugged his shoulders.

'There was no one hanging around in the lobby waiting to speak to her?'

'Not that I noticed. But, then, I wouldn't have. The whole place was packed.'

'With?'

'The Jane Austen lot. A lot of foreign professors and their ladies. They'd just come out of the convention room.'

'Mr Lovett didn't tell me about that.'

'Maybe not, but there were swarms of them all over the place.'

'In the garden?'

'In the garden, the dining room, the convention room. You couldn't move for them.'

★ ★ ★

The chambermaid at the hotel — a frank, friendly woman by the name of Anita — was quite helpful. She told Max she had knocked on Miss Messel's door at about a quarter past twelve on the day she died. 'I wanted to clean her room, but she told me to go away.'

'Politely?' Max asked.

'She just called out, 'Go away. I'm resting.''

'She didn't open the door?'

'No.'

'Did you hear anyone else in the room with her? Voices of any kind?'

'No.'

'So what happened next?'

'I went off round the corner to do number sixteen.'

'And?'

'Well, I let myself in, stripped the beds and then went to the linen cupboard to get fresh sheets. The others were in a hell of a state. God knows what they'd been doing.' Anita's face registered disapproval. Her good-natured expression changed to a finicky look. 'You never know what you're going to find in this job. Why, once — '

'Where exactly is the linen cupboard?' Max cut her short on the more lurid details.

'At the end of the passage on the corner.'

'Back towards Miss Messel's room?'

'That's right. And that's when I heard her talking to somebody.'

'In the corridor?'

'No. In the doorway of her room. I can't be sure that it was her, of course. I had my head in the cupboard. And sometimes you're in your own world. Guests come and go, but you don't take much notice. But her voice is, well — '

'Distinctive?'

'That's exactly it. She didn't sound like anybody else. Know what I mean?'

'Not exactly. Can you describe her voice to me?'

'It was . . . well . . . fruity. Husky. Sort of chocolate with a hint of arsenic.'

As descriptions went, it was pretty poetic. 'So what did you hear them say exactly?' Max asked.

'All I heard was her voice — if it was her. She said, 'What on earth are you doing here?''

'But you didn't hear the reply?'

'No, sorry.'

'So you can't say if it was a man or a woman?'

Anita shook her head. 'Sorry. I wish I could, but I can't.'

Max said, 'Can you show me the linen cupboard? And Miss Messel's room?'

The woman looked worried. 'I'd have to get permission.'

'Mr Lovett said I can go ahead and talk to anyone and go anywhere in the hotel.'

She still looked doubtful.

'And if it's Mrs Lovett that you're worried about, I believe she's gone off for the day.

Gone to visit her sister in Hereford.'

'Oh, right.' Her eyes brightened. Suddenly it was a different matter. She had stopped feeling uncomfortable about the request and went off to find her keys.

Room twenty-one, though looking out over the hotel gardens at the back of the premises, seemed tranquil enough that morning. There was a four-poster bed with pale green hangings. A greyish-green carpet. Wallpaper with creamy roses. The usual built-in wardrobe and a couple of painted chests stencilled with a leaf pattern.

Max admired the view out over the terraced gardens for a while. Roses in full bloom and a vine-hung pergola next to the dining room. Then he turned to gaze around the room. Not in use at present. Well, that was understandable. The police would have only just finished going over it. 'Did she always have this room?' he asked.

'Always. She insisted on it.'

Max wondered how you could insist when you weren't actually paying your whack. 'You wouldn't know how many times Miss Messel has stayed here in the last year?'

'Two or three times at least.'

'And she was working at the Theatre Royal each time?'

'I don't know. I never go to the theatre. She

came down to see that rock musician one time. Had a drink with him in town somewhere and brought him back here for supper. They were all talking about it. Craig got his autograph. I'm trying to think of his name. Sean somebody.'

'Sean Donahue?'

'That's it.' She looked pleased with herself.

Max gazed round the empty room. 'Did you clear this room up after the police had finished with it?'

'Yes. I did.'

'Anything interesting lying around the place?'

'No, sir. The police and Mr Lovett sorted it before I got there and I was glad, I can tell you. It was bad enough cleaning up after such a horrible tragedy. I couldn't stop thinking about it for ages.'

★   ★   ★

Craig was happy to agree that he had asked for Sean Donahue's autograph.

'You went up to them in the dining room?'

'That's right.'

'So what was their relationship, would you say?'

'The night I got his autograph she was all over him.'

'Really?' Hard to imagine the Flora Messel Elizabeth had described being all over any man. Easier to see her dangling them on a string. 'How long ago was this?'

'Last October. I'd just been up to one of his concerts in Bristol.'

'And what was Mr Lovett doing while she was 'all over' Donahue, as you put it? Did he join them for a drink?'

'Not that I know of.'

'But they were pretty close, Flora Messel and Mr Lovett?'

'I suppose.' His reply was guarded. Was he just unobservant? Or a touch on the dim side, taking nothing much in and therefore not giving much out?

10

Elizabeth parked the car outside number 10
Garrick Lane — a tranquil, undramatic
terrace on high ground to the north of Bath.
It was a light, warm afternoon. Incomparable
views down over the city. Everything drowned
in a soft light; the sky a luminous blue; the
lane at the bottom swerving round to a small,
spired church.

She walked up the steps to the tall
frontage. To the right of the door were a
dozen bells. She had to get out her glasses to
peer at the names, some of whose washed-out
writing was almost indistinguishable. Luckily,
Adams was fresh and clear. She rang the bell.

After a while, footsteps came running down
the stairs and the door opened. 'Can I help
you?' a voice enquired.

'Elizabeth Adams?'

'That's my name, but I answer to Buffy. It's
what I used to call myself when I was a
toddler and it seems to have stuck. You must
be Mrs Blair.' She stopped to stare at
Elizabeth. 'I know you. At least, I know your
face. You were on the train.'

'That's right.' Elizabeth took in that

85

extraordinary-coloured hair and her warm smile. Ms Adams was wearing a green silk shirt and a long skirt patterned with vine leaves. 'Small world.'

'Isn't it?'

'You'd better come in.' Something had caught her eye. She peered over Elizabeth's shoulder at the Martha Washington flyer on the back window of her car. 'I've seen that shop. Never been inside.'

'Try it some time,' Elizabeth said. 'I might even offer you a cup of coffee.'

'You run a shop as well?'

'I like to keep busy.'

'Right.' Buffy Adams studied her for a moment, then said, 'You'd better come in.'

'Thanks. I won't keep you long.'

She was led up two flights of stairs in what would once have been a grand, dignified house. Now isolated rooms, each with a number on the door, were separated by graceful passages. They were on the third staircase when Elizabeth had to stop and get her breath back. If I'd known, she thought, we'd have had our little talk on the doorstep.

'Sorry. You're not used to stairs?'

'I'm not used to staircases that go on for ever. You must be as fit as a fiddle. It's OK. You can go ahead now.'

On the fourth floor, a door stood open

straight ahead of them. Buffy said, 'Here we are.' The room was full of character and seemed too big for the furniture. There was an immense feeling of space. That was because of the two superbly proportioned windows that ran almost down to the varnished floorboards.

'Nice place,' Elizabeth said.

'They call it a studio. That way they get to charge you more. Coffee?'

'No, I'm fine, thanks.'

'Sit down. I'm glad you came. This whole thing seems so odd. It's been going round and round in my head.' Buffy Adams sat down herself.

'That's why you phoned James Lovett?'

'Partly. It's all so odd, don't you think? How we met on the train. How we were all there that afternoon. You, me, the little French girl, that poor woman who expired after the chicken sandwich. Well, perhaps poor's the wrong word. After all, she was famous. And filthy rich. She had it all.'

'I suppose you're right.'

'What I couldn't get over was the feeling that it was all pre-ordained. We were meant to be there that afternoon.'

'That's an interesting thought.'

'So I took myself off to my Mr Wilson.'

'You did?'

'He puts me under hypnosis. He's very good. You should try it some time.'

I don't think so, thank you.

'It helps you understand what's going on,' Buffy said. 'Helps you peer into your subconscious. Explains everything.'

'That must be comforting.'

'Yes, it is.'

At this moment, a black and white cat came prowling in from the adjoining kitchen. 'We've got visitors,' Buffy said to him. 'You like visitors, don't you? He's the most sociable cat I ever owned.'

'What's his name?' Elizabeth asked.

'Tam. Yes, you're such a beauty.' The cat jumped up into her lap and began rubbing himself against Buffy's shoulder. 'You know you are. And such a show-off.'

'Not the easiest place to keep a cat,' Elizabeth said. 'Up three flights of stairs.'

'I know. But I couldn't part with him when I moved here. We manage, don't we?' She addressed the question to the cat. 'Tam's a free spirit. I put him out first thing in the morning and he wanders. There's a garden at the back. He thinks it belongs to him, don't you?' She rubbed the cat behind one ear. 'There's a bed of cat mint. Cat heaven. And he loves to roll around in dirt and chase insects. We have to watch out for slug pellets, though, don't we?' She ruffled the cat's fur. 'You thought you fancied them and they gave you a nasty haemorrhage. You were very ill, weren't you?'

Hell's bells, Elizabeth thought, she's waiting for the thing to talk back. I nearly bought a cat. Glad I didn't. They're lovely creatures, but you might get to count on them too much.

Buffy put her face down to the cat and kissed its nose. 'And one Christmas you tried to eat some tinsel and it got stuck in your throat. What a fright you gave me. Talk about nine lives.'

How old was she? Early forties, perhaps. Older than I first thought. Elizabeth said, 'You were saying — you took yourself off to your Mr Wilson . . . '

'Yes. Yes, I did. And we had the most amazing session. Guess what I found out?'

'You'll have to give me a clue.'

'It turns out I knew her in a previous life.'

'Knew who?'

'Flora Messel.'

'Good God — really?'

'Really. It turns out that we lived near each other in a village in Umbria in the fifteenth century. Her father owned a *palazzo* and I worked in the kitchens there until the fire.'

'Kitchens. That was what you were trying

to tell Mr Lovett on the phone?'

'Yes. Only he didn't quite seem to be with me. Mr Wilson says I almost choked.'

'You did?'

'While under hypnosis. I could smell the smoke, you see. That was when I was trying to help the three younger children out on to the roof at the back. We didn't make it, though. We all perished in the fire.'

'Good heavens!'

Buffy said happily, 'I know. Tragic, isn't it? I felt quite emotional afterwards. But the thing is, it explains why Maria and I were sitting opposite each other on the train the other day. She wanted to thank me for trying to save her brothers and sisters. I'm convinced of it.'

'Maria?' Elizabeth's head was spinning.

'That was Flora's name when I knew her in Assisi.'

'Right,' Elizabeth said. 'You're really into this regression stuff?'

Buffy stroked the cat, which was now curled in her lap. 'I certainly am. It gave me back my life.'

'Really?'

'Really. I was ill and no doctor I ever went to could cure me.' She let the cat leap down from her lap. 'I'd had abdominal pains since I was a teenager and they kept saying there was nothing physically wrong. They put me down as a nutter.'

Well, now, I wonder why exactly.

'Then I met a man in France — but it's a long story. You won't want to hear it.'

'But I do. It sounds fascinating.' Elizabeth pinned on her interested face, but wondered if it was a mistake.

'Well, five years ago I went to Brittany on holiday — and I met this man. He worked as a waiter in the hotel I was staying at. And we had a bit of a fling and all my pain disappeared and I — well, I can't describe it. I became a whole new person.'

'Holiday romances can have that effect.'

'It was more than just that. I can't tell you. I was this sad, inward-looking mouse-like person, a real no-hoper, and then my whole personality changed. I bought new clothes, dyed my hair red. And a friend of mine said, 'You know why you're so different? You were in love with that guy in a former life.''

'The waiter?'

'Yves. That's right.'

You do pick them, Elizabeth told herself. Wait till Max hears. He'll have a ball. 'I'm sorry. I don't follow.'

'Well, as I said, when all my pains stopped, Mim — that's my girlfriend — she was really

91

into regression and she reckoned I must have let go of some trauma that I'd been through with Yves in a previous life. I was a bit sceptical at first.'

'You were?'

'Yes. Then I went under hypnosis and — you won't believe this — I found I'd been married for five years to Yves, just after the battle of Waterloo.'

A fruitcake. Definitely.

'I made that phone call to Mr Lovett because . . . well, I read that piece in the *Mail* and he sounded so distraught. Regression helps you go down pathways and open doors, I told him. I thought Mr Wilson might be able to give him some comfort. I'm so much happier now. You should have seen me before.' She went over to a cupboard and pulled out an old box. Fished through the photographs it contained until she found the one she wanted. 'There.' She brandished it under Elizabeth's nose. 'That's me ten years ago, before all this happened.'

A small, mousy person with a withdrawn air gazed out of the photograph. 'Interesting.' Elizabeth couldn't think of anything else to say. It takes all sorts, she reminded herself. Ordinary or extraordinary, we all inhabit the same planet. Maybe.

11

Nethershute turned out to be an elegant, substantial grey stone mansion, constructed in the 1820s, set in acres of woodland, with a beautiful walled garden. Ten miles from the city of Bath, it stood all by itself at the end of a long drive and positively stank of money. Old money, Max thought, admiring the blowing sea of cow-parsley in the fields all around and the deep shadows in the tops of the tall chestnuts. The morning's mist had cleared. All around, islands of greenery stood quietly on what might have been a painted landscape. It was three in the afternoon. No sun, but the house, the flat Georgian front, the stone pineapples, the long windows, the lawns had a feeling of warmth, as though all that beauty could keep the cold out. Had kept it at bay for a couple of hundred years.

He got out of the car and locked it. Tubs of flowers stood round the steps that swept up to the entrance. To the far side of the house, through a gap in the yew hedge, an elderly man was stooping over a rosemary bush, rubbing a handful of its sharp-pointed leaves through his fingers. He lifted them to his nose and took a deep sniff. He had no inkling that Max was watching; perhaps it wouldn't have made any difference if he had. That deep intake of aromatic fragrance was all that he cared about.

Max scrunched his way across the gravel and said, 'Hi. I wonder if you could help me.'

The man seemed untouched by Max's presence. He was in his eighties, lean, wiry, with very blue eyes and a thick head of white hair. He wore a red sweatshirt underneath a tweed jacket that had seen better days. He gave Max a good strong look, then scattered the rosemary to the wind. 'Clears the eyes,' he explained. 'Stops them watering.'

'Rosemary?'

'I've always suffered with my eyes. Conjunctivitis, Dr Matt do call it. I suppose that cream he gives me works, but I prefer the old ways. My mother used to distil the oil from the flowers on a glass in the sun and use it as a balsam. They say it helps a weak memory, but mine gets worse all the time.'

'Join the club.' Nice old codger, Max thought. One of the old school. 'I was hoping to speak to someone who knew Miss Messel. Flora Messel.'

'Then you've come to the right place.'

'You knew her?'

'Since she was a little girl.' A long shake of

the head. 'It's a sad thing that happened to her.'

'Very sad.'

'And who might you be, if you don't mind my asking?'

'Ask away. My name is Max Shepard.' He fished in his inside pocket and passed over his card.

'You'll have to read it out to me. I haven't got my glasses.'

'I'm a private detective, Mr . . . '

'Bowman. Thomas Bowman.'

'Well, then, Mr Bowman, I'm being paid to investigate Miss Messel's death.'

'And who might be daft enough to ask you to do that?'

'A friend of hers. James Lovett. He owns a hotel in Bath.'

'Oh, him.'

'You don't care for him?'

'He's no worse than most, I suppose.' A shrewd blue glance. 'So what would he be asking you to investigate exactly?'

'He thinks Miss Messel might have been murdered.'

If he was startled, he didn't show it. Perhaps, at that great age, he was past being shocked. 'And who does he think might have murdered her?'

'Well, now, that's what he's paying me to

find out. Any ideas?'

'I might have ideas, but I'm not so sure I should be sharing them.'

'It would help me a great deal if you did.'

'Family business is family business, that's what I say.'

'You're related to Miss Messel?'

'No. But I worked here for nigh on seventy years.'

'As what?'

'Head gardener.' He said it with some pride.

'Seventy years? Then you must feel like part of the family.'

'Sometimes you do and sometimes you don't. My father — he was gardener here before me — said that if they didn't keep their distance, you should. A man of great dignity, my father. He were a rose man. When he was here — well, I've never seen a garden with so many roses. We used to prune them for days and days. The whole house was covered in roses. Pergolas covered in them right the way down to the bottom. He used to get scratched to bits. Then there was the kitchen garden. Vegetables and sweet-peas. The shrubbery, two orchards, a paddock and tennis courts.'

'A lot of work.'

'You're right there. Mind you, there was a

cottage that came with the job. Part of your pay.' He tapped the ground with his walking stick. 'I was born here, you know. I can remember as a child digging weeds from that crazy paving with an old penknife.'

'Really?' Max said. 'You must have seen a lot of changes.'

'You can say that again. It's all trends now. Water gardens. That beastly decking stuff. Makeovers!' He snorted. 'Playing at gardening. In my days, it had a serious purpose — feeding a household. Now they all go to the supermarket for their radishes. They go to nurseries and buy their plants. They don't grow them.'

Max began to wonder if he would ever get to anything relevant. 'Miss Messel's father,' he said. 'I believe he married twice?'

'Married young the first time. Just starting out, he was, when he first came here.'

'Starting out in what?'

'In medicine. That was back before the war. 1935. Colonel Aubyn Messel. A bright spark he was back then. Miss Iris took one look at him and had to have him.'

'So Nethershute was his first wife's home? She lived here before her marriage?'

'That's right. A lovely girl, Miss Iris. A real lady. Society people, her family, the Whartons, but they weren't offish or snobbish.

97

Used to come out sometimes for a chat and ended up helping me plant roses.' His eyes grew shiny for a moment. 'Pity she ever set eyes on him.'

'Aubyn Messel? It wasn't a happy marriage?'

'As unhappy as they come, I'd say. Of course, the war didn't help. Took him away for years. Diverted the stream, so to speak.'

'In what way?'

'Other women. Plenty of them by all accounts. Miss Daphne was born in 1940. After the war, things seemed set fair for a while, but he was soon back to his old ways. She never said anything, of course. Miss Iris. It wasn't her way. But when the cancer struck — Miss Daphne would have been twelve — we all knew the root cause of it. Bottling things up does no good.'

He was right there. 'So Flora Messel's father — Aubyn Messel — inherited this house from his first wife?'

'Unfortunately, some would say. Yes.'

'And the second wife? Flora's mother?'

'He got mixed up with her soon after Miss Iris died.' The old man shook his head. 'Talk of the village, it was. He started bringing this Greek chorus girl down for weekends. Half his age, she was. And then he upped and married her and installed her here as mistress

98

of the place. Just eighteen months after Miss Iris was buried. The whole village was in an uproar.'

'I can imagine,' Max said. 'It must have been hard for the child.'

'Miss Daphne? I'm afraid there were a few tussles when she was in her teens. She ran off one night. They found her out on the main road trying to hitch a lift to London. Her father brought her back, of course, but things never got any better. She made that woman's life hell.'

'Even when the half-sister came along? Flora? It didn't improve matters?'

'Made things worse, if you ask me.'

'They didn't get on, Daphne and Flora?'

'How could they? Too many years in between. And the freak used to make such a fuss of the baby.'

'The freak?'

'It's what the servants — there was a houseful in those days — what they used to call the second Mrs Messel behind her back. She was always dolled up, you see. And painted like a fairground tart.'

Thomas Bowman stood gazing up at the big windows. One hand rested on the curve of his walking-stick, the other absently plucked at the rosemary bush. He was half with Max, half somewhere else. There was a smell of herbs and orange blossom. 'She ruined the child.'

'Flora?'

'Never once checked, never taught to say please and thank you. Indulged at every turn — with Miss Iris's money. That was what got people's goat.'

Max was getting the picture. 'So Flora wasn't popular here?'

'Not as popular as she would have liked to be.'

'So tell me something. How come the old man left the house to Flora? Surely Daphne should have had first claim. If it had come from her mother . . .'

'You tell me,' Thomas Bowman said.

He knew more than he was letting on. There was a look on his face. 'The contents of the will were never disclosed.'

'But you must know. Things get round. There must have been rumours?'

Caution was paramount now. 'You'll have to ask the lawyers,' Thomas Bowman said, moving crab-like away from him. 'Or Miss Daphne.'

I will, Max thought. 'It's a handsome old place,' he said.

'Ah, well, she spent a fortune doing it up.'

'Flora?'

'My son was working up here for almost a

year.' He paused like an actor. 'Building and refurbishments, if you ever need anybody.'

'I'll remember,' Max said. 'Did Flora Messel have any particular friends around here?'

'There's Dr Hutchinson's wife. She used to come up here for tea and such.'

'So where can I find her?'

'Down at Hay House. It's at the end of the village next to the church.'

'Thanks,' Max said. 'You've been most helpful.'

Thomas Bowman leaned on his stick and cocked an eye at him. 'So I'll tell Kingsley he might have a bit of a wait on his hands.'

'Kingsley?'

'My son. He'll be seeing to her.'

Kingsley was going to do what for whom? 'I'm sorry. I've lost you.'

'He'll do a good job, mind. Real quality.'

'Look, I'm sorry,' Max laboured on. 'Your son is the local builder?'

'And the undertaker.'

'You mean — ' Max heard himself gibbering. 'Miss Messel. Your son's in charge of the — he'll see to — he'll have her — '

'In his chapel of rest in Halt Street. In apple-pie order. He'll see to her properly, Kingsley will. Eventually. Tell your Mr Lovett not to worry about that.'

12

Money, property, Max thought as he drove on down to the village. The cause of so many arguments. So what if the half-sister is to inherit the house? Must check on that. It might have some bearing.

The village of Dutton Cary lay to the east of the deep valley that ran from the M4 motorway down to Bath. It consisted of a church, two farms, a pub called the Jolly Ploughman and a scattered group of cottages, built mostly during the reign of the first King George.

Deck-chairs on lawns, Max thought, willow pattern in window-sills, pewter tankards, no doubt, hanging in rows in the pub. God's in his heaven, all's right with Merry England.

Sleepy England.

He parked the car by the iron gate to the narrow churchyard, opened the door and listened to the small sounds that made up a flat afternoon silence. Air moving, trees sighing, sparrows chirruping. The odd baa from the odd sheep, muffled traffic from the motorway a couple of miles away.

Always that, these days, no matter how idyllic the setting.

He locked the car and looked round for a sign that said Hay House. There it was, across the road. A handsome front standing comfortably inside a clipped box and holly hedge. Double-fronted, honeysuckle round the porch, two small bicycles flung down next to it.

He crossed the road and saw that there was someone in the porch. A young man. Well, youngish. Early forties? Unruly brown hair and a blue checked shirt. Loaded with carrier-bags and an assortment of books and files, he was attempting to get his key in the lock and not succeeding. One of the bags was leaking groceries. Two tins of baked beans had just clunked at his feet.

'Need a hand?' Max asked.

'What?' He turned as Max walked up the drive. 'Well, if you could just take this for a minute . . . ' He handed Max one of the bags. 'I knew I should have made two trips, but it was too much effort.' He turned the key in the lock, shoved the door open and grinned. 'Mission accomplished. Thanks a lot. Now, is there something I can do for you?'

'I hope so. This *is* Hay House?'

'It is.'

'Then I'm looking for the doctor's wife. Mrs Hutchinson.'

'Ah. Now. Will the doctor do?'

'You're Dr Hutchinson?'

'For my sins. And you are . . . ?'

Max did the necessary introduction.

'A detective?' He looked Max up and down. 'I must tell Pauline.'

'Pauline?'

'Our receptionist. She's into Raymond Chandler. I've been trying to introduce her to Rankin, but no luck so far.' He had brown eyes, full of fun, kind but lively. 'Mind you, she's a lady of a certain age. Don't tell her I said that.'

'How much is it worth?'

'A lot. So — you want to speak to my wife. I'm afraid she's fetching the children from school.'

'Will she be long?'

'Shouldn't be. Want to wait?'

'If that's OK.'

'No problem. You'd better come in.'

Max followed him into the spacious hall. Dr Hutchinson dumped the files on the settle and took the bag back. 'I'm most grateful. Thanks.'

'You're welcome.'

Dr Hutchinson hesitated. Smiled but more seriously. 'I have to ask. It's not every day a detective turns up asking for my wife. Is it about the accident? Only it wasn't her fault, you know. The other silly devil came out of a side road.'

'It's about Flora Messel.'

'Flora?' He stuck the bag down with the others. 'Sad business. Tragic. But I don't see where Georgia comes into it.'

Max explained as best he could.

'A murder inquiry? Christ!' He was so taken aback that his face was slightly comic. 'You're joking?'

'I'm afraid not.'

'Are the police treating it as murder?' he asked.

'I wouldn't know. You'll have to ask them.'

'I can't honestly believe — Well, I know Flora wasn't everybody's cup of tea, but she wasn't *that* objectionable. Not when you got used to her little ways.'

'Little ways?'

'Well, she was high-handed, could be stroppy and rather enjoyed picking a fight.'

'You liked her?'

'You noticed. To be honest, I couldn't stand her. But murder? No, I don't believe it.'

'James Lovett, the guy who's employing us, seems convinced.'

'Obviously.' He paused, then said, 'Were they . . . ? No, we'd better not get into that.'

'Were they what? Having it off?'

'You don't mince your words.'

'No point. I can't tell you — yet — if they were having an affair. Was she prone to it?'

'Famous for it, if you believed the village gossip.'

'And did you believe it?'

'It rather depended on who was passing it around.'

He had a point there. Max said, 'Was Flora Messel your patient?'

'Yes, she was. But I can't disclose — '

'Of course not. I wouldn't expect you to. But she was an old friend of your wife, I gather?'

'Yes.'

'You didn't approve?'

'What makes you say that?'

'Your face.'

He sighed. 'OK, I didn't approve. Look, I'm only telling you this because I want to protect Georgia. Flora Messel was a tricksy lady. She used people when it suited her, then discarded them. My wife could never see that and I long ago gave up trying to convince her. They shared a flat when they were younger, when they lived in London. Georgia says they had a lot of fun and will never hear anything bad said of Flora. Fair enough, I suppose, but I'm just trying to put you in the picture.'

He looked as if he was about to tell Max something else. The shadow of something crossed his face, made it seem less vital and breezy. For the fraction of a moment, in the afternoon light of this family house, he looked like a man with a secret to divulge. Then footsteps came thundering up the front path, followed by young voices and that of a woman laughing. 'No, you can't bring home a rat. I don't care how fascinating it is.' The door flew open. Two boys rushed in followed by a small girl and a young woman in jeans and a floppy lemon T-shirt. 'Sorry, Matt,' she said. 'I didn't realise you had a visitor.'

'Actually, it's you he wants to see.'

'Really?' Georgia Hutchinson smiled at Max. She seemed a little surprised. An attractive girl, Max thought. Very fair, very slender, very stylish. The kind of girl who couldn't be flashy if she tried. 'Hello. What can I do for you?'

'I'm sorry to barge in on you. Max Shepard. I'm a private detective and I wondered if we might have a word.'

'A detective?' Her colour rose.

'It's about Flora,' Matt Hutchinson said.

'Flora?' There was suddenly an unsteady expression in her light grey eyes.

'I'll see to the kids,' Dr Hutchinson said. Already he was sweeping them away into the nether regions of the house. Before he went, he took his wife's arm. 'This is probably going to upset you. Try not to let it. I'm in the kitchen if you need me. OK?'

'OK.' Had any of it gone in? She seemed to be looking through him.

'Use the sitting room. I'll bring some tea,' he said. A shout and a squeal from the back of the house — the children were taking advantage. A door slammed. Something went crash. 'Right,' he said. 'Somebody's going to get it.'

The sitting room was half panelled and painted the colour of clotted cream. Chintz curtains, sofas and linen-shaded lamps. 'Do sit down,' Georgia Hutchinson said. Alarm was still written all over her face.

'Thank you. I'll be as brief as I can.' Max said. 'Look — there's no way to break this gently. I've been asked to investigate Flora Messel's death. There's a possibility — no more than that at this stage — that she may have been murdered.'

'Murdered?' Mrs Hutchinson's cheeks grew even pinker. 'I don't understand.'

'James Lovett — the man who owns the hotel she was staying at when she died — Mr Lovett thinks someone may have put peanuts in her sandwich deliberately.'

'I don't believe you.' It was an odd little

whisper, very affecting.

'So we're talking to anyone who knew Miss Messel and might shed some light on her tragic death. I was told you were a close friend of hers?'

'Yes.'

'This may sound odd, but my partner was travelling down from Paddington on the same train as Miss Messel the day before she died. She heard her make several calls on her mobile. I don't suppose one of them was to you, by any chance?'

'No.'

'And you didn't call her that day?'

'No. I hadn't heard from her for several weeks.'

'I'm really sorry to have troubled you. It's just that the calls she made that day may offer us some clue — might help us track down whoever it was who murdered her. If it was murder, of course.'

'Then it's not certain?'

'Nothing is certain as yet.'

'So it might have been a terrible accident after all?'

'It might indeed. Did she ever call you when she was away working, Mrs Hutchinson?'

'Sometimes. Yes, she did. Her way of life is — was — quite lonely, you know. Always on the move. A few weeks working with one set of people, then off half-way across the world to do another film or play. She used to say that talking to me kept her feet on the ground.' Georgia Hutchinson seemed in a daze. 'She'd call to tell me if she'd been to a fun party. Or to let off steam when things went wrong.'

'Can I ask if you know anyone called Foxy?'

'Foxy? Amelia Fox. Yes, she works for Flora's theatrical agent. I'm afraid Flora was a bit naughty. She sort of appropriated Amelia — treated her almost as a personal assistant. Anything difficult and she'd have Foxy haring all over London fixing things for her.'

'What kind of things?'

'Oh, travel arrangements, press interviews, booking restaurant tables, hotel rooms. Flora was always so cheeky — but she got away with it. When we shared a flat together in London, years ago, she used to say, 'I can't believe you're so nice, Georgy. Nice is boring. You only live once. Take what you want and don't worry about people so much.' It sounds awful, but she wasn't terrible at all. Just — '

Her eyes filled with sudden tears.

'Take your time,' Max said. 'It would just be a great help if you could tell me about her.

What kind of person she was. The private person, I mean, not the star of stage and film.'

'She was such fun.' Mrs Hutchinson scrubbed at her face. 'I know she put most people's backs up, but I can only speak as I find. She was a good friend over a lot of years.' Her eyes returned to Max's face. 'She can't possibly have been murdered. Can she?'

'I hope not.' Max looked sympathetic, then said, 'What can you tell me about her relationship with her father and her half-sister. An older half-sister, I believe?'

'Daphne? Yes. There was half a generation between them.'

'Did they get on?'

'Daphne and Flora? I'm afraid not. Apart from the age thing, they were very different people.'

'In what way?'

'Where to begin?' She thought for a moment, nervously, then said, 'Daphne is a very conventional woman. She's married to a country solicitor, she hasn't worked since she had the children — three boys — she's a local magistrate, a pillar of the WI and the local Tory Party. She's one of those brisk, provincial, unimaginative women you can't ever imagine being young or letting their hair down. She's as plain as a pikestaff — I shouldn't say that, but it's true, so I will. She's bossy, a touch smug. Always got a dog at her heels. Runs the household like clockwork.'

'Could you give me her married name?'

'Billington. Her husband is a partner at Billington and Crosbie. That's in Queen's Square in Bath.'

'And her home address?'

'Doome Down Barn, Upper Dutton.'

'You sound as if you know Mrs Billington well. Does she live near here?'

'Five miles away. But she practically runs the church here. All her family are buried in the crypt.'

'Her father?'

'Yes.'

'Tell me about him.'

'Aubyn Messel? Well, I didn't know him all that well. He was ill and confined to his bed for a number of years towards the end of his life. But village gossip has it that there were the most almighty rows between the old man and Daphne. She resented him marrying again after her mother died.'

'And Flora? How did she get on with her father?'

'She had him wrapped round her little finger.'

'They were close?'

'He doted on her.'

'That's why he left her the house?'

'I presume.'

'Seems a bit unfair. I mean, there were two daughters.'

'I know. Daphne hit the roof, or so I heard. Threatened to challenge the will.'

'But she didn't?'

'Not that I know of.' Mrs Hutchinson's hands were twisted together like a nervous child's.

'Was it a surprise? The will? Or had he told them what he was going to do?'

'It came as a complete shock, I think. I mean, everyone knew the old man was difficult. A law unto himself.'

'Like his younger daughter?'

'I suppose so.'

'Flora didn't feel obliged to redress the balance?'

'I'm sorry?'

'Share the house with her sister? Offer Daphne half its value?'

Her face impassive for the first time, Mrs Hutchinson bent to straighten a ruck in the rug. 'Not a chance. She loved the place too much.'

'So did Daphne, I imagine.'

'Yes. But Flora knew how to bring it to life. She was wonderful at that kind of thing.

Colours, fabrics, décor.'

So that's all right, Max thought, his face implacable. We may be selfish, greedy, constantly chasing round the world so that we won't actually be able to live in the place once it belongs to us. But we have this ever-so-clever gift for interior decoration. 'Look — I have to ask this. Please don't take it the wrong way. Just out of interest — where were you the day Flora died?'

'We were at an auction sale in Cirencester. There was a Chinese bowl I wanted to bid for and Matt had the day off, so we . . . ' For the first time, she looked straight at Max. Big grey eyes full of abstract panic. A hand went to her mouth. 'You're asking me for an alibi. You think I killed Flora.'

'Not at all. It's merely routine.'

'I can't imagine what motive you think I'd have. Look, I think I'd like you to leave now. I don't want to talk to you any more.'

Max, trying to calm her down, said, 'Of course I'll leave, if that's what you want.'

'It is. I do want.' She was standing now, gripping the arm of the chair, her voice rising hysterically.

'OK. Fine,' said Max.

Shaking like a leaf, she turned towards the door. 'I think you've got a cheek. Really I do.' They heard footsteps in the hall.

114

Max said, 'Look — I'm sorry to have upset you.'

'That's all very well. Coming here making accusations.' Her whole manner had changed. She was suddenly militant. 'Get out of here. Just get out of here! Now!'

'Sweetheart, calm down. The children — ' Expertly fielding his wife, Matt Hutchinson said to Max, 'I did warn you. Probably best if you leave now.'

Max could see that. He beat a hasty retreat.

13

Meanwhile, Elizabeth was walking away from Le Jardin des Plantes. She had wandered into the restaurant just before three thirty and had been shown the door (well, practically) by three thirty-five. Luc Valéry had refused to let her see the new waitress. What he had actually said was that Mireille wasn't there. But Elizabeth had ideas of her own about that.

When you did this job day after day, you got to know when people were lying. Or, in this case, avoiding telling the exact truth. Running rings round it. Barely touching base. Overacting and making all sorts of diversions in order to take you round the houses. Monsieur Valéry's very sexy, very Gallic smile had certainly been working overtime. No doubt he had meant well, had thought he was protecting Mireille from an over-zealous, hard-boiled old Yankee broad who was hassling the girl to death.

American-ness. Sometimes it made you stand out in a crowd when you didn't want to. As soon as you opened your mouth, they had you taped. How the Brits (and the

French, for that matter) love to pounce on a Yank, she thought. They like nothing better than to disapprove of you in the nicest possible way. Oh, Monsieur Valéry had put it as politely as possible when he asked if the Shepard Agency knew how business was conducted in this country. He wasn't sure about how things went on in California, as he wasn't a great fan of *LA Law*, and he was sure Elizabeth had the very best of intentions, but at the same time Mireille was a young girl in a foreign country and all these unnecessary questions could, if looked at in another way, be translated as harassment.

And suddenly, there you were — defensive and wrong-footed. 'I don't come from California,' Elizabeth had protested.

'But you know what I mean?' Luc Valéry studied her charmingly.

Oh, I know what you mean, Elizabeth thought. I'm a crass American materialist, a tasteless Hollywood type who eats little girls like Mireille for supper. In a giant burger, no doubt. 'Look, all I wanted was a quick word with her.'

'I'm sorry, that's not possible.' Monsieur Valéry's eyes flickered. A lie was coming. 'Mireille's not here, I'm afraid. It's her day off.'

And lies waste my time, Elizabeth thought.

'She's . . . gone off for the day with some friends.'

'Would that be from her exchange school?'

'I'm not sure. I didn't ask.'

'You wouldn't have any idea which school that would be?'

'I'm sorry, I can't help you.'

'You wouldn't have her home address? I mean, the address where she's staying in Bath? I wouldn't ask — only this is pretty important. A murder inquiry.'

'Murder?' He looked away across the tables. There was a painting on the wall above the fireplace. Vibrant colours, light shimmering through the garden of a ruined chateau.

'Yes. You may have heard. The actress. Flora Messel. It was in the papers.'

'We don't get much time for reading. Better not know about all the dreadful things happening in the world, I say. What you don't see, you won't cry over. In France, we have a saying. Newspapers are like cats. They piss all over everything. Now, I'm afraid I have a thousand and one things to do. So if you'll excuse me — I'll tell Mireille you called.'

'Thanks. May I leave my card? If you'd just — '

'My God, is that the time? I have to be in the kitchen. Mussels to prepare, vegetables to slice, menus to see to . . . '

It had been like trying to hold a conversation with the White Rabbit. Now Elizabeth let herself stand for a moment on the flagged pavement two doors along from the restaurant, gazing with an abstracted eye at the sleek curves of an eighteenth-century chair in an antiques shop called Portia's Box, and pondering what to do next.

She asked herself why Mireille Bucolin did not wish to speak to her.

Because she's frightened? Of what? Or whom?

Of course, she resents the fact that I inadvertently put the police on to her. And the Valérys might not be too pleased to have the plod sniffing round their restaurant. Perhaps they told her not to talk to me.

Would they get rid of her if she defied them, I wonder?

Mireille was there, Elizabeth thought, hiding away in the back quarters. I'll swing naked from that chandelier if I'm wrong.

She turned to retrace her steps back to the office. Seagulls let out protesting cries as they wheeled round the rooftops. A pale sun had come out in the alley — a fine, pleasant, busy little thoroughfare, dotted with bow-fronted shops that beckoned you to walk in.

She wished she could remember more of what Mireille had said to her when they got off the train that day. So what do you remember? What stands out? A flare of something — fear? — when I asked if she was staying with her friend.

What else?

Not sure. The expression on her face, perhaps, when I told her to enjoy her stay. Excitement? Anticipation, certainly. Wild anticipation.

About what?

That's for her to know and you to find out. And so I will, if I ever manage to get hold of her.

In the meantime, she had better get back to the shop. There was a collection of child-size quilts to display, not to mention the accounts to sort — always something to shrink from until absolutely necessary. Well, not shrink from exactly. She just shoved the job to the back of the pile if there was something to get more of a kick out of.

Which reminds me, she thought. You need to buy some flattie shoes. Wouldn't it be better to do it now while you're out? And wasn't that a shoe shop I saw back there, next to the shop with the Russian dolls?

It was when she turned to check that she saw someone in a mauve top slip out of the Jardin des Plantes and walk quickly away from it. Mireille. Elizabeth was sure of it. For those few seconds, across the length of the alley, she looked older, had the air of someone at once more knowing and less indecisive. Then Elizabeth called out to her. 'Mireille! Wait!' And the girl turned, slanted back, looked horrified, took to her heels and was gone like a gazelle.

★　★　★

Max said, 'So why didn't you run after her?'

'I did, but she can give me forty years.'

'You should get yourself fit.'

'I might say the same of you,' she said firmly.

'I'm fit.'

'Fit for the pub, most days.'

'I haven't been to the pub since . . . ' He stopped to calculate. 'Since Saturday night.'

'And today's Tuesday. Big deal.'

'Your trouble,' Max said, 'is — '

'Coffee, anyone?' Ginger said, gathering the mugs together.

Max looked at Elizabeth as much as to say, sod you, but Elizabeth had gone over to her desk. Dropping into her chair, she bent forward and flipped open a file. 'So,' she said, 'how did it go up at Nethershute?'

'Quite useful, actually. I picked up a lot of stuff about Flora's family. Oh, and I upset the doctor's wife.' He brought her up to date on the details. 'She went berserk. Assumed I'd got her on the suspects list.'

'And do you?'

Max said, 'Nah. She was just in shock. Hysterical because I told her her friend might have been murdered.'

'So who *would* you put on the list?'

'The half-sister.'

'If she inherits the house. Who else?'

'The ex-husbands. Rosemary Lovett? The pop-star boyfriend. Sean Donahue.'

'Sean Donahue?' Ginger said, in an awed voice. 'You're kidding!'

'Am I missing something?' Elizabeth asked.

'He's new wave.'

'Oh, really?'

'A bit of a maverick.'

'Right.'

'Dark hair, blue eyes, dramatic,' Ginger said. Then added, inexplicably, ' "Two Look Too".'

' "Hold Me While My Heart Beats".' Max was joining in. 'Funny, sexy. Not just love songs. They're on a different plane.'

'You don't say?' Elizabeth was feeling left out.

'I'll lend you one of his CDs,' Ginger said dreamily. 'If you have to interview him, can I come?'

Max didn't seem to hear her. 'Is rock poetry? That's the question he asks.'

'No,' Elizabeth said. 'So you do the pop star and I'll find the ugly sister.'

'Max — can I come?' Ginger asked pleadingly.

He looked at her. 'There are rumours that he's an obnoxious, drug-taking, beer-swilling prat.'

'No way!'

'A hell-raiser.'

'That's all right. I like hell-raisers.'

Elizabeth closed the file. 'Find out where he lives and arrange to see him.'

Ginger said, 'He bought a country house in deepest Gloucestershire.'

'Then let's hope he's in residence.' She pushed the file away, got up and slung her bag over her shoulder. 'Right. I'm off.'

'Already?' Max glanced at his watch.

'Don't worry. I'm not skiving.'

'Did I suggest — '

'You didn't need to.'

'So where are you off to, may one ask?'

'You may. I'm going to drop by the Theatre Royal,' she told him. 'I want to know how many enemies Flora Messel made there.'

★ ★ ★

'One day she'll pass herself coming back,' Max said, when Elizabeth had gone. He sat

123

looking into a point of space. A hand idly pushed back his thick, brown hair. 'I was wondering . . . ' he said.

'Right.' Ginger plonked the mug of coffee in front of him.

'You on your own tonight?'

'That depends.'

'On what?'

'On you, by the sound of it.'

'Will what's-her-name be there?'

'Oonagh?' Ginger said. 'She's all right, you know. No need to run away from her.'

'I'm not. I just asked if she'd be there.'

'Any particular reason?'

He looked cagey. 'I just wanted to talk to you about something.'

'I thought that's what we were doing.'

'No. I mean proper talking.'

Whatever that was. After a pause Ginger said, 'I'll call her. Find out.' She had a thought. 'We could always go to your place.'

'It's a tip.'

'Eat out, then.'

'I'm skint.'

She sighed. 'I'll pay.'

'No. You paid last time. Call Thingy. Tell her you want the place to yourself tonight. Invent a crisis . . . What's so funny?'

'I don't need to invent one. You are one. A walking crisis.'

14

Judy Dean, who was directing *The Doll's House*, leaned back in her bucket seat and said, 'Yes, I called them into the theatre for a rehearsal on Monday morning. Just to give them something to do, really.'

Way up at the back of the Theatre Royal, two junior members of the cast were hunched one each side of a slim Regency pillar munching sandwiches and going through their lines. Cut-glass chandeliers shimmered lightly above their heads. It was five to four and in the pretty, gilded auditorium, with its half-circles of red velvet seats, there was a sense of quiet pressure.

'Was she difficult to work with?' Elizabeth asked.

'She liked her own way.' They sat in the second row of the stalls, Judy Dean holding her mug, frowning, trying not to resent the precious time that was being eaten up. Elizabeth focusing hard on the questions that she needed to cram in before the interview was terminated. 'She had talent, but was temperamental.'

'She liked to make her presence felt?'

'It didn't always endear her to fellow actors.'

'Especially on a first night?'

'Exactly.' Ms Dean ran a hand through her spiky white hair. 'Everybody tries to stay calm, but no-one quite makes it. Most of them are eaten up with nerves. Going mad inside. So we didn't always need Flora's histrionics.'

'But you got them?'

A long sigh. 'You're not kidding. The rehearsal was due to begin at eleven. Flora was actually here at that point — '

Elizabeth nodded. 'Had she eaten anything?'

'Not that I know of.'

'So what happened next? At what stage did she leave?'

'About three quarters of an hour into the rehearsal. There were a couple of new members of the cast brought in at the last minute and still learning their lines and she exploded at one of them, which made the poor girl even more nervous. She burst into tears and that infuriated Flora even more. She went into a rant about unprofessional little halfwits who couldn't be bothered to do the job properly. She didn't see why she should waste her energy — not to mention her voice — at this time of the day. And she flounced off.'

'Was this a dress rehearsal?'

'No. We'd done all that the day before.'

'So there was no costume to take off or make-up? She left the theatre then and there?'

'That's right.' Judy Dean smiled wryly. 'She always liked a dramatic exit.'

Well, she had that all right, Elizabeth thought. Rather more of one than she intended. She sipped slowly at her coffee. 'So how are you managing without her?'

'Anna — the understudy — is doing a wonderful job.'

'But she's not Flora?'

'Less power,' said Dean. 'Less edge. On the other hand, they're forming a stronger team. Flora wasn't fond of giving away scenes to supporting actors.'

'I see.' Elizabeth said, 'Any of them dislike her enough to slip peanuts into her sandwich?'

The reply was disconcerting. 'All of them, if you're asking.' Her pleasant, clever face looked quite reasonable. 'Some joker actually said after she walked out of the rehearsal, I wonder if she'll be alive by the end of the week.' She laughed apologetically. 'I'm sorry Flora died in such a horrible way, but I have to say there's a possibility that only the audiences will miss her.'

Flora Messel's dresser, five minutes later, registered indecision, then looked at Elizabeth in the dressing-room mirror. 'I looked after her on several occasions over the years. She wasn't easy, but I've learned when to keep quiet and when to talk. That's the secret, you see.'

He was a pleasant, balding man in his forties with uneasy grey eyes. He had found it all quite . . . upsetting. He sat with his hands clasped around one knee, smiling with agonised politeness, wondering what he could say in response to Elizabeth's questions.

'Do I know anyone who might want to kill her? Plenty, dear, between you and me and that table leg. She made a career out of putting people's backs up.'

Elizabeth gazed at him pensively. His petrol blue shirt didn't quite match his electric blue trousers. 'Tell me about her routine on opening night.'

'Opening night? Well, of course, that includes the day that leads up to the performance and the whole chaos that goes on after it. I wouldn't use the word routine. I'd call Flora's arrangements a ritual. She was very superstitious. Most actors are. Now Miss Messel would always have the same thing for breakfast. A poached egg with one piece of white toast and one piece of brown. She'd go shopping first thing in the morning and buy herself a little good-luck present — '

'Did she this time?'

'Oh, yes. A very nice little pink lustre bowl. She loved her antiques, did Miss Messel. They tell me her house is stuffed with them. Anyway, once she'd pottered her way round the shops, she'd come down Trim Street, through Orchard Street and into Beaufort Square. Orchard Street was a must with her. A kind of rabbit's foot, if you see what I mean. She told me one day that Orchard Street put her in touch with Sarah Siddons. That was where the first theatre was, you see, the one Mrs Siddons made famous. She made her debut in Bath, you know, in 1778. It was a great triumph. Audiences went mad over her. Had fainting fits. And Gainsborough painted her portrait — Flora had a copy of the picture in her drawing room, she told me — and Dr Johnson wrote his name on the hem of her dress in the portrait, so that he might share a little of her fame. And Dr J was not a sentimental man, you realise — '

The Siddons lecture was getting out of hand. Elizabeth said, 'And when Flora had finished her walkabout and reached the theatre — ?'

'Well, if there was a rehearsal, she'd turn up here and drop her bags on that chair. She would perch herself on the trunk over there in the corner — Mrs Siddons is reputed to have kept her costumes in it — and she'd read her cards and telegrams. She'd pin them up on the wall, make a nice little arrangement, then ask for a jug of water for her flowers — '

'Flowers?' Elizabeth said. 'From whom?'

'From herself, dear. She bought them from the stall in Union Street. Roses and delphiniums in summer. Then the jug of flowers would go over there by the mirror — you get two bunches for the price of one that way. And she'd take herself off to rehearsal. Late. She was always late. You'll be late at your own funeral, I said.' He glanced down at the card he was holding in his hand with sudden confusion. 'The things you say.'

'So she didn't eat anything?' Elizabeth asked.

'She'd always have a chicken sandwich at 12.30. Anything heavier or earlier threw her on to the wrong wavelength, she said.'

'So she had nothing at all here?'

'I'd swear it on the Bible.'

'But you weren't actually with her?'

'Doesn't make any difference. I know her. Knew her. She was neurotic about her ritual.'

Elizabeth fished in her bag and brought out

130

a CD that Max had lent her. She held it out to show him. 'Recognise this man?'

'That's Sean Donahue.'

'Right. He wasn't hanging around the theatre the day Flora died, by any chance?'

'No, but he turned up to watch her performance the last time she played here. *Lady Windermere's Fan*. Last September. He sat in Row E and chewed gum like mad all the way through. Bit of a moron, if you ask me. I don't know why she was lowering herself. Of course, he was six or seven years younger. That was flattering. But he wasn't her class. He was a step down for her. Know what I mean, dear? Came from a council estate in Manchester. Whereas Flora was . . . well, quality.' He continued to consider the two of them. 'She liked hiding away on his country estate. Liked playing at being Garbo.'

'Playing at?'

'Well, between you and me, dear, she was always banging on about wanting to lead a quiet life and how much she disliked being stared at in the street. But don't you believe a word of it. Little Flora loved the limelight. In many ways, she needed it. She'd have gone on stage for free, just to have people look at her, believe you me.'

'The telegrams from friends, the cards and

131

gifts — are they still here?'

He shook his head. 'The police took them.'

'But from what you can remember, was there anything unusual? Different? Suspicious?'

'Hate mail, you mean?'

At this point, the door opened and Judy Dean stuck her head in. 'Charlie — I need you.'

'Five minutes,' he said.

'Now. Bring the cream silk shirt and the gold cane. And no, it won't wait!'

* * *

The shop was shut when Elizabeth got back at ten past five. Odd. She thought. Caroline didn't say she had to leave early. I shall have to call her.

She half expected to find a note of explanation on the counter, but found none. Even more peculiar. Another bilious attack? Elizabeth picked up the phone and dialled Caroline's number, but it went on ringing for ages. No-one at home, then, either.

Elizabeth thought, oh well, I'll try later. Really, I might have to have a word with her. But I can't understand it. She's usually so dependable.

She wandered round the place for a bit, then dug out the local phone directory.

Found a long list of Billingtons and went down them slowly with one finger. Bristol, Bristol ... Bath, Coombe End ... Midsomer Norton. Ah, here they were Billington J.

Doome Down Barn, Upper Dutton.

She made a note of the number on the back of her receipt book and dialled it.

'Yes?' The voice was female, formal, the product of a damned expensive education. Among other things.

'Mrs Billington? Daphne Billington?'

'Yes.'

'My name is Elizabeth Blair.'

'Yes.'

'I'm a private detective.'

Elizabeth practically heard the other woman blink. 'Yes,' she said flatly.

'I'm sorry to bother you, but I wondered if we might meet up and have a word some time. It's about your sister's death.'

'Flora?'

'Yes.'

'She was my half-sister.'

Now let's get that right. 'Yes, of course,' Elizabeth said charmingly. 'Would some time tomorrow suit you? Only I shall be in the area.' She found herself crossing her fingers.

'Why would you want to talk to me about Flora's death?'

'It's a little difficult to explain over the phone. I'd rather talk to you in person.'

A pause while Daphne Billington reflected, judged, made decisions. Then, 'Very well. I could see you tomorrow afternoon. Say three o'clock?'

'That would be splendid. Thank you so much.' Elizabeth beamed down the phone. You're intrigued, she thought. And distracted and a little bit worried. That's interesting. I like this job. Coming across all sorts of people. The nice ones and the nasty. The strong and the fragile.

Sometimes, quite frankly, I'd do it for nothing.

But don't tell Max that. She had one last thing to do before calling it a day and heading back to South Harptree. Little Mireille's address. She had to get hold of it, but she couldn't afford to walk openly into Le Jardin des Plantes and ask.

They wouldn't give it me for one thing, she thought. And for another somebody would call ahead and warn the girl that I'm coming. So a certain amount of subterfuge was called for. Which didn't always work, but she hoped it would this time . . .

15

Ginger said, 'You'd watch tiddlywinks if there was nothing else.'

'Sorry?' Max pressed a button and continued to watch the cricket without any sound.

'I said you watch sport wall-to-wall.'

'I'll turn it off,' he said.

Ginger folded her arms, leaned her head on the kitchen door, looked at him. 'Good.'

'At the end of this over.'

She said, 'I thought we had things to discuss.'

'We do.' Reluctantly Max flicked again and switched off the television.

'Now or while we're eating?'

'Over dinner. I'll open some plonk.'

He looked uneasy, she thought. Even sitting there gawping at men in white, he had radiated unspent energy. Legs jigging, fingers tapping. Made you feel tired to watch him. She wanted him to come right out with it, whatever it was. She didn't want to spend half the evening in limbo, waiting.

Max went through to the kitchen, found a bottle from the rack above the fridge and set about opening it. But he was taking his time. You could tell from the way he set about unpeeling the seal that he was in no hurry. Working on one tiny sliver of metallic foil, stopping now and again to turn the bottle and frown at it.

It was when he wasn't really with her, when he talked to her but didn't say anything, that she found him most attractive. Like when you fancy somebody, but you can't get to touch them. Getting isn't everything, she thought, that's why all those old black-and-white films are so powerful. They knew the secret. Less is more.

She was thinking this — looking at his brown fingers fiddling around with the cork — when he said, 'Something smells good.'

'Bangers and cheesy mash.'

'Great.'

'I'd have done something more exotic, but there wasn't time.'

'Bangers and mash is fine.'

'Good.'

'My favourite.'

'It's three kinds of cheese with a layer of mushrooms in the middle.'

'Can't wait.'

For God's sake, she thought. All this polite talking. What's wrong? Why aren't you your normal couldn't-care-less self?

The cork came out. The meal got served. They ate in the kitchen. For some minutes Max concentrated on his cheesy mash, forking it in as if his life depended on it. Then he refilled his glass, which didn't need refilling, and with a nonchalant air said, 'Something's different in here. You've been decorating.'

'No.'

'New blinds?'

'There aren't any blinds.'

He risked a glance in the direction of the windows. 'You're right. Funny, I could have sworn . . . '

Evening traffic rumbled beyond the windows. 'So how long have you been here?' he asked.

'Three years.'

'Really? I thought it was less. I remember coming here the first time. It was tipping down.'

'Max, is there a point to this conversation? You're bumbling.'

'Am I?'

'Yes. Why not spit out what you've come here to say and have done with it?'

'What I've come here to say?'

'Yes.' She looked suddenly unsure of herself and said, 'You want out. Is that it?'

'Want out?'

'Of the relationship. You and me.'

'Good God, no. What made you think that?'

'The way you were acting. All distant and absent. The way you made sure Oonagh was out.'

'What's wrong with that? Three's a crowd.'

Her face all closed up, she said, 'That's how it happened last time.'

'Last time?'

'When Tom dumped me. He asked me to cook a special dinner, made a great fuss about me being a brilliant cook and after that a charming little speech telling me he was moving out. He thought we needed more space. What he meant was that *he* needed more space.'

'Bastard.'

'What really happened was that he'd found someone else.'

'So you were living with him?'

'Yes.'

'How long?'

'Two years.'

He looked at her and said, 'So his loss was my gain.'

A slow flush filtered through her skin. 'That's a nice thing to say.'

The first natural grin of the evening. 'I'm a nice person.'

'I know you are,' she said. 'So if you're not about to dump me . . . ' Ginger could still feel the fear in her knees. She sat there waiting for it to go away. She felt both relieved and elated as she touched the floor tiles with her bare toes.

Max pushed away his plate. Threw her a rather jumpy once-over, then cleared his throat. 'I wanted to ask you something. You don't need to worry. Is there any more wine, by the way?'

'Wanted to ask me what?'

'Well, I wondered . . . ' Abruptly he drained his glass.

'Yes?'

'I wondered if you'd think about . . . ' He looked desperate. One hand had clamped itself tightly round the stem of the glass. He said, 'Well, it just occurred to me — sod it, that's not true. I've been thinking about it for ages — '

'Max, for heaven's sake.'

'OK. All right. I'll ask you and that'll be that. How about moving in with me? Sharing a place? OK, so I know mine's a pigsty, but we could find somewhere else. Or I could move in here. Of course, Thingy would have to go. That sounds bad. Take your time, of course, but will you think about it?'

'You're asking me to move in with you?'

'That was the general idea.' Max allowed himself to relax a little against the back of the chair.

Ginger was far from relaxed. She just sat there looking at him.

Now that he had finally got his big speech over and done with, Max was his old careless self. 'I kept wanting to ask you at the office. You know, drop it out casually. But I was afraid Elizabeth would walk in when I was in the middle of it. Then she'd have put her oar in.' He paused, glancing across the table at her. 'You OK?'

'I'm fine.' She swallowed.

Max was penitent. 'I sprang it on you.' He spoke more quietly. 'Look — take your time. Think about it. It's a big decision. Why don't I get you another drink?'

'Yes. Yes, please.'

'Right. Corkscrew. Where did I leave it?'

'I think,' Ginger said, 'I'd better tell you right now.'

'You don't have to.'

'I do,' Ginger said. 'I'm sorry, Max. I can't move in with you.'

* * *

Elizabeth, dropping her car keys into her pocket, said, 'It's just that I was worried

140

about her. Caroline never shuts the shop early.'

Rupert's long legs and handsome face came down the last few stairs. He stood at the bottom of the stairwell, his fair hair combed beautifully back from his forehead. One finger to his well-bred lips, he led her on tiptoe across the hall and into the sitting room. His expression was at once sober and elated.

He said, in a hearty whisper, 'She's resting. I won't disturb her, if you don't mind.'

'Not at all,' Elizabeth said.

'One can't be too careful.' He closed the door with pantomime stealth. The room was impeccably furnished with a Samarkand rug, a handful of cream silk chairs and a grand piano. Perfect, like the two of them, Elizabeth thought. Almost too perfect. Imagine eating buttered toast here.

With Marmite.

'So what's wrong?' she asked.

Rupert said, 'Nothing's wrong.' He stood with one hand on the chair arm. In twenty years, he would be a real stuffed shirt. At the moment, in his early thirties, Caroline's husband was a crisply starched shirt. Stiffly ironed. Not a crease on him inside or out, except for two tiny ones at the corners of his upturned mouth. Dear God, Rupert was

141

almost . . . Elizabeth had to take a second look to make quite sure. Yes, actually grinning. What on earth could have got into him?

'So?' Elizabeth said enquiringly.

'So . . . ' Rupert stood there like the Cheshire Cat.

'You don't mean . . . '

'I do, actually.' He waited until he had thoroughly worked up her expectations, then said in a boundingly proud voice, 'We're expecting a happy event shortly after the festive season.'

How did you manage it? Elizabeth wondered. Both so terribly, poshly child-like. Must have used a handbook. On an Empire sofa, possibly, to the accompaniment of Handel. 'Well, now, that's just wonderful! Congratulations to the both of you.' And heaven help you when the gloopy nappies arrive, she just managed not to say.

'Mummy and Daddy are thrilled. Caroline's parents too, of course,' Rupert said, with evident self-pride. He lifted a cuff-linked wrist and looked at his watch: what he saw alarmed him. 'Would you mind awfully,' he said, 'if we adjourned to the kitchen? Only I promised her a milky drink at eight thirty.'

'Actually,' Elizabeth said, 'I have things to

do. Now that I know things are OK, I'll leave you to it.'

'No, no. You must stay and have a dash of bubbly,' Rupert insisted. 'Just let me minister to my little girl and we'll have a jolly-up.'

* * *

As Max strode into the office next morning, Elizabeth said, 'Guess what? Caroline's pregnant.'

'Bloody obvious,' he grunted. The sun was shining, the sky was an airy blue. Max, having gone back to his own flat the night before instead of staying at Ginger's, wasn't in the mood for chatting. If he hadn't had to come in to pick up his bag of tricks and make a phone call, he'd have avoided the office for a day or two. But as it was, he had to walk up the stairs and face her.

Ginger.

What a load of crap she'd given him. All that stuff about not being ready to move in with him quite yet. Not wanting to make the same mistake again. And that voice she'd put on. Half buttering him up and half preaching. Boy, was she good at that. Must get it from her father. Is that why? he wondered. Because of the Reverend? No, can't be. She lived with the other bloke, after all. Bloody Tom. Didn't give him the runabout, did she? He could get his irons in the fire. Get himself well and truly rooted. No keeping that bastard hanging about on a string.

But me. I'm not good enough. Not permanent enough.

That's what he had yelled at her when their tempers had both flared. He'd finished up really losing it and telling her maybe he could do with a bit of space, too. And she'd said fine by her. He could sling his hook. So he had. It had been raining outside and the street had looked all shiny. He'd sat in the car for ages, toying with the idea of going back up there. But when he got out of the car and locked it, his feet turned the other way and he walked instead all the way down into town through black air and cold drizzle. And by that time he was feeling hurt rather than angry and the rain was getting heavier and one of his shoes had sprung a leak, so he ducked into the first pub he happened across and ordered a double brandy.

Not the answer.

His head, this morning, felt like a kettle that had just come up to the boil.

Elizabeth, standing in the shop doorway, was saying something about milky drinks.

'Sorry?'

She gave him a look, then said, 'One of those nights?'

But he wasn't to be drawn. 'You might say.'

'Ginger didn't look too hot either.'

He ignored that and kept walking towards the staircase, his legs heavy and a set expression on his face.

'I'm in charge of the shop this morning, but Caroline's coming in this afternoon.'

'Right.'

'When she stops throwing up.'

'Right.' He felt like throwing up too.

'So I'll hop up to see the Billington woman this afternoon. That OK with you?'

'Fine.'

'But first I'm going to try and get hold of Mireille's address.'

'How?'

'Not sure yet,' Elizabeth said. 'And what have you got in your diary?'

'Not a clue.'

One thing that could fairly be said for Max was that he didn't do things in half measures. Elizabeth shook her head. Must have been a thickish night.

Youth, she thought. Longing for it all to happen, and when it did, they didn't like it. Just as she was settling herself down to work, the phone rang. She picked up the receiver and said, 'Elizabeth Blair speaking. Can I help you?'

It seemed not. There was silence at the other end.

'Hello? Did you want Martha Washington or the Shepard Agency?'

Again nothing.

'Is anybody there?' Elizabeth asked.

The silence went on for a second or two, then there was a faint click. Whoever was at the other end had rung off.

Elizabeth dialled 1471 and got the recorded message: 'You were called today at 09.05. The caller withheld the number.'

'I hate that,' she said to herself. 'Somebody calls you and you never get to find out who it is. Probably a double-glazing salesman. Or BT trying to sting me with their latest scheme.'

But she wasn't convinced. Damn it, she'd be puzzling about it for the rest of the day.

16

Buffy Adams felt like a cat in the rain. Odd. Uncomfortable. A little shivery. She wanted to pick up her feet and run for cover. But it wasn't raining. It was a calm, still, mysteriously moonlit night. She had come down to the garden for air and for . . . What? She wasn't sure. But back up there, on the third floor, something — again she didn't know what — was threatening to overwhelm her. It had all felt suddenly unfamiliar.

She thought: I didn't belong there. It's like when I was a child playing let's-pretend. Sometimes it would all run out. I couldn't hold the story, the characters in my head any more. Yes, that's what it felt like. I've run out of things to do here in my life in Garrick Lane. It's waste-ground. I should be somewhere else. Someone else.

Suddenly she was not at all comfortable in her skin.

She stood staring at a strand of large-leaf ivy on the stone wall in front of her. Better get rid of that. A single leaf could kill Tam if he tried to chew it. So many common plants, she thought, that are lethal to cats. Oleander, morning glory, lobelia, lily of the valley. Wisteria pods, narcissus bulbs, rhododendron. Abruptly she reached over and tugged out the ivy by its roots. No wonder it was a killer. It smelt revolting. Somehow worse in the clean, pure air of night.

Then there are your Christmas plants. Mistletoe, amaryllis, Jerusalem cherry, holly. It's a wonder cats survive at all, let alone proliferate.

She threw the ivy into one of the dustbins that stood half hidden behind a length of larch fencing tacked to the wall and moved slowly back up the path. Yes, it had happened before, this feeling of being a shadow of a person. Almost as if you were walking on a vapour. Like being a ghost. Unclaimed. Inconsequential.

But somehow . . . somewhere . . . she would find herself again.

Glancing up at the lit windows of the house, she thought, I'm about to tangle with something new. She'll help me. Maria. Flora . . . I can feel her. She's trying to tell me something, but I'm not picking up very well.

As one of the old trees above her head shifted, she thought she caught the words: *Not here*.

But where?

The cat, Tam, brushed suddenly against

her legs. While she bent to stroke him, her mind went on compulsively. Not here. Then some place, perhaps, that Flora knew. Familiar ground. Somewhere where the vibes would be stronger.

The cat had stopped purring. Walking alone, proud, disdainful, he began to lead her back to the house. I wonder, Buffy thought, following behind, do they survive death too? Cats? If so, Tam, who were *you* before?

* * *

Johnny Billington had married Daphne thirty years ago, give or take a few months. He could never remember the exact date of their anniversary. Got himself into trouble every damned year because of it. But dates didn't matter, he told himself. He remembered the day itself. Nothing flashy about the weather, just as there had been nothing flashy about the wedding. A clear sort of a day. Septemberish. Leaves all over the lawn, the gardens sunny. Dahlias and those small, tawny chrysanthemums — the clustery ones — in the church. He still made a point of bringing them in for her whenever he thought the anniversary might be looming.

She had told him off for using that word.

And, of course, you could see her point.

Johnny didn't mind getting his ear wigged now and again. In fact, he'd got quite accustomed to it. Before they met, no one had much cared what he did or how he did it, so it was almost a relief when the rather fierce Daphne Messel had walked up to him (at a rather splendid Christmas party at Nethershute) and told him that his tie needed straightening.

Good old Daphne. Blunt, but a tower of strength all his life. In those days, he hadn't a clue where he was heading. But Daphne had seized hold of him, turned him round a few times and faced him in more or less the right direction.

When she'd accepted his stammered-out proposal of marriage, he couldn't believe his luck. All at once, he became (in his own eyes, at least) a man of substance. A man who, now that Daphne Messel had seen something in him (though God knows what), could stop feeling inadequate and make something of himself.

They had bought Doome Down Barn when the children were small. Practically pawned the family silver (what was left of it) in order to do so. Back in those days they hadn't a bean. But having no initial funds, he reflected now, squinting through the window of his first-class carriage at the bare, smooth downs of Wiltshire, could cut both ways: you only fully appreciated money when you made it yourself. Having done that with the legal practice that he had rather surprised himself by making a success of, well he was entitled to sit back and enjoy it.

He glanced down at his watch — five minutes past three — and wondered what Daphne would be doing back at the Barn. Having tea, no doubt, with one of her friends. The dreaded Olivia (otherwise known as Bobby) probably.

An energetic woman, Bobby. Snappy of mouth and square of jaw. Johnny usually ran when he saw her coming.

But like to like, he thought. No one had ever called his Daphne a weeping willow. His eyes softened as he imagined her sitting with her Doulton teacups and her bag of embroidery in the conservatory he'd had built for her at the back of the Barn.

With any luck, he'd be there himself in a couple of hours. Johnny Billington leaned back in his seat. A civil, rather remote-looking man in gold-rimmed glasses and a sober suit and tie. Not the most passionate-looking man in the world. Mild. Equitable, for the most part. But a man of surprising emotional depths. More intricate than you could ever have imagined.

151

Elizabeth said, 'Mrs Billington?'

'That's right.'

Georgia Hutchinson had been right. Mrs Billington was as plain as a pikestaff — except for her very blue eyes. A brighter blue than her famous sister's. Well-scrubbed skin, tangerine lipstick. Solid thighs and solid arms inside a sober navy blue linen frock. Her springy, greying hair was drawn back in a tortoiseshell band. Thirty years ago, it would have been a tawny brown. Thirty years ago, Elizabeth thought, so was mine.

'I'm Elizabeth Blair.'

'You'd better come in.'

Doome Down Barn was an ancient stone building with a huge arched entrance and iron lacework gates. The house stood in the middle of a cobbled and herb-filled yard. There was a courtyard feel about the place. A sunny yellow hall led into a huge sitting room with patio windows then back into a shady conservatory with light filtering in from the orchard outside.

'Have a seat. I'll fetch the tea.'

'Tea would be great.' Elizabeth prepared to wallow in quiet luxury for a few moments. She flopped into the deepest of sofas. Watched the light flickering through the trees,

152

admired the tall Greek Revival lamp, the pink checked cushions in the window-seats, the orange lilies outside the open door.

The house relaxed around her. A very pleasant house. Plush would be a better word. Pity about the loud fabric (cheery yellow lemons and red plums) covering the chairs. But you couldn't win them all.

'So — what's this all about?' Daphne Billington put the tea tray down on the table and unloaded the teapot, two china cups, two tea plates to match, milk, sugar and a glass stand with a fat jam sponge-cake. 'You mentioned my half-sister.'

'Flora Messel. Yes,' Elizabeth said. 'This is a touch difficult. I don't want to alarm you, but we've been asked to investigate her death.'

'By whom?'

Elizabeth told her.

'But why on earth does this Lovett man want you to investigate?'

'He thinks she may have been murdered.' Behind them a burgeoning clematis threatened to climb in through the window. Elizabeth watched her hostess closely. Daphne Billington's eyebrows went into an arch and then down again.

'You are joking?'

'I'm afraid not.'

'So what grounds does he have for this claim?'

Elizabeth gave her the basic facts as she knew them. Mrs Billington sat and listened. For one moment Elizabeth thought she was going to get angry, but then her expression changed and, abruptly, she smiled.

'Something's amusing you.'

'Not really. It's just — well, this may be indiscreet of me, but I should tell you that my half-sister and I weren't close.'

'I had heard.'

'Had you indeed? Then you may as well know at this stage that Flora was a little cat. I used to joke that one day somebody would murder her. That's what struck me as funny. I wanted to kill her hundreds of times. Oh, my God. I've just realised. You came here because you thought — you may have got me on your list of suspects.'

Elizabeth said, 'I have you down as having the strongest motive. I believe your half-sister inherited a house that once belonged to your mother. That must have upset you.'

'Yes. I was very angry about it.'

'I can imagine.' Elizabeth watched Daphne Billington slowly filling her cup. 'So why did your father do such a thing? I'm sorry to ask, but it helps to have the full picture.'

'Why did he leave my mother's house to

Flora? Because she was his favourite. And because she was prepared to flatter him and pet him into giving her practically anything she wanted. Whereas I'm Joe Blunt. Always have been, always will be. I told him the truth and not what he wanted to hear.' She picked up a small, bone-handled knife. 'Did you ever see Flora on stage, Mrs Blair?'

'Only in some film or other.' Elizabeth struggled to remember its title. All she could recall was a scene in which Flora, playing someone's Parisian mistress, stood outside a lighted window in long grass with bare feet.

'Well, she was talented. She had an aura, a great charm when she chose to exert it. And our father always fell for it hook, line and sinker. She could twist him round her little finger. Anything Flora wanted, Flora could get.'

'Did he tell you he was going to leave her the house?'

'No. It was a great shock.' Daphne Billington had cut her piece of sponge-cake into tiny squares; she pushed one around her plate, picking at the crumbs. 'My father and I had our differences over the years. I resented him marrying again and I never got on with my stepmother. I thought her vulgar and I said so.'

'But you still expected your share of the house?'

'I never doubted it. Not once. It belonged to my mother's family and he knew how much it meant to me.'

'When was the will made?' Elizabeth asked.

Daphne Billington looked grim. 'He made a new will three months before he died and no one knew a thing about it. They found it in one of the drawers of his desk.'

'Signed and witnessed?'

'Yes. Witnessed by his housekeeper and the nurse who was on duty at the time.'

'A nurse? He was ill?'

'He'd been ill for a number of years.'

'And what was wrong with him exactly?'

'Old age, basically. He'd had two hip operations and then a knee operation, which didn't work. And he was just generally frail.'

'Of both mind and body?'

'Not of mind. No. Otherwise we'd have contested the will.'

'I'm surprised you didn't.'

A small shrug. 'My husband said we'd never prove anything and it would cost a small fortune. So, in the end, his judgement prevailed. In some ways I wish it hadn't. I would have felt better — less frustrated — if I'd been able to do something instead of sitting around feeling bitter. Bitterness eats into you.' She looked beyond Elizabeth, at the garden. 'Several of the villagers said they were going to club together and fight the will in court. All the cottages are owned by the estate as well, you see.'

My, my. Are they indeed? 'They didn't fancy Flora running the show?'

'They're very loyal to the Wharton family. They didn't think it right. So they got a meeting together. Someone rang and asked me to come along.'

'And did you?'

'How could one not? I grasped the nettle and went over there to talk to them.'

'So what happened?'

'Not much. It seems that Flora managed somehow to charm them out of it. She always knew how to wheedle.' She put down her cup. Some deep-felt resentment flickered for a moment in her eyes.

Elizabeth popped a piece of her cake into her mouth. Then she cast a glance down at her list of queries. Keeping her eyes fixed on the list, she said, 'So, who inherits Nether-shute now that your half-sister is dead?'

'I do. And before you say anything else, I realise that puts me in a very dodgy position.'

'A very pleasant position, I'd say. But yes, I have to say it also gives you a powerful motive for murder.'

'If it was murder.'

'If it was murder, which we have yet to establish.'

'Well, if you want my opinion, it's a load of nonsense.'

'You may be right.' Elizabeth moved to the next question. 'Could I ask where you were on the day your half-sister died?'

'Certainly you may ask. I've nothing to hide. I was in a hotel in Tetbury. I went to a needlework exhibition there with my friend, Bobby. Ask her if you don't believe me. She can vouch for me all day. I was still there in a tea shop when Johnny rang from the office to say that Flora had died. I went home at once, of course. Johnny thought it best.'

Elizabeth said, 'So when was the last time you saw Miss Messel?'

Daphne sent her mind back. 'She came over here the Sunday after my father's funeral. She claimed she wanted to put things right between us. That she felt terrible about inheriting the house, she had no idea why he'd done it, but she didn't want me to be cross with her. All a total sham, of course. I told her that if she wanted to put things right, she should let me have my share of the house. But she wasn't having any of that. Dear me, no! She didn't feel that guilty. All she wanted was to salve her conscience. Not that her conscience was ever a very large receptacle. It never seemed to stick around for long and you certainly never saw it in action.'

Elizabeth said, 'You were very attached to Nethershute. I can understand why. Was Flora as fond of the house as you were?'

'I can't see how. If she'd cared at all about Nethershute, she'd have been there more often.'

'So how often was she there?'

'Once in a blue moon. She'd come and go. It broke my heart to see the old place sitting there empty, like — like a stage-set for her precious showbiz friends to weekend at. It was always a family house. There have been Whartons at Nethershute for centuries.' When Mrs Billington was upset, her voice rose, her vowels became even more chiselled. 'My children should have been there. A house needs people to care for it.'

'But Miss Messel seems to have cared for it. She spent money on it.'

'Money!' Abruptly she tossed her tea down. 'What's that got to do with anything? She didn't even stay in the house when she was working in Bath.'

'Apparently she was always drained after a performance. Too tired to drive.'

A dismissive laugh. 'It's only ten miles, for God's sake. A quarter of an hour by car.'

True. Elizabeth said, 'Can I ask you something else? Did your half-sister inherit money with the house?'

'Money?' Daphne practically hit the roof. There was a definite flair for drama in the Messel genes. 'There was money, once upon a time. Wharton money. But my father spent all that years ago, mostly on keeping his new wife in her little luxuries.'

'I see. So Flora inherited a house but no money with which to maintain it?'

'Oh, that wouldn't bother her, I can assure you. She could always get hold of money. Men practically threw it at her. Dear little Flora always fell on her feet.'

Elizabeth did not reply to this, simply started packing things back into her bag and sliding the zip across. 'So you'll be moving back to Nethershute before too long?'

'After things have been settled. Which might take time.' After a pause, she said, 'Johnny's not too keen on the idea. He's very much attached to this place. But he knows Nethershute is in my blood. And it's our children's future.'

So all's well that ends well, Elizabeth thought.

For some.

★　★　★

An hour later, towards the tail end of that afternoon in early summer, when the café tables and the streets were emptying and the hotels beginning to fill up, Elizabeth picked up an evening paper, tucked it under her arm and made her way purposefully up the narrow alley with its black, wrought-iron palings towards number 14 Elliott Buildings. The house, though unpretentious, had a Regency balcony on the first floor and the remains of an easy, aristocratic look. Tall windows remained obstinately upper-class, though framed in dirt and draped with uncongenial net curtains.

Yes, this was it. Two shabby pillars, steps littered with pigeon droppings and a front door that had once been handsome. Might even be so again with a lick of the right-coloured paint and a good soft cloth and some Brasso on that lovely old knocker. Make it feel like home again. Give it back its dignity. It's a gentleman's house, but gone downhill.

One of these days, Elizabeth thought, as she climbed the steps and looked for the bell, I'll move into town. Buy one of these sad old places and bring it back to life. Wouldn't that be fun now?

You think you can afford it?

Maybe not, but what's the point in always

playing safe? You take out a bigger mortgage. Live a little. Nothing wrong with that. Is there? She found the bell, pressed it hard, stood back and looked at the house with a speculative eye.

Yes, you really could be made very fine again. Flowers, lights in the windows, a few good pieces of furniture. Not to mention the odd quilt or two to lighten the gloom . . .

'Yes? Can I help you?' The words, spoken with some abruptness, snapped uncomfortably into her daydream. The woman was a dull-looking type in a navy trouser suit. Mousy hair, old while still young, mouth like a trap.

'I certainly hope so. I'm looking for a girl called Mireille Bucolin. A French girl. I was told she had a room here.'

Well, not told exactly. The French waiter, the previous night, had needed coaxing to give out details of Mireille's address. Elizabeth had lain in wait, two doors down from the restaurant, for over an hour, tucked back into a shop doorway, until the boy in the distinctive green T-shirt had emerged. Had followed as he crossed the street and loped away down the pavement, swinging his rucksack over his right shoulder, a tall boy with dark hair in a little quiff like Tintin. Elizabeth had caught up with him as he turned into the abbey churchyard.

'Excuse me,' she had said rapidly, 'but would you be Mireille's friend? What a stroke of luck! I was wondering how I was going to get hold of her.'

'Mireille?' The boy stopped and turned.

'Yes. The little French girl who works with you at Le Jardin. I was hoping to catch her as she left, only I must have missed her.'

'It's Mireille's night off.'

'Then I guess that explains why she wasn't there.' Elizabeth turned on her Yankee grin. 'Oh, damn it, now what am I going to do? I promised to get this to her tonight.' Pulling the package out of her pocket, she stood there looking at it. 'It's a present for her mother's birthday. Something she ordered from my shop.'

'I could give it to her tomorrow,' the boy said.

'Too late, I'm afraid. She needed to pack it up tonight. I don't suppose you have any idea where she lives? If it's in town, I could take it round.'

The merest hint of hesitation. 'Elliott Buildings, I think.'

'Any idea what number?'

'I don't know the number, but it has a postbox right outside the door. She was telling me how handy it was.'

'That's wonderful. Thanks a bunch. I can't tell you how grateful I am.'

So here she was. Mireille's landlady (God, she looked hard) uncrossed her arms and said, 'What is it you want her for?'

Elizabeth, cheerfully beaming, trotted out the story about the shop purchase, even embroidering it a little. 'I had to get it in specially and they only delivered it late this afternoon.'

'Really?'

'I'm so sorry to call so late, only it has to get there by Monday and I told her it would take at least a week.'

'I suppose it would.' The woman looked at her grimly.

'So is she in? Could I see her?'

She thought about it. Not a single expression crossed her face. 'I'm afraid not.'

'But it's urgent. I won't keep her long. I just wanted to hand the package over myself.'

A faint twitch of the mouth that might have been a smile. 'Not much chance of that,' she said drily.

Elizabeth said, 'She's not in?'

'She most certainly is not. She did a moonlight flit.'

'You mean she left?'

'Owing me rent. The little madam. If I ever catch up with her, she'll know it.'

17

'Here's the turning,' said Ginger, pointing to a narrow lane just before the next bend. 'According to his directions, it's half a mile down to the house.'

'There's no sign,' Max told her.

'Probably deliberate. He wouldn't want the groupies to find him.'

Max swung the car into the lane, which had deep potholes, hedges that swept against the sides of the car and tall grass down the middle. 'Bloody hell! You'd think he could afford to have the road done.'

'Just look at the cow-parsley!'

Max tried to steer the car round a dried mud crater and swore as he went into it. 'Damn the cow-parsley. Are you sure this is right?'

'Positive. I wrote it all down. He said it's a bit overgrown but he likes it that way.' Ginger peered ahead through an ocean of cow-parsley. When they had bumped on for a bit, she glanced warily at him and said, 'I hope you're not going to sulk all day.'

'Who's sulking?'

'You are. You've hardly said a word all the way down.'

'Nothing to say.'

'There's plenty you want to say.'

'You can read my mind, I suppose?'

Ginger said, 'Like a book. You think the silent treatment will wear me down.'

'I don't know what you're talking about,' he said, being deliberately obtuse.

Ginger thought about counting to ten and rejected the option. 'Sometimes, you know, you can be a complete prat.'

He met her glance with an open blue gaze. 'I love it when you throw compliments around.'

'In that case, I'll throw a few more. You want to be right all the time. You don't know the first thing about women. And you're not half as funny as you think you are.'

'Anything else?' he enquired, changing gear with a jerk and accelerating over a particularly long clump of grass. The lane seemed to be degenerating into a cart track.

'You think you're so clever. I'll tell you something. I made the right decision the other night. It would drive me up the wall to live with you.'

Max said, 'So I won't bother — ' The car lurched, hit a bump and shot sideways, grazed a rusting piece of farm machinery half buried in the nearside ditch. 'Shit!' he said.

Ginger returned to her cow-parsley admiring and smiled while he wrestled the car out of the deep rut. The lane, which ran now through high woods, closed in around them. There was a beechy, ferny smell underneath the spreading branches.

★ ★ ★

Stanton Manor, Sean Donahue's country seat, was separated from the woods that surrounded it by high stone walls. The house had a rather beautiful if stocky-looking eighteenth-century façade. If the orchards and gardens seemed overgrown and forgotten about, the terraces in front of the glittering windows were well tended.

Donahue was sitting on the front terrace, staring out over the lawn to the shade of the woods. He was a strikingly dark man, hollow-cheeked, almost haggard-looking. An almost-handsome Heathcliff in a white shirt and designer jeans. The reflections of the Virginia creeper behind him gave him a romantic green pallor. He came out of the trance as Max slammed the car door. Came slouching down the steps, hands in pockets.

'Max Shepard?' The blue eyes were penetrating, his mouth sarcastic-looking.

'That's right.' Max held out his hand.

Donahue ignored it. Unfazed, Max said, 'This is my assistant, Jane Dickinson.'

Donahue said, 'You're the girl who called me?'

'That's right,' Ginger said, thinking that he was shorter than she'd imagined.

'Good of you to see us,' Max said quickly.

'Oh, I'm quite a nice guy,' Donahue said in a mocking voice, 'contrary to rumour.'

There was a silence and Ginger began to wonder whether they were to conduct the interview standing there on the gravelled drive. She had expected to take an instant liking to him, but at the moment she wasn't aware of him as anything more than a slightly menacing guy who looked bored out of his head.

'Nice place you've got here,' said Max conversationally.

'I've gone respectable,' Donahue said. 'Didn't you know?'

He's enjoying putting us at a disadvantage, Ginger thought, keeping us standing here. Well, blow that for a game of soldiers. 'I read somewhere,' she said, 'that you were born in a council house in Manchester.'

'You heard right. Two mouldy bedrooms, outside lavvy, backyard you couldn't swing a cat in and an inspiring view of the crap floating in the canal.'

'I was born in Manchester,' Max said.

'The posh end?'

'Not that posh.'

'Bet you didn't sleep on an old sofa stuck out on the landing?'

'Not exactly.' Max was looking nervous.

'I bet you had fish knives and soup spoons?'

'Can't remember,' mumbled Max.

'Well,' said Donahue, 'that's that sorted. Coffee on the terrace?' he suggested.

'Right. Thanks,' said Max.

They followed their host up the flight of steps. At the top, pinks flowered in terracotta pots.

A girl with long blonde hair brought out the coffee. Her pretty smile came out and went in again. She unloaded the tray on to the blue-painted table and took the empty tray back in through the open french windows.

'OK. So you wanted to talk about Flora?' Donahue settled himself, elbows propped on the arms of his canvas chair, fingers lightly meeting. 'What's going on?'

Max told him. Donahue listened hard, his legs stretched under the table, and let it sink in. 'You think she was murdered?'

'Mr Lovett does.'

'Then he's a fool. But I knew that anyway.'

'Could you elaborate on that?'

'He was a fool about Flora. Besotted with her. He drove her mad.'

'Did she tell you that?'

'All the time. She used to laugh at him. Poor old Jimmy. That's what she called him.'

'But she stayed at his hotel. Why do that if he drove her mad?'

Donahue laughed. 'You're not that naïve. The room was a freebie. Flora took all she could get out of life.'

'I see,' Max said. 'Then they weren't having an affair?'

'Good God, no!' Donahue reached for the coffee pot. 'Who told you that?'

'Can't remember.' Max took the mug of coffee that had been pushed towards him. 'We heard that you were involved with Miss Messel yourself.'

'Depends what you call involved.'

'To put it bluntly, you had an affair.'

'We had something going.'

'For how long?'

He didn't instantly reply to this question. But then he said, 'You do want to know a lot. For about a year.'

'So it was over at the time Miss Messel died?'

'God, yes. Months before.'

'And whose decision was it to end the relationship?'

'Mine. She was getting a bit heavy. Wouldn't let me breathe. And I couldn't stand her pretentious friends. Arty-farty theatricals. It caused friction.'

'I see.' Max took a long sip of his coffee. It was good. The expensive stuff. 'So could you tell me when you last saw Miss Messel?'

'It must have been . . . let's see now.' Donahue examined the air in front of him. 'It would have been December. She was down here for a Christmas break and she asked me to meet her in town for a drink.'

'So you met where?'

'At the hotel. Lovett's.'

'She was staying there?'

'No. She was at Nethershute, but we had a meal at the hotel.'

'So you were on good terms at that point?'

'Until about half-way through the evening. Yes.'

'And what happened half-way through the evening?'

'I told her I wanted to call it a day.'

'You wanted to end the relationship?'

'That's right.'

'And how did she react?'

'How do you think? She wasn't too happy. In fact, she gave me hell.'

'There was a scene in the restaurant?'

'Not a scene exactly. She got very actressy. I tried to calm her down.'

'Did you succeed?'

'For a while.'

'And how did the evening end?'

'We got pissed together. I called a taxi and offered her a lift home. She refused and said she'd spend the night at the hotel.'

'And did she?'

'As far as I know. You'd better ask poor Jimmy.'

Funky music began to filter out of the house behind them. The blonde came drifting out through the french windows and floated down the steps with a pair of secateurs in her hand. Flora's successor? Ginger wondered. Younger, more beautiful, more vibrant. That's how it goes.

Donahue suddenly caught her eye as if to say, 'So who are you looking at? Is she anything to do with you? Well, fuck off, then.'

Wondering how she could have got her former hero so glaringly wrong, Ginger found herself going back over the history of his life as she knew it. Art student. Gigs in London. Picked up by some radio journalist who offered to manage his band and make them regulars on the pub-rock circuit. Then a record deal with Pye and a lucrative

172

ninety-week chart run for the label. His band had supported another act in the USA, but ructions in the dressing rooms meant that he'd never quite made it there.

He was known in Britain for his cult singles. Had signed with Polydor as a solo artist. Had also made his film début. A cameo role in an art-house movie called . . . She couldn't remember. But most of all, he played a wonderful clarinetty sort of piano and wrote songs like an angel. Michael, she decided now. The one always spoiling for a good fight.

'Can I ask you something?' she said.

'You can ask, I might not answer.'

'Where did you meet Flora?'

He said, 'In a hotel bar. Some kind of fringe festival. It was three a.m. We were drinking with a whole crowd of people. Models, hangers-on. And in the middle of them all, Flora appeared. She was doing some kind of experimental theatre just for fun. She was like that. A wild child. Couldn't stand being pigeon-holed. I'm a loner as well. We just hit it off.'

'Did you meet her family?' Max asked.

'Not exactly.'

Max waited.

'I didn't meet them, but I felt as if I had. She used to talk about them.'

Max said, 'What impression did you get of them?'

'She was close to the old man. Oh, she used to wind him up. He was a real old Tory. A Little Englander. When she got married the first time to this French guy, her old man went mad. She didn't care. She thought it a huge joke. Told him if he didn't behave, she'd give him a half-French grandchild.'

'And the second husband? How did he go down?'

Donahue leaned back, his hands clasped behind his head. 'Even worse. Trevelyan's a bit of a leftie. The old man couldn't stand him.'

'Miss Messel had a sister, I believe?'

'The delightful Daphne.'

'You met her?'

'Once.'

'And?'

'And that was enough.'

'You didn't like her?'

'She's a roaring snob. That about sums her up.'

'I gather they didn't get on, Daphne and Flora?'

'The only thing they had in common — apart from their father's blood — was a gift for riling people and a love of Nethershute.' He shifted in his chair, stretched his arms, brought his hands down to his knees and eyed them with an impatient air. 'That it? Any more questions? No? Then, if you don't mind, I've got things to do.'

Perhaps it was the disillusioned look on Ginger's face that made him lunge at her with a sudden snappy question. 'What's up? Not had your money's-worth?'

'I didn't say that.'

'You didn't have to.' He flashed her a look of irritation. 'I've been fairly civil. I'm not pissed. Or off my head with cocaine.'

'Put all that behind you?' Ginger asked. Max was frowning at her. But what the hell? She wasn't going to be browbeaten.

'Too bloody expensive,' he said, 'in more ways than one. Anyway, my work was suffering.'

'I like your work.' She hadn't meant it to come out like that. Like, I love your music, but you're a pain in the butt.

'I'm deeply grateful.'

'Think nothing of it.'

For the first time he almost smiled, looking full at her with his dark blue eyes. And for half a second, he was another person entirely. But not for long. 'I take it this has been a private conversation? You won't go running to the press? If you do, I'll get my lawyers on to you.'

Max said hurriedly, 'You can rely on our confidentiality. That's what I tell all our clients.'

'Good. Only there are journalists who go white at the sound of my name.'

'I wonder why,' Ginger said.

Max threw her a black look and said, 'There's just one last question, Mr Donahue. Where were you the day Flora Messel died?'

'I was at my other house in London. The first I heard of Flora's death was on the television news that evening.'

'It must have been a great shock.'

'What do you think? I was devastated. I mean, we'd split and everything, but . . . ' His eyes had gone bleak, 'You don't expect a thing like that. It knocks you for six.'

★　★　★

'Shan't take you again,' Max said, when they had got back to the office.

'Any particular reason?' Ginger asked, with a mixture of sweet and sour.

'You were deliberately putting his back up.'

'It was up already.'

'I don't care.'

'Well, I care! In my opinion — '

'I don't pay you to have opinions.'

'My God, you're pompous!'

'Children . . . children,' Elizabeth said, rather threateningly. 'Neither of you seems to be in a particularly good mood.'

'He doesn't pay me enough to be in a good mood,' Ginger said.

Elizabeth asked to be filled in on the visit to Donahue. She sat listening to the report thoughtfully. 'Odd pair,' she said at last. 'Flora and Donahue. They sound as if they deserved each other. So,' she said, with a sudden change of topic, 'anyone got any idea where little Mireille might have cleared off to?'

'Mireille?'

'That's right. She seems to have walked out of her lodgings.'

'So ask at the restaurant.'

'I did.'

'And?'

'They haven't seen her since she left work the day before yesterday.'

18

'Anybody notified her parents?' Max asked.

'They called her father, but he didn't know anything about a change of address.'

'It's only a couple of days. Does she have friends? Boyfriends?'

'Not that anyone knows of.'

'Do the police know?'

'Madame Valéry reported her missing this afternoon.'

'And?'

Elizabeth shrugged. 'They said they'll make enquiries. But she's a teenager. They're always bunking off.'

'She'll probably turn up, then, in a day or two.'

'I certainly hope so.'

★   ★   ★

Elizabeth stood in the shop window a half-hour later, unhooking a Strippy Saw-tooth and hitching at a corner of its border, which had wedged itself under the display stand. The sun, slanting in at an angle, was warm on her back. I liked the girl, she thought, but there was something odd going on. She couldn't be involved in this murder — if it is a murder — could she? She'd only just arrived in Bath. And she didn't know Flora Messel. I'd swear to it. Well, she might have flung her the odd glance. Might even have half recognised her, like I did. But anything else? No. Sitting there right next to each other on the train for over an hour . . . it would have shown.

Unless the girl, too, was a consummate actress. But, no. I don't believe it. Not at that age.

OK, so let's take her at face value. She didn't know Flora, but she picked up Flora's book by mistake and went to return it. She met the actress briefly at the hotel.

Maybe saw someone else as well. The murderer.

If there is a murderer.

No. You're pushing it all too far. It's pure speculation.

* * *

The next morning Caroline was back in the shop. She looked as if she might fade out again like a television screen at any moment, but she was determined to be useful if not too audible.

'You OK?' Elizabeth asked, wanting her to sit down.

'I'm fine.' She said it in a gentle whisper, not daring to raise her voice.

Elizabeth glanced at her, apprehensively. She looked immensely fragile this morning, almost too delicate to talk to. The early-morning sun was very bright. Caroline didn't have to say that she would feel more stable if it went behind a good, muzzy cloud.

'Sure?'

'Honestly.'

'OK. But if there's anything you want . . . '

'Thanks.'

'If you need me, just — '

'I have your mobile number.' She smiled peakily and vanished into the kitchen, emerging a minute later with a bottle of fizzy water in her hand. 'You don't mind?' she asked.

'My dear girl, feel free.'

Upstairs Ginger and Max were studiously ignoring each other. This is going to be a dilly of a day, Elizabeth thought. Already it has a feel about it. Like it wants to go straight back to bed and pull the blankets over its head. 'Delightful atmosphere round here,' she said to Max. 'Do I take it that you two are not on speaking terms?'

'Take it how you like,' Max said.

Ginger's face looked up from the envelope she was opening. 'He's in a strop because I won't move in with him.'

'Into his flat?'

Max said, 'Tell the whole world, why don't you?'

'Elizabeth's not the whole world. She's family.'

'And your flatmate?' Max said. 'Bloody Oonagh? Is she family?'

'No. But she's a friend and I was fed up with your attitude and she's a good person to talk to.'

'So what else did you tell her about while you were at it?' Max stood on the other side of the desk, looking tense and furious. Things were obviously not tickety-boo. His ego had been well and truly punctured, given one hell of a clump.

'Nothing,' Ginger said shortly.

'Who are you trying to kid? You've been chopping it all up into little pieces together. What I say. What you say. What we get up to in bed, I shouldn't wonder. I've heard about these shrinks — '

'You know your trouble?' Ginger glared back at him. 'No brains. You're just a walking ego.'

* * *

Elizabeth beat a tactical retreat. It seemed prudent.

A quarter of an hour later she was walking into the entrance hall of Lovett's Hotel and approaching the reception desk. Rosemary Lovett stood flicking through a pile of papers on the shelf behind her.

Elizabeth said, 'Hi. Remember me?'

'Mrs Blair,' she said coolly.

'Elizabeth — please. Is your husband around?'

'I'm afraid not.' A purse of the lips. 'He's not well.'

'Oh dear. I am sorry. Nothing too serious, I hope?'

'He's been doing too much. But that's nothing new.' Mrs Lovett, who had finished rifling through the papers, gazed back at Elizabeth. 'Is there something I can do for you?'

'Possibly.' Elizabeth said, 'I wanted to ask him something that slipped my mind. I understand that Miss Messel had a visitor around lunchtime on the day she died. A French girl . . . Mireille Bucolin apparently turned up here to return a book she'd picked up by mistake. A pale blue paperback.'

'I don't recall any French girl.'

'Were you on reception that day?'

'Until about one o'clock. Yes. But we were frantically busy with the Jane Austen convention. You'd have had a hard job picking out anybody.'

Elizabeth asked, 'Is there a side door?'

'No. There's a small entrance in the lane at the back, but I hardly think she'd have found her way around there.'

'I did hear that one of your waiters ... Craig ... showed Mireille up to Miss Messel's room that day.'

'Really? Well, I have no knowledge of it.' Again she sent out a cool, forceful glance.

Elizabeth stood thinking for a moment or two and then said, 'Could you tell me what happened to Miss Messel's personal belongings?'

'The things she left in her room? Certainly. Her sister came and fetched them.'

'Did she now? Was there a lot of stuff?'

'Rather a lot — yes. Two Italian leather weekend bags and a holdall.'

'So who packed the bags? You or Miss Messel's sister?'

'The sister — Mrs Billington — packed it all up.'

'An upsetting task, I should imagine, under the circumstances.'

'She didn't seem unduly upset. Or if she was, she didn't show it,' Mrs Lovett said. 'Is that all? Because I have rather a lot on my plate.'

But Elizabeth was not yet prepared to duck out. She pinned on her warmest smile. 'I won't keep you long. So you didn't happen to see a pale blue paperback among Miss Messel's belongings?'

'I told you. Her sister packed everything up.'

'You didn't even go up to her room to pack a bag for her when she was taken off to hospital?'

'No. James went with the ambulance, but he was in too much of a state to think about things like that and I had a hotel to run.' Was there a slight touch of Cockney under the carefully modulated voice?

'Of course,' Elizabeth said understandingly. At this point the question she had to ask would wait no longer. She continued to look steadily at Rosemary Lovett with shrewd green eyes. 'Could I be very cheeky and ask you rather a personal question? How did you get on with Miss Messel? I suppose what I mean to say is, did you dislike her as much as everyone else seemed to?'

She considered. The element of flattery in the question did its work. 'Flora was a pain in the neck. I hated her on sight and I went on

184

hating her. I made no bones about it then or now.'

More candid than one could have hoped. Perhaps there was a chance after all of getting underneath this contemptuous woman's skin. Contemptuous and unhappy, Elizabeth thought. There's a sense of isolation about her.

'Then her habit of staying here when she was in town must have been . . . '

'A thorn in my flesh? You're very quick.' She seemed to find the line of questioning amusing.

'But she still came. And paid nothing for the room, I understand?'

'You understand correctly,' she said caustically, 'Are you married, Mrs Blair?'

'I'm a widow.'

'But you were married?'

'Yes.'

'Happily?'

'Very happily.'

'Then you were lucky.'

'Very lucky.'

'Your husband was a sensible man?'

'As sensible as they come. He was a country lawyer.'

'Ah, well . . . ' The note of irony again. 'He would never have gone off the rails.'

'He took the occasional illicit fishing trip.

That was about as far as it went.'

'Lucky you.' For a moment she looked envious. Then she said, 'My husband went to drama school. Did he tell you?'

'I did hear.'

'Yes, well, the trouble with James is that he never got over his theatrical yearnings. He only ever had a minor talent. He'll tell you that himself. He never made any money at it. I kept him for years while he played the odd minor role. Left alone, he'd have given up and come back down to earth. But he bumped into Flora again and that was it. She put the stars back into his eyes.'

It was said with an edge. Bitter, Elizabeth thought. Ferociously so. You're as tough as hell, but it haunts you, this taste your husband had for another woman. 'They were having an affair?'

'Oh, I shouldn't think so for one minute.' The reply was of a startling directness and accompanied by a smoky laugh.

'But I thought . . . '

'It would have been simpler if they were. Then there might have been a chance of it dying a death. But Flora preferred to pull his strings. He slept with her once or twice when they were students and poor old James has been living on it for the rest of his life. Sad, don't you think?'

For him and you, Elizabeth decided. The quiet of the hotel lobby was scented with the aroma of breakfast coffee.

'The answer to your question, Mrs Blair, is that I put up with Flora staying here because I got bored to death with arguing with him about it. If it kept the peace and distracted him for a few days and he was better-tempered for a while afterwards . . . ' A flap of the hand. 'Well, so be it. That's what I thought. Any more questions while you're at it?'

'Yes. You had an argument with Miss Messel the night before she died. Is that true?'

'Who told you?'

'One of the staff.'

'Yes, it's true. She was on her high horse and she'd had too much to drink at dinner and she was offensive to one of the staff. I caught her on the stairs later and I told her I found her lack of manners disgusting and that if she didn't respect my staff I wouldn't have her here again.'

'And what was her reaction?'

'She just laughed. I really think she got pleasure out of upsetting people. And she liked to do it in public with an audience to hand. Like when she gave that boyfriend of hers the push. She had to do it in the restaurant with other diners listening — '

'Boyfriend? Which boyfriend?'

'The pop star. Sean Donahue.'

'But surely he was the one who finished the relationship?'

'Is that what he's saying? Then he's a liar. I heard what he yelled at her as he stormed out . . . '

19

It was still early. A soft, slow morning. The streets were as yet uncrowded, save for the odd delivery lorry rattling into the courtyards behind the great houses that had turned themselves into hotels. The sun kept emerging from a cloud, pausing and going back in again.

Sean Donahue, Elizabeth thought. Writes weird and depressive lyrics. Lives in a very desirable property in the country.

Stanton Manor. Nethershute. All this prime property. How do they do it?

Mr Donahue told us a big, fat lie about who ended his affair with Flora Messel. Now why would he do that? To save his injured pride? Because he would rather be seen as the dumper rather than the dumpee? There was also of course, another more sinister scenario. If Flora had given him the elbow, we have a pretty powerful motive for murder. Anger. A desire for revenge. I think we might have to check Mr Donahue's alibi. Make quite sure he was in London the day Flora died.

Still walking, she went on turning it over in

her mind. Flora's credit cards, she thought suddenly. Were they ever found? Must check up on that, too. So many little scraps to be chased after. I'm like the guy with the spiked stick in the park over there. Collecting all sorts of odds and ends to be turned out of the bag later.

She decided against going back to the office. No way, she thought, until those two youngsters have got over their funny spell. She strolled very slowly back to where her car was parked. I'll go home, she thought. Give myself the rest of the morning off. A spot of thinking was called for and for that she needed peace and quiet.

★ ★ ★

Mireille Bucolin was wearing the same lavender sweatshirt she had worn on the train, but with a short, tight skirt. She looked in control of herself, but her fingers would keep fiddling nervously with the loose end of her watch-strap.

'Why won't you tell me?' the boy asked. They spoke swift French, leaning together on the wrought-iron railings by the side of the river.

'There's nothing to tell.'

'You think I'm stupid? Look — your

father's frantic. He keeps calling the restaurant. Let me tell him you're OK, at least.'

'No. Not yet.' She was adamant. Panicky at the very thought.

'You're being stupid. You know? Really stupid.'

'That's your opinion.'

'Yes, it is. And I'm right. You're in big trouble. If you get caught — if the papers get hold of it — well, you'll have messed your whole life up. And for what? If I had my way — '

'What? What would you do?' She sounded defiant and scared at the same time.

'Look — Mireille — I'm trying to help.'

'I know that. But you can't. I have to go. I'm already late.'

'You can't go.' His voice became more urgent. His hand gripped her arm. 'I won't let you. I'll go to the police and tell them what I know.'

'You don't know anything,' she said fiercely.

'I'll find out.'

'No. You won't,' she said, twisting her arm away. 'It's nothing to do with you. It's my life.'

* * *

191

He sits waiting for her in the car, scribbling something into the notebook that rests against the steering-wheel. A phrase comes into his head. He writes it down, thinks about it for a moment, frowns and then scratches it out again. An impatient tapping of fingers. His gaze fixes itself unseeingly on the park across the way. Then, in a self-assured movement, he lifts a wrist to glance at his watch.

She's late.

Five minutes more he sits there. Then he spots her trailing up the hill towards him. She looks very young, very clean, very prim and proper. Unless you know better, he thinks. Which I do. Oh, most certainly.

She spots the car, opens the passenger door, climbs in and shuts the door behind her.

'*Ca va?*' he asks.

'*Ca va.*' But she's unhappy, uneasy. Her cheeks are very pale.

'OK. Let's go,' he says in French.

'I don't know if — '

'If what?'

Flax blue eyes, pure and grave, glance across at him. She sits gazing at him as if she has never seen him before.

'Mireille? What's wrong?'

'It's all going wrong. I'm afraid.'

'Of what?'

'Of the police. This detective.'

'Look, we talked it through. There's no need — '

'How do I know that?' Her fingers are shaking as she pushes her hair back from her forehead. 'I don't know that. I want to call my father.'

'That's not a good idea. Not yet.' He puts a hand on her knee. 'It's OK. I'll look after you.'

She sits there bolt upright in the seat next to him. 'Louis thinks I'm mad,' she blurts out.

'The boy at the restaurant?'

'Yes.'

'I shouldn't have let you see him.'

'I had to. I told you. I left my address book in his flat.'

'You're hopeless.' His voice softens for a moment. 'You didn't tell him — '

'No. Don't worry.' She sounds weary. 'I didn't tell him anything.'

'You're sure?'

'Positive.'

'That's OK then.'

'No. No, it's not OK. I want to go home.'

'Well, you can't. Not just yet.'

'Why can't I?'

'Because we need each other and you're

panicking for no reason.'

She shakes her head violently. 'I won't tell anybody. I promise.'

'We'll talk about it later.' He turns the key in the ignition and the engine springs into life.

★ ★ ★

Rain was falling when Elizabeth woke the following morning. She could hear it dripping from the guttering under the eaves and spattering against the half-open window. She got up and closed it, noting as she did so that Dottie had ambushed the milkman again and was having a good old chinwag with him. The poor guy was getting soaked, whereas Dottie, in her blue dressing-gown, was snug and dry underneath her porch.

Elizabeth dropped back before they could catch sight of her. Walked barefoot over warped boards to the bedroom door. She had reached the half-landing between the two front bedrooms when the phone rang.

Back into the bedroom.

It was Max. 'Guess what?' he said.

'I haven't a clue. Why don't you tell me?'

'Andy called. A body's been found in the staff cottage at Nethershute. Want to take a trip up there? I'll pick you up in half an hour.'

20

Thomas Bowman had found the body when doing his rounds the previous evening. Max had asked for him in the village and had been directed to his cottage at the back of the church. He thanked his stars that he had happened across him on that earlier visit, because the police had cordoned off Nethershute and were saying nothing until the official news conference later that day.

Thomas told his tale sitting on the wooden seat in his garden. His philosophical-looking face managed to look placid yet interested at the same time.

He told them the same story he had given the police. He was in the habit of keeping an eye on Nethershute, taking his usual walk around the grounds, no special time or route. Just acting as a watch-dog, you understand. Miss Messel had given him a set of keys, and after her death, the solicitor had been happy for him to be employed in the same capacity. Eyes and ears. Not as sharp as they used to be, but good enough, as events had proved.

Elizabeth said, 'So let me get this right. The

staff cottage had been empty for several months?'

'Ever since she moved out.'

'Who?'

'The Coote girl of course. Virginia Coote. That was her name. She worked for Miss Messel.'

'In what capacity?'

'General dogsbody. Well, she called herself housekeeper and personal assistant, but some folks do like to raise themselves up, if you know what I mean.'

'So she generally looked after the big house. Is that what you mean?'

'That one never looked after anything except her own interests.'

'Right. So, this housekeeper — what age would she have been, by the way?'

'A young thing. Early thirties.'

'And how long had Miss Coote worked at Nethershute?'

'Let's see now. Three years? Maybe four.'

'And she left — when?'

'Eight or nine months ago. I remember because young Joshua — that's my great-grandson — had just been born. Miss Flora came knocking on the door to say how pleased she was and that's when she let on that the girl had taken herself off.'

'Taken herself off?'

'They'd had a bit of a set-to, her and Miss Flora, and Ginny had walked out. Well, between you and me and that gatepost, she were a bit like that.'

'Like what?' Elizabeth sat admiring the pink rambler that stretched itself along the length of the cottage window.

'Well, you know — drugs and such.'

'Drugs?'

'I never saw it myself, but it was common knowledge that she got a bit lit up now and again. Or should I say switched off? What you will.'

Beside her, Max sat carefully composing his face.

'Can we get back to last night, Mr Bowman? You were doing your rounds. And I gather from what your neighbour told us that you found a body?'

'That's right.'

'Bit of a shock, I expect?'

'It might have been when I was a younger man. It's a bit of a licker when you're younger, but when you get to my time of life — well, I've seen a corpse or two in my time. And with Kingsley in the business, so to speak . . . I help him out, you see, when he's short-staffed.'

'Ah, yes. Kingsley.'

Elizabeth looked mystified.

Max said, 'Mr Bowman's son is an undertaker.'

'Is that so?'

'So you were letting yourself into the staff cottage — what time would this have been. Mr Bowman?'

'Sevenish. I often take a walk in the evening. And I thought I'll just take a look round the cottage. Pick up any letters or junk mail. There were one or two bits inside the front door. I gathered them together and it was then I noticed that someone had been in there. The kitchen was in a hell of a state, if you'll pardon my language. Dirty dishes in the sink. Half-eaten food on the table. You've never seen such a mess.'

'Had it been tidy on your last visit?'

'The week before? As straight as a new pin. So that's when I decided to take a look round upstairs. And I found her — '

'Her?'

'The body.' There was nothing much in the old man's blue gaze. 'I stopped at the top of the stairs to get my breath back and I noticed that the front bedroom door was ajar.'

'Was that unusual?'

'It was. I always shut the doors to cut down the risk of fire. And I'd shut it the week before.'

'So?'

'So I went over and I pushed the door open. And that's when I saw her?'

'Her?'

'She was half in and half out of the bed. Sprawled as if she were asleep. Only there was vomit all over the bedclothes and she was at a funny angle. And — well — she was dead. I knew as soon as I saw her. I shut the place up and came back here and I called the police.'

'Not the ambulance?'

'No point. She were as dead as a doornail.'

'Who was dead, Mr Bowman?'

'Why, the Coote girl, of course.'

'But — you said she left nine months ago.'

'So she did.'

'Had anyone seen her since that time?'

'Not that I know of. Not in the village. It would get around, you see.'

'I'm sure it would,' Elizabeth said, pushing the facts as she had heard them round her head.

Max had pulled a tablet of chewing-gum out of his pocket and was unwrapping it. 'Did she have any friends in the village?' he asked.

'Friends? Ginny Coote? Not here. Not the sort.'

'Not sociable?' Max asked.

'She were a townie. She didn't mix with the likes of us. She had her car and she took herself off to the bright lights.'

'London?'

'Bristol.' Thomas Bowman put Max right on that score.

'So what kind of car was it?'

'Ah, now you've got me. It were small and red. But as to the make . . . ' He shook his head.

'So was there a car parked outside the staff cottage when you found the body?'

'Now that's a point. You've got me there, young man. No, there wasn't. Odd that.'

★ ★ ★

'What do we do next?' Max asked.

'The sister, I think, don't you?'

'Flora Messel's sister?'

'She might fill in some more background detail about Ginny Coote. Accidental overdose, do you think, or something more sinister?'

'Better wait for the post-mortem, I suppose.'

'Yup. Any theories passing through your brain?'

'None that I'd care to run with. How about you?'

'Pass. Think it's connected with Flora's death?'

'Could be. One accidental death seems

OK. Two is more dodgy.'

'Uh-huh.' Her mind was moving on. 'There's one more person I'd like to call on while we're here.'

'Who's that?'

'The doctor's wife. Bosom friend of Flora's by all accounts.'

'Can't imagine Flora being bosomy.'

'Neither can I. But people are often a layer deeper than you think.'

'That's very profound.'

'Isn't it? So . . . I'd like to sound out the doctor's wife.'

'Don't ask me to come with you,' Max said. 'She threw me out of the house last time I dropped by.'

'OK. I'll be ten minutes or so. What will you do?'

'Well, there's always the pub,' Max said cheerfully.

* * *

Georgia Hutchinson's smile wasn't that welcoming, but as Elizabeth had told her she was Max's partner at the Shepard Agency, it wasn't surprising.

'I know you won't want to talk to me, but I'm desperate. I need all the information I can get about the girl who's

201

been found dead up at Nethershute and the police won't let anyone near.' She stood there on the doorstep looking as if all her bounce had gone. As if her energy had just run out.

'Why me?' A fine movement of her long lashes. She was a good-looking girl. Very posh, very thin, very polite.

'Max tells me you were a friend of Miss Messel's. I just thought you might know something about the dead girl.'

'Oh, no. I didn't know her at all. I'm sorry. She just worked for Flora.'

'As what?'

A light shrug. 'She took care of things up at the house.'

'You've no idea where she came from? How Miss Messel came to employ her?'

'From an agency, I should imagine.' A clock struck in the house behind her.

'I just wondered. Only she doesn't sound the usual type. I did hear — well, drugs were mentioned.'

'I can't tell you anything about that.' She looked thoroughly apprehensive. She was eager for Elizabeth to be gone. 'You must ask elsewhere. I'm sorry.' The door banged shut.

★   ★   ★

'So what did you make of her?' Max asked.

'Scared.'

'That's what I thought.'

'She knows things about Flora — about the set-up at Nethershute that she doesn't want to tell. We've got to do some more digging, Max.'

'Go on, then,' he said resignedly. 'Tell me where.'

'I think we'll go back to James Lovett. He's known Flora for years. Don't know why I didn't have a longer session with him in the first place. Let's get back to the office. And talking of the office, did you make it up with Ginger?'

'Make what up?'

'Oh, come on, Max. I've known you too long. Things aren't going very well, are they?'

He sat there staring out through the windscreen.

'Want me to talk to her? Have a heart-to-heart?'

'If you like.'

Must be bad, Elizabeth thought, if he's letting me butt in. 'OK. Leave it with me.' She put out a hand and patted his arm. 'Don't worry about it.'

'I'm not.'

He wasn't telling the truth. Small lies, she thought. They shelter us from the chilly wind. From a trickling fear about the future.

★ ★ ★

Back at the office, she called Sean Donahue's number. It rang and rang. She was about to put the phone down when a woman's voice answered. 'Yes? Hello?'

'I'd like to speak to Mr Donahue, if he's available.'

'I'm sorry. He isn't. Not at the moment.'

'Ah.'

'Can I take your name and number? He might be able to call you back. But it won't be today.'

'Pity. It's rather urgent. Are you his wife . . . girlfriend . . . secretary?'

She wasn't going to answer that one. 'If you'd like to leave your name and number.'

'My name is Elizabeth Blair. I'm from the Shepard Agency and I'd like to finished the interview that my . . . assistant . . . conducted with Mr Donahue the other day.'

A pause. Then the voice said, 'Mr Donahue didn't say anything about you coming back.'

'No? Well, I don't imagine he tells you everything, whoever you are. Tell him to call me, will you? Sooner rather than later. I'll give you my number.'

One of those stroppy moods was descending on her. They did on occasion. It was in the genes. Her mother, while not exactly argumentative, had liked a tilt at a good windmill. A quick wiry woman. Elizabeth sat there remembering her. Imperious might be a better word. But cheerful with it.

Ginger sat tapping away on her keyboard, apparently heedless of Elizabeth's presence in the room. What am I going to say to her? Elizabeth thought. How best to begin?

If truth were known, she was nonplussed by Ginger's decision not to move in with Max. The two of them are made for each other. Any fool can see that. There's no doubt she's head over heels in love with him. I've got eyes.

But the path of love was not always easy. A series of chicanes, more often than not. Elizabeth cleared her throat. 'Mind if we have a word?'

Ginger's fingers stopped tapping. She looked up.

'What's all this about you turning the boy down?' In for a penny, Elizabeth thought. No utter use pussyfooting around.

'Turning him down?'

'His offer. A roof over your head. A share of

his duvet. The God-given chance to spend your weekends struggling with the mouldy contents of his kitchen sink.'

Silence.

'He's pretty miserable, you know.' Elizabeth parked herself sturdily on the corner of the desk.

'I'm sorry, Elizabeth. It's private.' Ginger's forehead was creased.

'OK. Sorry to have butted in.'

Ginger flushed scarlet. 'Oh, sod it. Of course you want to know what's going on. You're stuck here in the middle of it.' A long, deep sigh. 'Sometimes I wish it had never started.'

'You and Max.'

No reply.

'You don't mean that,' Elizabeth said.

'No. But I was happy before, when we could have a good fight and it didn't really mean anything. You know?'

'I think so. Now it means too much?'

'Far too much. I can't cope. Can't concentrate.'

'Don't worry about it.' Elizabeth's eyes had a humorous gleam. She said, almost by way of a sideline, 'That's a new pot plant in the window.'

'I thought it would cheer the place up.'

'That bad?' Elizabeth said. 'Look — a

trouble shared is a trouble halved.'

The girl flushed, hesitated. 'It's difficult here. He might walk in.'

'Some other time, then?'

'Yes. Some other time.' Suddenly Ginger said, 'Come round for supper tomorrow night?'

'I'd enjoy that.'

'I'd say tonight, but I'm trying to arrange something with Max.'

'Sounds like a good idea.'

'He's got this thing about my new flatmate — Oonagh.'

'He does?' Elizabeth's surprise must have showed.

'No, not that kind of thing. I mean he disapproves of her. He's never even met her, but he's frightened of her. It's getting to be a fixation and it's driving me up the wall, so I thought I'd try and do something about it.'

'Such as?'

'Well, I've asked Max to come round for a talk this evening. What I haven't told him is that Oonagh's going to be there. And her boyfriend. He's a vet.'

'Really?'

'A lot older than her, but quite nice. I thought if Max got to know her, if we all had a drink together, he'd realise how stupid he's being. Only don't tell him they'll be there or he won't come.'

'Right.' A strictly formal reply, if a little sceptical. Elizabeth had a sense of danger looming. But her rule was never to interfere. Not unless it was strictly necessary.

She made a swift exit before she could change her mind and be tempted.

21

James Lovett looked dapper, but distinctly unwell, Elizabeth thought, when she went to talk to him that afternoon. He had managed to get up from his sickbed, but only just. He wore a sharp blue blazer and striped shirt as before, but his face was a colourless mask that was almost painful to behold.

He looked like a man whose light had gone out. At once remote and vulnerable. Elizabeth had seen that look before, after funerals when the reality of a loss was beginning to sink in.

Night happens suddenly, she thought. Poor sod.

'Don't you see?' he said abruptly. 'This second body. It's proof.'

'Of what?' Elizabeth asked.

'That Flora's death wasn't an accident.'

'It's a possibility. Did you know Miss Coote?'

'I knew her.' His voice was dry.

'So tell me about her.'

'Virginia Coote? I remember her laugh. She had the loudest, most vulgar laugh you ever heard. A dirty laugh.' His face creased with sudden disgust.

'So I gather you're not sorry she's dead?'

'I have no feelings about it,' he said.

Fibber. 'So how did Ginny Coote get the job in the first place? Through an agency?'

'Good God, no. What agency would employ scum like that?'

'Then how —'

'The girl latched on to Flora at some showbiz party. Started bragging about how she used to cook and organise for some City type who had a chalet in Switzerland. True as it happened, but it turned out he'd sacked her for incompetence and worse. But she made up some cock-and-bull story about him trying it on with her. Sexual harassment.'

'Which Miss Messel believed?'

'Not sure. Probably not, but that was Flora. She made instant decisions. Foolish decisions at times.'

'And this was one of them?'

'Yes. I thought so. I told her I thought the girl unstable and untrustworthy. I tried to warn her —'

'And what was her reaction?'

'She just laughed. 'Let her have a go,' she said. 'I like young people around.' Ginny Coote seemed to amuse her. Flora didn't seem to care what went on while she was away filming. The wild parties —'

'In the house? At Nethershute?'

'From what I hear. Flora gave Ginny permission to swim in the pool, so she had the keys to the place and it went on from there.'

'So anything could have been going on?' While the cat's away, Elizabeth thought.

He looked miserable. 'Flora was far too trusting.'

Trusting? Flora Messel? Elizabeth didn't think so. She might take in stray cats, but she would have some perception. Oh, yes, Flora would have known what was going on. Might even have been involved in — what? Drug-dealing? Whatever else that led to?

Now there's a thought.

She said, 'So you think the two deaths may be connected. Does that mean you suspect foul play? That Ginny Coote may have been murdered?'

'I shouldn't be surprised.'

'Why do you say that?'

'She knew a lot of dodgy people.'

'Seriously dodgy?'

'Like who?'

He had no real idea. Could name no names. He just knew by gut instinct.

'Did she have a boyfriend? Boyfriends?'

He didn't know that either, though various seedy-looking young men — leather jackets, drove like maniacs — had been seen with her in the village.

'OK,' Elizabeth said, with a slight feeling of exasperation. 'So can we talk about Sean Donahue?'

'That bastard.'

'You didn't like him?'

'I loathed him.'

'Your wife said Flora finished the affair. That he kicked up a fuss in your restaurant the night she told him.'

'That's right. I asked him to leave. He was using foul language.'

'Threatening her?'

'I suppose so.'

'You didn't mention this last time we spoke.'

'Didn't I?' He sounded vague.

'It might have helped.'

'I suppose so. To tell the truth, I was in a state.'

And you aren't now?

'I don't have much recall of what I said when we last met.'

That much was obvious. 'So the affair with Donahue was another of Miss Messel's bad decisions?'

'Yes.'

Possibly a fatal decision? 'Did he cause any more trouble after that night?'

'She had one or two abusive phone calls from him, I believe.'

Well, thanks for not telling me that, either. 'Anything else? Any physical threats?'

'Not that I know of.'

Something was bugging her. Something that filled her with curiosity. 'Wasn't it a mite tactless of Miss Messel to bring Donahue back to your hotel if she knew you were, shall we say, stuck on her?'

'No. Not really. We never talked about how I felt about her.'

'Really?'

'It would have embarrassed her.'

You think?

He said, with some emphasis, 'It was enough that she was my friend. I never really believed it, you know, and now that she's gone, it seems even more of an illusion.' One shaky hand went to his temple.

'But you went on loving her secretly?'

He said simply, 'I loved her so much. Still do. I knew she would never love me back. That would have been too much to expect.'

It seemed cruel to question him further on the subject. Elizabeth said, 'By the way, you wouldn't know if her missing credit cards turned up?'

'Sorry,' he said. 'You'll have to ask someone else. Her PA. Her solicitor.' He had turned deathly pale. Elizabeth felt a prickle of concern for him. 'Are you OK?' she asked.

'Do you want me to fetch your wife?'

'My wife?' He said it as if she no longer existed.

'I thought you might need someone.'

'My wife's . . . in London. Gone for the day. Shopping.'

'Just one more question,' Elizabeth said. 'It's a bit delicate.'

Warily he waited.

'Your wife. Rosemary. Does she cook?'

'I'm sorry?'

'Does she ever help out in the hotel kitchen?'

He still wasn't with her. She would have to go further. 'Is your wife a jealous woman?'

'Jealous of what?'

'Do I have to spell it out?'

He was with her at last. 'Jealous enough to put peanuts in Flora's sandwich?' He shook his head vehemently. 'No. Rosemary's not like that. Not capable of such a thing.'

'We're all capable of it, Mr Lovett, if we're pushed far enough.' It was the one thing she'd learned for certain from working in this business.

'In any case, Rosemary didn't go near the kitchen that morning.'

'You can vouch for it?'

'Of course. Ask anybody.'

Elizabeth thought back to her interview

with Sandra Shaddock. Wondered if Rosemary Lovett could have put pressure on the girl to lie for her. Tell them I tampered with Chef's sandwich and you'll lose your job. But was the flat-faced, dozy-looking little Sandra capable of such subterfuge? Elizabeth had her doubts.

★ ★ ★

'So,' Ginger said at eight forty-five that evening, 'here we are. I'm so glad you two have met at last.'

'Mmn,' said Oonagh, 'It's about time.'

'Long overdue. Great wine.'

'Steve's favourite.'

'Think he got lost?'

Too much to hope, Max thought. Wild evening. I'll kill Ginger. Weird woman, Oonagh. Even weirder than I imagined. Black, cropped hair. Eyes like currants. A fierce sort of a face. God, this wine's strong.

'He probably had to work late.' Oonagh's voice was weird too. Irish, very fast and very elaborate. It swooped around like she was trying to carve patterns in the air with it. 'He'll be along presently.'

How long's presently? Max wondered. His eyes were glazing.

'More wine?' Ginger said.

215

'Why not?' He held out his glass.

Oonagh plonked hers down on the table. 'So tell me, Max. What do you get out of being a detective?'

'A headache, mostly.'

She laughed, but then she was off again, chucking words around like they'd just been invented. 'You must see as many neurotics as I do. Poor sods with no one else to turn to. Sad souls swallowed up by dark gods.'

'I had someone searching for his tractor,' Max said.

She didn't seem to have heard him. 'Of course, it's like therapy. Somebody has to do it. At least, I suppose so. But don't you sometimes wish you could spend the day talking to normal people instead?'

If only, Max thought. He caught Ginger's eye. She was daring him not to behave himself. 'What's normal?' he asked.

'Good question. Someone brought it up at the seminar. We frame our lives in normality, but forget to look at the hidden picture. Quite a common phenomenon. One that causes all sorts of problems, wouldn't you agree?'

Max didn't know if he agreed or not. He didn't understand a word she was saying. He wished she would shove off and find her missing boyfriend (and three guesses why he was missing) so that he could join Ginger on

216

that very squashy sofa.

Dusk was beginning to fall, but the peachy light of a summer's day still lingered in the high corners of the room. He wanted to be alone with Ginger. He wanted it with an intensity that was only heightened by the strong red wine that had begun seeping into his brain.

'Put some music on, Max,' Ginger commanded.

'Like what?'

'Something cool and jazzy.'

'Right.' He got up and went over to the music machine.

'Excuse me one moment,' said Oonagh. 'I'll try Steve's home number again.' She went off into her bedroom with her mobile.

'Can't you get rid of her?' Max hissed, as soon as the door was safely shut.

'No, I can't. I asked them to spend the evening with us.'

'Why?'

'Because you're always so horrible about her.'

'Well, that makes complete sense.'

'You know what I mean.'

'No I don't.'

'You're not being very grown-up, Max.'

'No? So maybe I don't want to be grown-up.'

'That I find easy to believe.'

A sudden spurt of anger went through him. After all, he was the one who had asked her to move in with him, to take the relationship to a new, deeper stage. It wasn't on to accuse him of childishness. He said, 'So what's grown-up about getting me here under false pretences?'

'I did not!'

'You made out it would just be the two of us.'

'I didn't exactly say that.'

Max said, 'I suppose you thought if there was company, we wouldn't have to talk about it.'

'Talk about what?' Ginger asked.

'Now who's being infantile?'

The door opened. Oonagh emerged, mobile in hand. 'Can't get a signal in there,' she said. 'I'll try on the landing.'

Ginger waited until they were alone again, then said furiously, 'I am not trying to avoid the issue.'

'Could have fooled me.'

'Oh, that's typical. We have to do things your way. When you say so. Never mind what I want. Well, I have news for you. I don't have to wag my tail and jump through the flaming hoop every time you flick your fingers. So you can come down off your high horse.'

Max looked as if he would have pointed out the mixed metaphor had he known the correct term for it. He stood there looking down at her.

'I'll tell you something else,' Ginger went on. 'I wouldn't ever choose to live with a man who's so insensitive to other people's feelings.'

'Insensitive? Me?' He smiled, knowing that it would wind her up even more. He liked the way she went all pink and steamy when she was really fuming.

'Supercilious bastard!'

Max lifted his glass and drained it. He was feeling better. Scoring more points, on the whole, than she was, so he could afford to stop feeling sorry for himself. 'The thing is,' he said magnanimously, 'I've just realised something. It's probably not your fault.'

'What's not my fault?'

'The fact that you've been so . . . intran . . . intrans . . . obstinate.' Good word, Max, if difficult to get out. 'It's her influence, of course.' He nodded towards the door. 'The mad leprechaun. Bloody feminist, I suppose . . . ' He was having trouble with the sibilants. They tended to slur. 'Tell by the look of her. If I'd been living with her, I'd have changed too.'

'Max!'

'There's something about ugly women.' He took another mouthful and waved his glass in the air. 'And I've just realised what it is. They poison the minds of the other ones. The stunning ones. And you're very stunning. Did I ever tell you?'

'Max — '

'No, no. Don't try to deny it.' He had a thought. 'You know what would help? If she shaved her eyebrows.'

'For God's sake — ' Ginger said.

He was now well into his flow. 'Or put a bag over her head. Yeah. That'd do. You know what amazes me? That she's got a boyfriend. I mean, I had her down for a dyke.'

'Max — '

She had a funny look on her face. Not the furious one that had been there for the last five minutes. More a kind of horrified fascination.

'Mind you, he hasn't actually turned up. Maybe he doesn't exist. Maybe she invented him. Whaddya think?'

Before Ginger could answer, he became aware of a movement behind him. He turned. The door that gave on to the landing was half open and Oonagh was standing in it. From the look on her face, she had been standing there for some time.

'I think,' said Ginger, 'you'd better get out of here. Fast!'

22

Pierrepont Mews had an air of cosy distinction, first thing on a city morning. Elizabeth never tired of strolling into it. No cars, no bars, nothing big, nothing brash, nothing blaring. Just cobbles, old-gold stone, Regency rooftops and a sense of timelessness.

She fished out the shop keys and fitted one into the lock. It clicked and turned. The mail behind the door flapped back. Bending to pick it up, she leaned across to shove back the basket of appliquéd napkins that blocked her way, then dropped the mail on the counter. Not too many bills, thank the good Lord. Time enough to sift through them later when the coffee pot was on. Outside, George Godwin was opening up the Music Box. Give him five minutes and he'd be trotting along for his breakfast — bacon butty from the café around the corner.

The door tinkled behind her.

A customer? This early?

'This *is* the right place,' a voice said thankfully. 'I know you said Pierrepont Mews, but I didn't bother to write it down and my street map got thrown out for the

221

recycling lorry by mistake and I wasn't sure I'd be able to find you.'

Buffy Adams, attired this morning in a yellow velvet top and a flimsy blue skirt that would have looked better on a twenty-year-old. 'Are you open?' she asked.

'Yes, we are.'

'I know it's early, but this is my best time of the day. I'm hopeless after lunch. Something subdues me. They say it has to do with the time you were born. What do you think?'

What do I think? Elizabeth thought she needed coffee pronto. She thought she would take refuge in the kitchen for a brief space and rattle mugs around before facing up to being tackled at this hour by her new friend with a semi-detached grip on reality. She said, 'Would you care for a coffee?'

'Love one. Thanks.'

'Okey-dokey. Take a look round while I get organised.'

Ms Adams took her up on the offer, talking non-stop as she did so. 'It was in my mind to come yesterday, but I had to work. I was supposed to have the whole week off, but one of my colleagues had a job interview and no one else could fill in. Oh, that's a pretty thing.'

'What is?' Elizabeth stuck her head back round the door.

Buffy was fingering the quilt in the window. 'The Cat's Cradle?'

'Is that its name? I love that cherry pink. My mother used to sew. I'm useless. So where's the detective agency you were telling me about? I couldn't get over your having a finger in both pies. The one thing so safe and comfy and the other so potentially . . . well . . . dangerous. Is it dangerous? Chasing after criminals?'

'Intermittently,' Elizabeth said, as she put the coffee pot on the hob and lit the gas with a match.

'I think you're quite astonishing. Really.'

I might return the compliment, Elizabeth thought. Is it going to be one of those days? Because if so, I might go straight home again. Get back under my quilt.

'I'm really into detectives. I love all those old black-and-white movies. Philip Marlowe. *The Maltese Falcon*. They freak me out.' From the front of the shop came all sorts of eager little exploratory movements and exclamations.

'I bet some of these quilts are old. Really old,' she called out.

'The oldest is eighteen hundred and two.'

'Think of that! Think of all the tales it could tell.'

'One or two.'

'I felt sure I'd like it here. You know what?'

'What?'

'You and I must be on the same wavelength.'

Elizabeth's eyebrows shot sky-high. 'You think so?'

'I'm sure of it.'

Elizabeth fished for milk in the fridge and dispensed some into a jug. She found the sugar and two mugs. 'Plain biscuits or chocolate digestives?'

'Chocolate, please.'

The shop bell tinkled. Thank God, Elizabeth thought. She stuck her head out to see who had come in. 'Caroline!' she said, smiling madly. 'Great! Coffee's on.'

'Not coffee,' Caroline said. 'Not for me.'

'Tea?'

'Not tea either.' The mere mention of it was obviously making her feel queasy.

Buffy Adams said, 'Anyway, I had this funny feeling the other night.'

'You did?' Slowly Elizabeth shook her head.

'One of those moments when the past seemed to be calling to me.'

'Oh, really.'

'You'll never guess what I did?'

'You're right. But I guess you won't keep me in suspense for long?'

'I went round to the Theatre Royal and I had a good long chat with the girl in the box office.'

'Good Lord!' Elizabeth appeared now in the kitchen doorway.

'I wanted to know how Flora was on that last morning. If she had any premonitions about what was about to happen to her. I'm very interested in all that, you see. Whether the new life you're about to be pitched into sends out any signals. The box-office girl was very nice. She told me all sorts of things. Did you know, for instance, that when Flora was doing a play here in January, she had something really horrid sent to her in the post?'

'No.' Elizabeth was suddenly alert. 'I didn't know that.'

'Well, they tried to hush it up. I don't think it was exactly the kind of publicity they wanted.'

'So what was it? This thing she got in the post?'

'Well, apparently it was rather a bizarre funeral wreath. White lilies with a pig's heart attached.'

A muffled gasp from Caroline. A sudden heaving sound. She came past Elizabeth at a fair old lick, heading for the toilet.

'She doesn't look very well,' Buffy said.

'She's pregnant,' Elizabeth told her.

'How fantastic. And absolutely awful at the same time, of course.'

Like someone else I could mention, Elizabeth thought.

'The rumour was it was sent by an ex-lover.' Buffy's eyes were avid.

'The wreath?'

'That's right.'

Elizabeth put the jug of coffee on the counter. The ex-lover. 'It wouldn't have been Sean Donahue?'

'Sean Donahue? You don't mean the pop star?' Buffy asked, dazzled.

'No. No, of course not. It couldn't have been him.' No need to put any more crazy images into the girl's head. There were enough floating around in there already.

★ ★ ★

Half an hour later, she called Max to give him a hurried account of what Buffy Adams had told her.

'Every fruitcake has its silver lining, wouldn't you say? Flora ended her affair with Donahue last December and in the New Year she gets this revolting parcel complete with cryptic message. Typed. 'You'll get what you gave me.''

226

'Is that what the fruitcake told you?'

'Uh-huh. Seems to me we should make Mr Donahue a priority. Of course, we don't know the wreath came from him. But I'd bet my last dollar on it. Max — are you still there?'

'Yes, I'm here.'

'Everything OK?'

'Fine.'

He didn't sound it. More lovers' quarrels? 'Listen — will you tell Ginger I'm out this afternoon on Martha Washington business? Should be back by five.'

'Ginger's not in today.'

'Oh, really? Is she sick?'

'No idea. She just didn't turn up.'

'So did you call her?'

'Yep.'

'And?'

'And she's not answering.'

'That's odd. Hadn't you better go round.'

'Can't,' he said. 'I'm off to Belgium.'

'Belgium?'

'I've had a tip-off about the tractor.'

'Right.' It *was* going to be one of those days.

Next she rang Le Jardin des Plantes and asked to speak to Jill Valéry. A door slammed in the background, there was the sound of distant voices, the phone seemed to go dead and then, a minute or two later, a woman's voice said, 'Yes?'

'Madame Valéry, this is Elizabeth Blair. Do you remember me?'

'The detective?'

'That's right. I'm really sorry to trouble you again, but did Mireille turn up yet?'

'No. No, she hasn't.'

'I'm sorry to hear that. Listen — she told me she was on an exchange trip with a local school last year. I don't suppose you have any idea which one?'

A pause. Then, 'St Brendan's, I think she said.'

'Thanks. That'll be a great help.'

'The police have already been up there. I don't think anything came of it.'

'Well, it won't hurt for us to go over the same ground.'

'I suppose not.'

A short silence. Elizabeth said, 'Can I ask you something?'

'Go on.'

'Did Mireille ever talk about any friends she may have made last time she was here?'

'No. No, she didn't. She was quite a private girl. Guarded, even. Know what I mean?'

Elizabeth knew very well what she meant.

Madame Valéry said, 'That's what worries me most. She could have been in big trouble and she wouldn't have told a soul.'

Her third call that morning was to St

Brendan's School. 'I'd like to speak to the Head of Languages. Is that possible?'

'I'm sorry, Mr Collins is teaching at the moment.'

'Then could I make an appointment to see him as soon as possible?'

'I'll give him the message, but I can't promise anything. We're in the middle of exams.'

'Tell him I won't keep him long, but I need to speak to him and it's pretty urgent.'

'And this is about . . . ?'

'I'm afraid I couldn't possibly tell you over the phone. If you'd just get hold of him for me. Here's my number.'

So, she said to herself as she slammed the phone down, that just leaves Ginger. But as she was due to have supper at Ginger's flat, that particular problem could safely be shelved for the time being.

★　★　★

Elizabeth moved absorbedly among the tables at the auction rooms. Now and again she would stoop to examine a puckered seam, admire a delicate piece of feathering, jot a lot number or a comment down in her catalogue.

For days now she had been looking forward to this sale, which included a small collection of Durham quilts. The catalogue had explained that, though known collectively under this name, they were actually made throughout the north of England as well as in Scotland and Wales. Second half of the nineteenth century and into the twentieth. Wholecloth quilts, made from plain lengths of fabric which showed off the fine stitchwork to perfection.

Fine pieces of work. It couldn't be denied. So why do I feel a mounting sense of disappointment? she wondered, as she turned the corner into an aisle lined with fine old pieces of furniture. Is it just that they're all so very plain? Maybe.

Maybe. Take Lot 116, for example. A pure white, austere little number, its central motif quilted with flowers and feathers. Fresh, clean, virginal, sensible. Looks as if it should be in a convent. So that's good, isn't it? There's nothing to detract from the flawlessness of the stitches. Not sure. Accuracy isn't the be-all and end-all. Give me a botched-up mess of stitches on a bed of patchwork any day.

White was all very fine on a balmy summer's day. But when a north wind came whistling round your nether regions — well, hang austerity. Give me a mess of colour. Something to cheer your cockles. That red

Paisley, for instance. Berry red. Her eyes lit up. She leaned forward to touch it. Now that is something!

Lot 120. She ran a finger down the catalogue. Welsh. 1880–1900. Llanybydder. She marked the number with a cross. We'll have a go for that one. Hope there aren't too many dealers to push the price up. Hello! What's that, tucked away at the bottom of the pile? A Crazy Patchwork. Let's see now . . . Lot 125. Welsh again. Silk plaids adorned with feather stitch. On a central panel of red velvet, in gold thread amid wisteria blossoms, was embroidered:

When Land is Gone and Money Spent
Learning is Most Excellent.

How true. How profound. It wasn't in pristine condition, but what the hell? You won't want to sell it on, she thought. So what? Stop being a kill-joy. Out came the pen and down went another mark on the catalogue.

There was a half-hour before bidding started. She fetched herself a cup of tea and sat there in the crowd, gazing absently at the table on which the Welsh quilts were displayed.

Her mind was restful yet quietly active. It

kept drifting back to what Buffy Adams had come out with that morning.

The wreath that had been delivered to the Theatre Royal. Would Sean Donahue really have made such a dramatic and public gesture? Pretty stupid, surely? Childish?

But ditched lovers don't always act like grown-ups, she thought. He would have done it on blind impulse and only worried about the stupidity of it afterwards. If so, he was lucky that Miss Messel hadn't reported the matter to the police. According to the girl at the box office (Elizabeth had called in there during the lunch-hour) Flora had gone a bit white, but had simply dumped the thing in the bin with impressive *sang-froid*.

That was Flora all right. Not easily fazed. Elizabeth remembered her arrogance when asked to stop using her mobile on the train. 'Couldn't you move?' she had drawled. She certainly wasn't the type to run when threatened. So what *would* she have done about it? Phoned Donahue and given him hell? Probably. With what consequences?

If it was Donahue who had sent the wreath. There were other contenders. Rosemary Lovett. Ginny Coote, the sacked house-keeper. Daphne Billington, even, the wronged sister . . .

But whoever had sent it, Flora would have

hit back. Of that, Elizabeth was certain. In any kind of dispute, big or small, she would most definitely have given as good as she got . . .

★　★　★

Elizabeth got back to the shop at five thirty, carrying the red Paisley quilt and the Crazy Patchwork. She had paid more for them than she had intended, but had been unable to help herself.

A thing of beauty is a joy for ever, she reminded herself. The old supportive mantra. It had got rid of her conscience on more than one occasion.

Caroline had departed, leaving a note on the counter: 'Sold the Cat's Cradle to your funny friend. She came back this afternoon. Quite a hoot. By the way, she wants to see you. She's found out something else and it's urgent. Oh, and a Mrs Lovett rang. Said to forget the Messel case and would you send your bill?'

23

While Ginger was whisking the walnut dressing for the salad, Elizabeth dialled the number for Lovett's Hotel. Rosemary's voice came on the line, sharp but calm. 'Mrs Blair.'

'Yes. I got your message. As I understand it, your husband no longer needs our services?'

'That's right. I really can't let James go on with this ridiculous wild-goose chase. He's a bag of nerves. In a dreadful state.'

'Yes, I could see that.'

'Then you'll understand why I've prevailed on him to leave it all alone. What's done is done. I keep telling him, it was nobody's fault, certainly not his, and I'm not prepared to let him go on torturing himself.'

'It's his decision, of course.'

'Yes, it is. So if you would let us have your bill.'

Elizabeth walked over to the window. Took time to put together her reply. 'I can send a bill . . . certainly. But as it was your husband who hired us, I'm afraid we would need to speak to him personally before quitting the case.'

'I told you — my husband is ill.'

'Even so.'

'He's in no fit state to talk to you.'

'It would only take a moment.'

'No. No, I can't allow it.'

'Then I'm sorry, but we'll be continuing our investigations.'

The line went dead. Ginger came barefoot out of the kitchen carrying a blue bowl containing the freshly tossed salad. 'You look puzzled,' she said.

'Mmm. Why would Rosemary Lovett want us off the case?'

'Ask me tomorrow.'

'You mean, no shop talk?'

'I get enough of it all day,' Ginger said.

The lemon and garlic chicken was smelling remarkably good. A chocolate cake was sitting on top of the fridge. Elizabeth said, 'So this is what you've been doing all day? Conjuring up a feast.'

'Why not?'

'Why not indeed?' A moment lapsed. 'Max has gone to Belgium. Did he tell you?'

'Nope.'

Another pregnant pause. 'I see.'

'What do you see?'

The lie of the land? The change in your expression? All the things that can go wrong in the mating game? 'That your love life

235

doesn't seem to be running too smoothly.'

'You can say that again.' Ginger plonked the salad on the table and swished on back to the kitchen.

Elizabeth followed her. 'Want some advice?'

'No.'

'Well, you're going to get it anyway. Don't let the anger pile up. It can be destructive.'

'So you're taking Max's side?'

'I'm not taking sides at all. All I'm saying is unload it — bawl at him — have the most spectacular row if you want to.'

'We've had that already.'

'But don't let it go on for ever. It corrodes. Believe me, I know.'

'How can you know? You had a wonderfully happy marriage.'

'Ginger, we were married for thirty-five years. You think in all that time we never had a row?'

'I can see that but ... ' There was something fiercely guarded about her. She was still keeping things to herself. But why would she tell me? Elizabeth thought. I'm not her mother. 'Would you want to live with Max?' Ginger asked.

Now there was a question.

'I'm sure I could,' Elizabeth said cautiously. 'If I were your age.'

'Oh, yes?'

'If I happened to be in love with him. Which you are.'

No denial of that, at least. Ginger fetched two plates out of the cupboard.

Elizabeth said, 'I'll give you another reason why he's so touchy about the subject.'

'What's that?'

'A lot of girls have let him down. Silly little girls. Until you came along, he didn't always choose well.'

Ginger said, 'I know all about that. But I got hurt too.'

'Not by Max?'

'No. I lived with someone for three years. He went off with another woman.'

'And you're scared it'll happen again?'

'I suppose so.'

'For what it's worth, I can't see Max letting you down.'

'No?'

'No.'

Ginger's gaze was fixed on her wine glass. 'Sometimes I think that too. But then he'll do something really impossible. Like last night. He upset Oonagh. He was really obnoxious.'

The story was related. Elizabeth tried not to find it too comical. 'He's impossible,' she said, 'but I love him to bits. And so do you.'

Ginger smiled suddenly, looked almost as if

she might relax. Lifted a hand and pushed back a strand of red hair, fixed it into a green plastic slide, tweaking at it with delicate fingers.

'OK,' Elizabeth said. 'So that's settled. Now, do you think we could have something to eat? I missed lunch and I'm ravenous.'

'I'm sorry.'

'I'll forgive you, as long as it's on the table in five minutes.'

Over dinner she told Ginger about Buffy Adams. 'She's a nice girl, but as mad as a hatter.'

'She bought your quilt.'

'True.'

'So you got something out of it. And you won't have to bother with her any more if you're off the case.'

'True.'

'So now what's wrong?'

'Nothing's wrong.' Elizabeth made out she had lost interest in the Messel woman, because she was tired and no longer felt like talking shop, but it was not strictly true.

The events of the last week or so were not going to be dismissed so easily. Flora's distinctive voice went on reverberating in your memory and you wanted to keep listening, even if it threatened to drive you mad.

Another very distinctive Messel voice was cutting into the peace and quiet of a cottage garden up at Nethershute.

Daphne Billington said, 'How did she get in, do you imagine?'

'Must have kept a key, ma'am.'

'I've asked you not to call me that, Tom.'

'Old habits die hard, ma'am.'

Didn't they just? Twice or perhaps three times that afternoon, Daphne, mooching around the staff cottage, had fancied herself a child again collecting a jam jar from Tom's lean-to pantry and hanging over the pond at the back of the cottage to fish for sticklebacks.

It was ten past four and it had just started to rain, a patchy, melancholy drizzle that turned the woods a darker green and the pots on the orchard wall a deeper shade of terracotta.

'Well, that's the kitchen straight,' Daphne said.

'It were a fair old mess.'

They did another companionable turn of the garden together.

'Flora was never a judge of character,' said Daphne.

'If you say so, ma'am.'

'I do say so. Careless. Taking on a housekeeper and not bothering to get proper references.'

'Doesn't pay these days,' Tom said. 'All sorts of rogues around.'

'Yes, well, they won't be around again. Not here. Things will be run as they were in my mother's time.'

'I shan't grumble about that, ma'am.'

Daphne's gaze went up to the open latticed window. 'That's my next job. Getting the bedroom back to what it was.'

'But not today, ma'am?'

'No. I've done enough for one day.'

Tom moved ahead of her up the path.

'Tomorrow afternoon, I thought,' said Daphne. 'I'll come armed with a few boxes and we'll have a bonfire.'

24

Elizabeth was standing against the filing cabinet in the office, one elbow hooked over the open drawer, next morning when the telephone rang. She reached behind her and picked it up. 'Shepard Agency.'

'I'd like to speak to Elizabeth Blair.'

'Speaking.'

'Good morning, Mrs Blair. St Brendan's School here.'

'Well, good morning.' I've never spoken to a school before, Elizabeth thought. Now there's a novelty.

'You wished to speak to Mr Collins, our Head of Languages.'

Elizabeth took off her spectacles. 'Yes. Yes, I did.'

'Well, he can fit you in after school today. Would three thirty suit you?'

She remembered looking down at the file card, all messed up with Max's crossings out, as she stood for a moment making the decision.

'He can only give you half an hour, so if you could be on time . . . '

241

'Yes. Right. Thanks a lot. I'll be there on the dot.'

When the phone went down, she said to herself, You must want your head seeing to. I know. Stupid, isn't it? I've got more work on my hands than I can cope with. I may not get paid for my time. So what's it for? Because you're the biggest snoop on the planet? Because you can't bear to let go of a case until you have it all properly tied up? No. Because a young girl has gone missing and that gets to me. So let the police deal with it. But will they? Anyway, what's half an hour? It won't hurt.

It wouldn't hurt either to find out about the missing credit cards. That was the other thing that kept niggling away at her for no real reason. She shoved the file back into the cabinet and slammed the drawer shut. Watched a young woman cross to the far side of the mews manoeuvring a baby buggy. The baby was yelling his head off. Poor little mite. Are you kidding? Poor mother. Absently Elizabeth said to Ginger, 'What's Andy's number? Find it for me, there's a good girl.'

He sounded half asleep.

'Hi,' she said. 'How are you?'

'Elizabeth?'

'Who else?'

She almost heard him groan. 'You're all I need.'

'You're not having the best of days?'

'Bloody awful. What can I do for you?'

'Well, I wondered if you could tell me if Flora Messel's credit cards turned up.'

'Christ! You're still on that?'

'Not if Rosemary Lovett has anything to do with it.' She filled him in on the state of play. 'I just called by the hotel, but the receptionist delivered the message that Lovett's ill. Not fit to see anybody for the next day or two.'

'If you ask me, he's pretty strung up.'

'Meaning?'

'On the point of a nervous breakdown. Look — Elizabeth, I'd get on with something else if I were you. We interviewed all the hotel staff, checked anything that seemed at all suspicious and came to the conclusion that Lovett . . . well, let's say he's not in a fit state to see things straight at the moment. The death was accidental.'

'You may be right. It's just that the credit cards are niggling at me. You know how things do.'

'No.'

She believed him. Nice boy, but if he were a horse, Andy would be wearing blinkers. 'So you don't know if they were found?'

'Sorry. I haven't a clue.'

'Then perhaps you could put me on to Foxy.'

'Foxy?'

'The person that Flora Messel called on the train that day. I told your boss. He must have got in touch with her. The number would have been recorded on the mobile.'

'I'm sure it would, but her mobile went missing.'

'How? When?'

'Hang on a minute. I'll have to check. I'll call you back.'

Ginger gave the impression she had thoughts to divulge.

Elizabeth said, 'I know. I'm loopy.'

'That would just about sum it up.'

'Just bear with me, there's a good girl. And make us a cup of coffee.'

Five minutes later, Andy called back. 'Miss Messel's mobile was at the hotel until her sister came to collect it along with all her other stuff.'

'And then what?'

'The sister said she took Flora's belongings back to Nethershute.'

'She had a key?'

'No. She rang the gardener.'

'Thomas Bowman?'

'Right. He has a key and let her in. She says she put the gear up in Flora's bedroom, but the mobile had gone missing by the time we went up there to check on her calls.'

'Was anything else missing?'

'No. The sister checked.'

'Odd.'

'Mmn.'

Elizabeth said, 'OK, so the mobile went missing. But you could still call the mobile-phone company and get a printout of her last calls.'

A pause. 'Yes.'

'Yes, what?'

'Yes, well I was supposed to do it — Gleeson did tell me to — but we're changing offices and we're short-staffed and this other case came up that had higher priority, so — '

'So you didn't get around to it?'

'That's about it,' Andy said. 'Look, I'll get the printout for you. OK?'

Elizabeth said, 'Our wonderful police force.'

'But it won't be today. I can get you that Foxy's phone number. Lovett gave us her details.'

It was better than nothing. 'Go on, then.'

'Her full name is Amelia Fox. She worked for Miss Messel's agent but, from what I gather, Flora practically took her over as her own PA.'

'OK. Thanks, Andy.'

'Don't mention it. Just tell Max he owes me a pint.'

Standing there, her mind racing, she wondered why anyone would want to steal Flora Messel's mobile. After all, these days they were ten a penny. A casual thief would have helped himself to a much bigger haul.

Someone didn't want her recent calls to be traced. Was that it? The same someone who had called her on the train and accused her of being bolshy for not wanting to do lunch?

Someone who had been abandoned by her? An old lover? Someone very angry, of that there could be no doubt.

And what was it that Flora had flung back? 'The world moves on. It's time you did too.'

⋆   ⋆   ⋆

Elizabeth didn't get through to Amelia Fox until she was back in the shop after lunch. At first there was some misunderstanding about the reason for the call. 'You're from Flora's credit-card company?' Ms Fox enquired, her voice at once smoky and sexily precise.

'No. Look — this is a trifle complicated. My name is Elizabeth Blair. I sat opposite Miss Messel on the train the day before she died. I heard her call to ask you to cancel her credit cards and it's been driving me mad ever since. Did you ever find them?'

'No, we didn't. But I cancelled them as soon as she told me.'

'So no one had used them? It's been bothering me, you see.'

'No one had used them.' A slight hesitation. 'Who did you say you were?'

'Elizabeth Blair. I run a quilt shop in Bath.'

'I see.' The voice relaxed. Ladies who sew. They're always trusted.

'Well, I'm certainly glad you cancelled them.' Elizabeth laid the fervency on with a trowel. 'Only I've been thinking about it nights. You know?'

'Of course,' the beautiful voice said. 'If you don't mind my asking, how did you get my number?'

'Sort of indirectly from Miss Messel's friend, James Lovett.'

'Oh. James. Yes.'

'He's in a dreadful state.'

'I can imagine.'

'So tragic, her death. I'll never forget that last journey of hers. When I see her in my head . . . ' By now Elizabeth was well into her busy-sewing-bee persona. 'What I remember most clearly is how she could put people in their place. My aunt Cooper from Pennsylvania was like that. Never one to miss out on the last word. Why, when that cat of a schoolteacher who lived next door to her — '

'Look — sorry. I'm not quite sure where — '

'I'm rambling on again. I do apologise. What I was trying to say was that I admired — envied, even — how Miss Messel dealt with that nuisance call.'

'Nuisance call?'

'Someone called her on the train and was positively pestering her for a lunch date. I suppose it's the down-side of being a celebrity. They think they own you. Fans, theatre buffs, the odd stalker.'

'Look, Mrs Blair — whoever you are — I don't think Flora was being stalked.'

'No?'

'No. I would most certainly have known about it. She would have told me. We were close friends. Anyway, if she was using her mobile, there's no way a nuisance call, as you put it, could have come from a stranger.'

'No?'

'No. The phone was new. She'd only bought it the day before. She was very busy with rehearsals, so she asked me to send her new number to a very close circle of friends. No more than half a dozen. The list she gave me is sitting here on my desk.'

Now, Elizabeth thought, we have a

problem. You've dug your hole and you're well and truly stuck in it. The avid, dizzy-headed, excitable Mrs Blair adopted for the purposes of snooping can hardly ask for the names on that list.

Damn and blast!

Some other way would have to be found.

* * *

It was four thirty-two as she was ushered into an empty classroom at St Brendan's.

'Grab a chair,' said Daniel Collins. Rather a solid-looking young man with sandy hair who would talk when prompted, but it was a bit like having a dog and making him perform by throwing him biscuits.

'Thanks. Good of you to see me.'

'Not at all,' he said, with a fleeting smile.

'I know you're busy. Exams, I believe.'

'Yes.' He had propped himself on one corner of the desk.

'The worst time.'

'Yes. Masses of marking. So — Mrs . . . er . . . '

'Blair.'

'Mrs Blair. What can I do for you?'

'I'm a private investigator.'

He looked as if he'd just taken a gulp of brandy. 'Good Lord!'

'Yes, I do seem to have that effect on people.'

'So what are you investigating?'

'A young girl's disappearance.'

'A girl from this school? I hadn't heard — I mean, no one told me. The headmaster normally informs us if anyone goes missing.'

'Not a pupil. No. A young French girl. Mireille Bucolin.'

'Ah.' Now he was with her.

'You remember her?'

'Mireille? Of course. Nice girl. Came over last year with the exchange group.'

'She hasn't been here since? On school premises?'

'Not that I know of. I certainly haven't seen her around. Did you ask elsewhere? The fifth-year pupils, for instance?'

'That's really why I'm here. I wondered if you could put me in touch with any friends she might have made here.'

'Let's see now. Five R.' He sat pondering. 'It's quite difficult. At that age they tend to go round in gaggles.' His thoughts visibly swung one way and then another. 'No, I really can't think of anyone.'

'No teenage romances?'

'Plenty, I suspect, but the staff would be the last to know.'

'So could you at least tell me who Mireille

stayed with last year?'

More deep thought. 'Davina, I think. Davina Longbridge.'

'So can you give me Davina's address?'

'Not at this moment. Davina's family moved to Norfolk — I think it was Norfolk — at the end of last year.'

'So I'd have to see the headmaster?'

'Or someone from the office. Yes.' Something seemed to be threatening his rather absent-looking expression. 'But the Head's away at a conference and I rather think Mrs Mason — the school secretary — has gone off home early. The dentist.'

'Damn!'

'You wanted something today?'

'If at all possible.'

He said, 'I'm afraid it isn't. There's nothing I can do until the morning when the office opens.'

★ ★ ★

The hallway leading to Ginger's flat was quiet. Max had taken the stairs two at a time, glancing at his watch halfway up to check that he wasn't too early. Five forty-five. Yes, she ought to be home.

He felt more cheerful. Jaunty, almost. The tractor had been traced to a container truck heading for a garage fifty miles south of Paris. Funny old business, paying a small fortune on the black market for a knackered lump of farm machinery.

He hadn't actually brought the thing back with him. The *gendarmerie* didn't move that quickly. But moves were afoot to return it to its original owner and he had a photograph of its number-plate in his pocket, which would no doubt cause Mr Youlegreave to cough up a nice fat cheque.

There's no accounting for taste, he thought, switching the Cellophane-wrapped bunch of roses to his left hand while he fished in his pocket for the latchkey Ginger had given him.

Yes, there it was. He ran a hand through his hair and straightened his jacket before inserting the key in the lock. For all his bounce, he was a touch nervous, though God knows why. It's not as if I intended bloody Oonagh to hear what I said. I wouldn't deliberately have insulted her.

That's not the point, Ginger had said.

Among other things.

He would just have to hope the flowers and the speech he had been preparing in his head would do the trick.

OK. Deep breath. Action stations.

25

As he eased open the door, someone got up from the sofa. A bloke. Late forties? Bearded. Light brown hair, receding. He wore a green striped jumper — the sort sported by ornithologists — cords and scruffy brogues.

Max looked taken aback.

'Sorry. Did I startle you?' His companion stood taking him in with a pleasant smile. 'Let me guess. You must be Max.'

'That's right.'

'Stephen.' One hand was extended in a genial handshake.

Oonagh's chap. The missing supper guest. Max's face cleared. 'Pleased to meet you,' he said. Make him feel welcome, he thought quickly. Get the old chat going. Play it right — frank, friendly, man-to-man — and it might go some way towards placating Oonagh. Not to mention Ginger.

'So,' he said, with a friendly grin, 'it's her turn to keep you waiting?'

'Sorry?'

'Getting her own back, is she? They always have to make you suffer for your misdemeanours. I remember a girl I went out with in Manchester, years ago when I was young and gullible. I was never on time and it drove her barmy. She never believed I had to work late. Always accused me of being out with some other bird.'

Stephen made an appropriate noise of understanding.

'I remember one night, when I was seriously late, Kelly — that was her name — went berserk and poured a pint of beer over me.'

'Really?' Stephen's eyes were interested and sympathetic. From Oonagh's room came the sound of a radio.

'Yeah.' Max quite enjoyed hearing himself tell the story. He dropped the roses on the table and loosened his tie. 'Mind you,' he said, 'I don't know what I was doing with her in the first place. That's a lie. She was hot stuff and you know what it's like when you're eighteen and you can't get enough of it and somebody hands it to you right on a plate.'

'I do seem to remember,' Stephen said. 'I can just about go that far back.'

Max said, 'Sorry — I didn't mean to imply — I wasn't saying — ' His voice suddenly sounded abnormally loud. He had a thought. A drink. That's what we need. 'Can I offer you something?' he asked. 'A beer? Something stronger?'

'Not for me, thanks. It's a little early.'

'Sure?' I'd need a drink, Max thought, if I had to sleep with Oonagh. Still, he's pretty affable. Shame, really.

'No. Thanks all the same. But don't let me stop you.'

'Better not,' Max said. 'I'm in the dog-house as it is.'

'Hence the flowers?'

'Hence the flowers.'

Stephen looked amused. 'So how did you land up in the dog-house?'

Max couldn't very well divulge what he'd said about Oonagh, so he opted for vagueness. 'Oh, you know. Women. You can't seem to have a straight conversation with them. They ask for the moon and when you get it for them, they don't want it.'

'Bad as that?'

'Yeah.' Max lowered his voice. 'Where is she?' he asked.

'Ginger? She popped out for some milk.'

The coast was clear. Max, having changed his mind and fetched himself a beer, found himself launching into laddish confidences. 'Well, we've been seeing each other — sleeping together — for months. And it was going OK. You know? Flying along. Mad, passionate nights, great sex, a lot of laughs in the office. We work together, you see. So I thought,

Maybe it's time to take it a step further. I asked her to move in with me. But she turned me down flat.'

'Really?'

'That's women for you.' Max's mood was beginning to swing. 'It crossed my mind — you don't think there could be somebody else?'

'A rival for your affections? Oh, no. I wouldn't think so. Ginger's not the type.'

'They're all the type,' said Max. 'Believe you me, mate. Look — are you sure you won't have a drink?'

'No, really. Look, there's something I perhaps should have told you . . . '

Max knew it! Ginger had been blabbing about their problems to Oonagh.

'Something you might want to know . . . '

What the hell was coming? Max felt a stab of alarm. Behind him the door opened. He turned his head to see Ginger standing there with a carton of milk in her hand.

'You're back,' she said. 'How was Belgium?'

'Flat.' He felt flat, too. All his earlier buoyancy had gone out of the window.

Ginger didn't seem to have noticed. Her eyes were on the roses that lay on the table. 'How lovely,' she said. 'Are they for me?'

At any rate, she was in a better mood. Max

wanted to be alone with her so that he could ask a few loaded questions. But Stephen continued to stand there like a pig in the middle.

Closing the door, Ginger waved a hand first in Stephen's direction, then at Max. 'Have you two met?'

Stephen said, 'We haven't actually been introduced.'

Ginger looked at Max. 'We can put that right,' she said. 'No problem.'

Max thought he could do without the sodding formalities.

But Ginger was going to insist on them anyway. 'Daddy, this is Max. Max, this is my father . . . Stephen Dickinson.'

★ ★ ★

Daphne Billington slipped on her jacket and stood regarding her husband who still sat, toast in hand, at the kitchen table.

She said, 'I suggest we meet at twelve thirty.'

'Whatever suits you, dear.'

'Any later and the place will be packed out. And then you'll get in a flap and your stomach will start playing up.'

'You're right, of course.' His eye fell on a particularly interesting paragraph in the business section.

'The Poacher, then. Twelve thirty.'

'Righty-ho.'

'You didn't hear a word I said, did you?'

'Mmn?'

'Johnny!'

His head came up, the paper went down. 'Poacher. Twelve thirty. Sorry. I'm a bit fuzzy this morning.'

'A bit fuzzy any time of the day.' She leaned over and dropped a sharp kiss on the top of his balding head. 'Right. I'm off. See you later.'

Outside, the sun was already warm, the sky a light blue. Daphne walked along by the herb bed to where her car stood at the back of the old stable. She unlocked it, threw her bag on to the passenger seat and tucked first her legs and then her skirt in. Noticed a smudge of yellow on the stone flags in front of her. Rose petals. Nothing ever so lovely.

For a moment she sat there. Then started the engine.

Her thoughts, as she eased the car out through the gate and down the hill, rushed around here and there. Nethershute. The estate-agent chappie. The letter she had just written to the solicitor. What, if anything, to do about that business a couple of days ago.

Odd. Definitely.

That story she had been told. I don't believe a word of it.

Daphne leaned forward to forage for a tape and prepared to insert it in the slot. All too pat and somehow contrived. I asked one, maybe two questions and got a hundred answers.

She was approaching the bend on the steepest bit of the hill. Come on, Daph. Concentrate. Slow down.

Her foot reached for the brake, but hit the floor instead.

There was nothing there. The car skidded, bounced off the hedge and accelerated down the hill . . .

★   ★   ★

Elizabeth was in the office before Max the following morning. She put the kettle on and threw a couple of teabags into the pot. For some reason the clock on the mantelpiece had been turned to face the wall. Elizabeth turned it round. It was ten minutes fast. One of Max's little ruses for getting off work early. She checked with her watch and put the thing right. It was as she poured the tea, while she was getting to work on her in-tray, that the telephone rang. She reached over and picked it up.

259

Max's voice said, 'I just heard something on the news. Flora Messel's sister died yesterday morning. Car accident. It seems her vehicle might have been tampered with.'

26

Elizabeth dumped the pile of letters back in the in-tray. Wondered why she didn't feel more surprised.

'Elizabeth? Are you there?'

'Yes, I'm here.' She was trying to remember something Daphne Billington had said to her when questioned at Doome Down Barn. 'I'm Joe Blunt. Always have been. Always will be?' So who had this brisk Joe Blunt upset that they should have interfered with her brakes? 'Did you call Andy?'

'No. I'm not sure we're still on the case.'

Elizabeth glanced at her watch and saw that it was ten minutes past nine. 'So where are you?'

'I'm at home.' A hesitation in his voice. 'Is Ginger there?'

'Uh-huh. Do you want to speak to her?'

'Er — no. No, it's OK. I'll be in later. Got to go now. Court hearing at eleven.'

Now why would he want to rush off like a scalded cat?

'That was Max,' she said, when she had put the phone down

'Where is he?'

'At home.'

'So is he coming in?'

'He says he'll see you later. He sounded weird.'

'He is weird,' Ginger said.

'Uh-huh?' It was turning out to be a useful noise to make. 'Weirder than usual?'

'Definitely.' Ginger tipped the tin of paper clips out on the desk and fished out a particularly small one. 'Take last night . . . He turned up out of the blue at my place with a bunch of roses.'

'Lucky you.'

'Only he didn't actually give them to me.'

'No?'

'No. He dumped them on the table while he was talking to Daddy and when I said — '

'Your dad came over?'

'Yes. He drops in when he's in town.'

'And you introduced him to Max?'

'Not exactly. They sort of collided with each other while I was out buying milk.'

This was interesting. 'So how did they get on?'

'Like a house on fire, according to Daddy.'

'And according to Max?'

'I haven't had a chance to find out. No sooner had I put a foot inside the door than he shot off.' Ginger looked worried. 'You know my dad's a vicar?'

'Yes.'

'Well, the only thing I can think is that Max couldn't take it. He had a chat with him and got cold feet.'

'I don't believe that for one minute.' At least, Elizabeth thought, I'm trying not to believe it. The boy's made of sterner stuff than that. Surely?

She gave up trying to work out what was going on between those two. Her mind went back to Daphne Billington. Attempted to fit this latest incident to the two earlier deaths. There has to be some connection, she thought. Not necessarily. Might just be a coincidence.

I don't believe in coincidence — at least, not to that extent.

So what do we have here? Three women who all, at some stage, lived at Nethershute. All with abrasive personalities. All at odds with each other. Not exactly true, she decided. Daphne Billington didn't know the Coote girl. Can you be sure of that? No. Not unless we ask the husband.

Elizabeth got up from the desk and wandered to the window. The sky was overcast. A bank of cloud was nudging its way in from the coast. The weather forecast had predicted rain.

It was as she turned from the window and

263

paused for an instant to survey the clutter of telephone directories on top of the piano that she remembered Amelia Fox's list. She hesitated, picked up the phone, put it down again and then, finally coming to a decision, dialled Andy's number.

'DI Cooper.' He sounded as if he were flipping through a wedge of papers.

'Hi. It's Elizabeth. Would you do something for me?'

'Elizabeth. Do I have a choice?'

'Of course. Listen — did I ever tell you how much we appreciate all your help?'

'Cobblers,' Andy said. 'OK, spit it out. I'm busy.'

'OK. I have a slight problem. There's a certain lady who has a list of phone numbers I'd dearly like to get my hands on. Only I can't ask her.'

'You're too shy and retiring?'

'Something like that. But you could ask. Make it sound sort of semi-official.'

'One of these days,' he said, 'you'll get me fired.'

'Great. Then you could come and work for Max and I could retire.'

'Work for Max? God forbid. So who's this woman you want me to ring?'

Elizabeth got on with the day's work, nipped out to buy a sandwich for lunch;

wondered if she should just take a little outing to the library to change her books. Would anybody mind? What if she stopped off at Starbucks on the way?

Before she could answer either of these questions, there was a rap on the door.

'Come in.'

The door banged open. A dark man in a black leather jacket strode into the office. Handsome, Elizabeth thought, but somewhat past his sell-by date. Also a little too long-haired Bohemian for my taste. 'Good morning!' she said cheerfully. 'Can I help you?'

'Is this the Shepard Agency?'

'It is.'

'Then you would be Elizabeth Blair?'

'That's me.'

'The big-mouthed American who was bothering my girlfriend on the phone the other day?'

In her cubby-hole behind the filing cabinet, Ginger looked startled.

'Your girlfriend?' Elizabeth asked.

'That's what I said. I understand you insisted on speaking to me.' A deep scowl was cut into his face.

'Mr Donahue!' Elizabeth looked at him with what she hoped was a sufficiently conciliatory smile. 'Yes, I did call and I spoke to a young lady who seemed . . . well, a little evasive . . . '

'She was evasive because I've trained her to be bloody evasive when we get nuisance calls from oddballs and nosy-parkers with nothing better to do than invade my private life.'

'Now listen here — ' said Elizabeth.

'No. *You* listen here. I've just about had enough of this crap establishment. Who the hell do you think you are?'

He's been drinking, Elizabeth thought. There was a reckless look about him, not to mention a distinctive whiff of stale alcohol. I wish Max was here. What do I do if he gets really offensive? Get Ginger to throw the fire bucket at him? Yell blue murder out of the window? Call the police?

Donahue advanced on her with an even less fetching expression. 'And as if that wasn't enough, you decide to pass my address and phone number to an even bigger nutter.'

'I'm sorry?'

'You will be, believe you me.'

'Look, I called to make another appointment with you. But what we offer here is a confidential service. I most certainly did not give your phone number to a third party.'

'No?'

'No.'

'You're a bloody liar,' said Donahue.

'I most certainly am not!' For one second Elizabeth thought it was going to come to fisticuffs. 'So who I am supposed to have given your number to?'

'A madwoman.'

'A madwoman?'

'A gibbering, out-of-her-skull, red-headed madwoman.'

The penny dropped. 'Buffy Adams?'

'So you did send her?'

'No, of course I didn't. She came to see me. And I may have mentioned your name . . . ' Oh, God, she thought. That's all it would take.

'In connection with what?'

'In connection with a parcel that was sent to Flora Messel at the theatre in January. A wreath decorated with a pig's heart. There was a rumour going round that it might have been sent by an ex-lover. And I . . . might just have happened to mention your name.'

He took two steps towards her. His face was alarmingly close. 'You told her I sent Flora that wreath?' He was practically shaking with anger. 'You demented, stupid old tosser — '

Elizabeth said, 'But you did send it?'

'Can you prove it?'

'No. But I could hazard a damned good

guess. You were mad at Flora for ending the affair — '

'No. I told your friend over there. I was the one who ended it.'

'That's not what Mrs Lovett told me. She heard you shouting at Flora in the hotel dining room because you'd just been given the elbow.'

'Then she's a liar.'

'I don't think so. I think you were as mad as hell at Flora and still totally obsessed with her. Obsessed and mad enough to wish her dead.'

'For God's sake — '

'And to attempt to harm her by putting peanuts in her sandwich . . . '

Donahue's voice said, 'No.' His voice was still harsh, but he was no longer angry. He now looked as if someone had stamped on him hard. 'No, I'd never wish her dead. I loved her too much.'

Elizabeth gazed at him for a moment. She noticed that his eyes were bloodshot and there were deep bags under them. 'Sit down. You look shattered.'

'I am shattered.' But he didn't take the chair she pushed towards him. He walked, instead, over to the window and stood staring out blindly.

'Buffy Adams . . . ' Elizabeth said. 'I didn't

give her your phone number or tell her where you lived. She must have done some detective work of her own. I'm afraid she's — '

'Two notes short of a tune?'

'Not quite on the same planet as the rest of us.'

'You're not kidding.'

'So what happened? Did she call you?'

'Several times. Then, when I refused to speak to her, she turned up on my doorstep.'

Elizabeth groaned inwardly.

'When I opened the door, she launched into all sorts of nonsense about glimpsing Flora through a mist and wanting to pass on a message and would I mind if she stepped inside?'

'I'm sorry.'

'And then she mentioned your name. Kept going on about how glad she was you'd met on the train and how you'd pointed her in the right direction.'

'I'm sorry. But I honestly didn't tell her where you live.' She hesitated, then said, 'You *did* send the pig's heart?'

'All right, yes, I did. Stupid of me, but I was in a stupid mood at the time.'

'Can I ask you another question?'

'You can ask. I don't have to answer.'

'True. The day before Flora Messel died, did you call her on her mobile?'

'No.'

'But I imagine you called her plenty of times when the relationship was thriving?'

'Yes.'

'But that would have been on her old number?'

'Her old number?'

'She bought a new mobile two days before she died.'

'Did she?' She couldn't see his face, but his voice didn't change.

'You didn't know?'

'How would I? As you so delicately put it, Flora had just given me the elbow.'

Elizabeth said, 'Sorry about that. So tell me something else. Did you know the Coote girl? The one who was found dead in Flora's cottage at Nethershute?'

'Ginny? I knew her. You couldn't miss her. She was a bit of an exhibitionist.'

'Did you like her?'

'Didn't have to.'

'Even so?'

'She was a loud-mouth and a tart. God knows why Flora took her on.'

'Any idea how or why she died?'

'She drank too much and popped pills. She was an accident waiting to happen.'

Which reminds me. Elizabeth said, 'Did you hear what happened to Daphne Billington?'

'No.' He turned from the window.

'Somebody tampered with the brakes of her car.'

'You're having me on.'

'No. I'm afraid she died yesterday morning.'

'Christ!' He looked thoroughly shocked. 'What's going on?'

'I was hoping you'd tell me.'

He gazed at her for a moment. 'So Lovett isn't as stupid as he looks?'

'Sorry?'

'Taking you on.'

'Actually. I'm not sure if we're still on the case. Mrs Lovett didn't approve.'

'That bitch. She hated Flora.'

Perhaps, Elizabeth thought, with some reason.

* * *

The trouble with having two interlocking jobs was that there was never time to do ordinary little chores like cooking and shopping and a million other things that bored you to death but had somehow or other to be fitted in around the edges of a working day.

Milk, she thought suddenly, towards the end of the afternoon. And, come to think of it, there wasn't a single loaf in the freezer.

Damn it, she would have to call at the supermarket on the way home.

By this time, Max was back in the office, but he seemed morose and hadn't a word to say for himself that wasn't absolutely necessary.

Elizabeth shrugged on her coat, looked round for her bag. 'How did you get on in Court?' she asked.

'Total cock-up.'

'Great. I'm off.'

'Bit early, isn't it?'

'Listen, I've been here all day. Unlike some people. I've done my share.'

'Where's Ginger?'

'Dentist. By the way, she thinks you're acting a bit oddly. Want to tell me why?'

'No.'

'OK. I've had just about enough for one day. I'm bushed. But first thing tomorrow morning, I shall expect to be told exactly what's going on. We can't run an office like this. Cranky boss and no goddamned organisation. You'd better cheer up smartish, my boy, or you and I will have a serious falling out.'

'So what's new?' he muttered.

Elizabeth got out. She walked to where she had parked the car, climbed in and dropped her bag on the passenger seat before letting rip by slamming the door and revving extra hard on the accelerator.

* * *

The supermarket was heaving and there were only a few trolleys left in the bay. She grabbed one and doggedly pushed the thing around the aisles, picking up bread and milk and pasta and vegetables before heading for the wine section. She had been working like a dog all week and deserved a treat.

'A Merlot. Yes, why not? She dropped the bottle in her trolley and then, as an afterthought, added a good Chardonnay. She was about to steer herself back to the checkouts when she spotted a face she recognised.

'Hi!' she said.

'Oh, hello.' It was Daniel Collins. He looked at her then looked away.

'I'd forgotten that St Brendan's was just around the corner. Don't you hate it?' Elizabeth asked.

'St Brendan's?' He stood there looking bashful over his basket, which contained a bottle of wine, a box of chocolates and a ready-made chicken korma for two.

'No. Food shopping. Boring as hell. Still, you look as if you're in for a fun evening.'

'I'm sorry?'

'Dinner for two. How I wish someone would do that for me.'

'Er . . . yes . . . well.' He began to edge backwards away from her.

'I rang the school secretary, by the way. She promised to come back to me with that girl's new address, but I haven't heard anything. Perhaps you'd remind her tomorrow in case it slips her mind.'

'Yes, of course. No problem.' He sloped off down the aisle with his basket. Odd guy, Elizabeth thought. Was he lost in thought or embarrassed because I didn't hear back from them?

Out in the car park, she unloaded her bags from the trolley, dumped the thing in its shelter and made her way back to the car. It was as she eased herself into the driver's seat that she saw Collins again.

He was fifty yards or so away from her, inserting his key into the car door and glancing right and left in what could only be described as a shifty manner. Checking that no one was looking. She was sure of it.

Automatically, she slid down in her seat. He hadn't seen her. One last swift recce and he was in the car and starting the engine.

She knew that she was out of her head to follow him but, like a lot of things in her life, it was an instantaneous decision.

She simply couldn't go home without knowing why he was being so secretive.

27

Max sat waiting for Ginger in the poshest Italian restaurant in town. He looked edgy, constantly fiddling with the Campari and soda that the waiter had put in front of him. He wore a sharp blue shirt and his new linen jacket — the one that had carved a massive hole in his credit card — but his stomach still had a sinking feeling.

Shortly after five thirty he'd plucked up the courage to call Ginger at home to ask if she would meet him at Il Casale. She had sounded surprised, had asked if he'd come into a fortune, had laughed when he said no, but the bank manager had very kindly offered to subsidise him. She had even asked if he'd meant to leave his roses behind.

So she didn't know.

The Reverend Stephen hadn't told her.

Which makes it worse, he thought wretchedly, because now I'll have to tell her myself. And then the balloon will go up. Why in hell's name didn't he say he was her father? Max closed his eyes and groaned as he remembered all that laddish stuff he'd come out with. *She was hot stuff and you know what it's like when you're eighteen and you can't get enough of it and a girl hands it to you on a plate.*

I'll never be able to look him in the face again.

We've been sleeping together for months . . . Great sex.

Oh, God.

From his window-seat Max looked out on to George Street. Tall old terraces opposite, made even taller by the flight of steps that led up to them. Cafés and bars. Still blue sky. Tourists strolling.

And then he'd gone on about all the booze Ginger had in the flat. It couldn't be worse, really. Well done, Max. How to win friends and really impress her old man.

At that moment Ginger walked in through the door. His heart lurched. She looked fantastic in something greenish and clingy. And she'd done something to her hair . . . For once it was flat and smooth like a curtain of beaten copper.

As she reached the table, he shot to his feet.

'You look nice,' she said, stretching on tiptoe to drop a kiss on his cheek.

'So do you.'

'My God — is that a compliment!' She curled herself into the chair opposite. 'So what's this in aid of?'

'Does it have to be in aid of anything?'

'When it costs as much as this place . . . yes.'

'Drink?' Max asked, stalling for time.

'The usual, please.'

'Gin and tonic with lots of ice,' he told the waiter.

She sat there looking at him.

'What?' Max asked.

She said, 'Sometimes I quite fancy you.'

You won't, Max thought, when you hear what happened last night. He's a gent. I'll say that for him. Keeping it under his clerical hat.

The waiter came back with the gin and two menus. They took their time about choosing. At one point Ginger was going to have the *crostini* and *ravioli* but then she changed her mind and went for the *bruschette* and *tortellini*.

After the waiter had taken the order, she relaxed and sat there playing with one silver ear-ring. 'So what *is* it all about?' she asked.

'I . . . Well, I owe you an apology.'

'For tearing off without a word last night?'

'For a lot of things.'

She said, 'I'll wake up in a minute. You never apologise.'

'I have been known to.'

'When?'

He tried to think. It wasn't easy.

'See what I mean?' She was laughing. Max wished he could laugh.

Ginger took a long sip of her gin and sat gazing at him over the top of her glass. 'Can I ask you something?'

'Go on.'

'How did you get on with my father?'

Here it was. The big one. The sixty-four-thousand-dollar question. A trickle of sweat was running down his back.

'Max?'

'He was OK.'

'So you liked him?'

'Yeah. He was great.'

'But?'

'But nothing,' he protested weakly.

Her sea-grey eyes remained on his. 'But you can't get past the dog-collar, even though he wasn't wearing it.'

'It's not that. Really.'

'What then?'

The waiter arrived with the wine. He made a great show of pouring a sample and Max was forced to go through the motions of tasting it. 'Great,' he said, nodding sagely. 'Thanks. You can leave it.'

Ginger said, 'I know he can get boring about Africa.'

'He didn't mention Africa.'

'He worked there, you see, when he was a young man. And his sweaters are awful. He really doesn't care what he looks like . . .

Max was beginning to feel hunted. The time had come, but the thought of telling her made him wince. You could get away with it, he told himself. Say nothing. She'd never know. But for once principles, amazingly, took over. 'It's not Africa and it's not the sweaters.'

'So what is it?'

'I . . . Look — I've got a confession to make.'

The waiter reappeared with *bruschette* in one hand and *antipasti* in the other. 'For the signorina?' he asked.

'The *bruschette*. Thanks.' Ginger waited until he had gone off again and said, 'What kind of confession?' She didn't attempt to touch the contents of her plate.

Max took a huge gulp of wine.

'It's bad, isn't it?'

'Pretty bad. In fact, worse than that.'

'You'd better tell me,' she said.

So he did. Every last bit of it.

For a moment the silence was deafening. Then the balloon went up. 'You told my dad your ex-girlfriend was hot stuff?'

He nodded.

'And that we had great sex?'

280

'But, you see, he didn't tell me he was your dad. 'I'm Stephen,' he said. So I assumed he was Oonagh's Steve. I'm sorry, Ginger. I'm really, really sorry. Look — I wouldn't have done it on purpose, would I?'

'You might have,' she spat back. 'You're stupid enough.'

He couldn't argue with that. 'I won't ever be able to look him in the eye again.'

'I hope not. God, I hope not. And you told him the flat was full of booze?'

'Not exactly. I didn't mean it to sound like that.'

'You never mean to do anything. You never think. That's your trouble. You're incapable of putting your brain into action before you open your mouth. In fact, I don't think you've got a brain.'

Max said, 'Have something to eat. You'll feel better.'

'I won't.' She was pushing her chair back.

'You're not leaving?'

'Give me one good reason why I shouldn't.'

'I love you. I really want to make it up to you.'

'I bet you do!' She picked up her bag so abruptly that she knocked the cruet off the table. Her eyes were shining with either anger or tears. 'I just bet you do. Well, it can't be done, Max. You're a joke. A complete liability.'

And turning with the greatest dignity, she swept out of the restaurant.

★ ★ ★

Elizabeth, meanwhile, was hunkered down in the driving seat of her car, which was parked at the end of a cul-de-sac towards the university end of the city. Daniel Collins's route had taken them up Entry Hill, left at the roundabout and half-way along Danvers Road, where he turned left and parked opposite a house in Danvers Terrace.

Here again, on getting out of the car, he had glanced all round as if to check that he was not being observed. Elizabeth, skulking still on the main road, had waited until he went into the house before parking her own car in a steep lane that led down to sports pitches behind a patch of allotments. From here she could sit and observe without being seen.

She knew she was being obsessive, but there was something about his behaviour in the supermarket. Something shifty. He'd been alarmed at bumping into her. Had shifted the basket on his arm to a different angle so that she wouldn't see what was in it.

Too late, boy. I don't miss many tricks. Too

long in the tooth. Too many hours spent noting little quirks of human behaviour.

He was up to something. Some grubby little affair, I shouldn't wonder. She thought, sometimes I wonder about you, Elizabeth Blair. Turning yourself at the least opportunity into a peeping Tom.

Look — we'll give it ten minutes. OK?

OK, but you need your head seeing to.

She turned on Radio 3 and sat there listening to good music. She fished around in the glove compartment and found an abandoned bag of toffees. Tweaked one out of the bag and peered up at the house Collins had gone into. And that was when she saw someone appear at the upstairs window.

Female. Young.

Elizabeth leaned forward and peered hard. It was.

Mireille. She would swear to it.

28

Daniel Collins developed a stammer when taken by surprise. 'You m-must be mistaken,' he said. 'Mireille isn't here.'

'No?' Elizabeth stood on the doorstep looking at him.

'No. I really d-don't know what you're talking about.'

'Mr Collins — I saw her at the window. So wouldn't it be easier if you levelled with me?'

'L-levelled with you?'

'Yes. I may be an interfering old busybody, but I'd like to know why you've got Mireille hidden away here when her mother is imagining her raped and murdered and buried somewhere in an English wood.'

'Her mother died ten years ago.'

'You're remarkably well informed,' she said.

He had the air of someone who knew he had put a foot wrong. 'She . . . she was telling me when she was over here last summer.'

'But she's not here now?'

'No. That was my . . . my girlfriend that you saw at the window.'

Then you won't mind if I speak to her?'

'Actually, I'd rather she wasn't involved.'

'Any particular reason?'

'She's . . . married,' he said quickly.

'And are you married, Mr Collins?'

He flushed. 'I don't see what that has to do with you.'

'Well, under normal circumstances it wouldn't. But if you've got Mireille upstairs — '

'I told you. I haven't.'

'Then you won't mind if I call my friend, Andy, who's a policeman, and have them take a look around the place?'

He knew when he was cornered. 'D-don't do that. Don't call the police. What do you want? Money? I haven't much, but — '

'All I want is to see Mireille and talk to her for a moment or two.'

'You'd better come in,' he said at last.

The house was small and modern — three bedrooms, Elizabeth would guess, with a kitchen and bathroom. It looked like a student squat. All a bit frantic. The sitting room contained a couple of sofas with striped throws, half a dozen wild posters, a coffee table covered in mug rings and two elephantine red floor cushions.

'Have a seat,' Collins said sullenly. 'I'll be back in a moment.'

He disappeared back into the hall and up

the stairs. Elizabeth crept to the doorway and heard him speaking to someone in a low voice. Then a door slammed and two pairs of footsteps started tramping around above her head. It took him at least five minutes to get her to come downstairs.

Mireille looked tired standing in the doorway with a wary expression on her face. Her glance went all round the room before finally settling on Elizabeth.

'It's OK. I'm on my own,' Elizabeth said.

'Please don't call the police,' she said, and promptly burst into a flood of tears.

Daniel Collins made a good job of comforting her and mopping her up. This isn't your average teacher-and-exchange-student relationship, Elizabeth thought, that's for sure. It's much more intimate. As he stood holding Mireille, he stroked her hair.

Elizabeth waited until the girl had herself back under control, then said, 'I think we could all do with a cup of coffee. Why don't you make one, young man, while I talk to Mireille?'

He hesitated, assented, went to the door and then came back again. 'I'd really rather be here.'

'To vet what she says? It's gone past that, don't you think?'

'I don't know what you mean.' His eyes

were dark and rather handsome. But perspiration shone on his forehead.

'I think you do,' she said. 'You're in a bit of a pickle, wouldn't you say? A man in your position shacked up with a pupil half his age.'

'She's not my pupil,' he said.

'Not at the moment . . . But last summer when she was here and you were in charge of her welfare . . . How old would she have been then? Fifteen? Sixteen?'

That hit the target. His hands were clasped tightly together to stop them shaking. 'I w-wasn't sleeping with her then.'

'I only have your word for that.'

'It's the truth, I tell you!' He was frightened out of his wits.

'But you're sleeping with her now?'

Silence.

Elizabeth said, 'How old are you, Mireille? Seventeen?'

He said, 'Leave her alone. I'll tell you.'

It was the old, old story. The lightning bolt. The *coup de foudre*. Boy meets girl. Or in this case ten-years-married, slightly-bored Head of Languages meets girl. Eyes lock, pulses quicken, sparks fly. While Mireille, at Collins's nod, disappeared into the kitchen to make coffee, he attempted to explain the affair to Elizabeth. It was not what he'd ever intended and, of course, he ought to have known better. But it had been so immensely flattering . . . a girl as pretty as Mireille hanging about waiting to talk to him in the school corridor or the car park. So beautiful, so gloriously fresh, her eyes brightly beckoning him to go that one step further.

Elizabeth said, 'So she was over here . . . when?'

'March last year.'

'For how long?'

'Two weeks.'

'You're a swift operator, Mr Collins,' Elizabeth said drily.

'Look — I told you.' He seemed irritated. 'Nothing happened on that first trip except a strong attraction.'

'And when she went back to France?'

'She began to call me on her mobile.'

Mobiles, Elizabeth thought. How did Adam and Eve ever get it together without one?

'And you called her back?'

'Not at first. No. But she kept ringing me.'

'Didn't your wife object?'

'She always rang in school hours. Mostly during the lunch-break.' His voice was growing more firm. 'She kept asking me to come over and see her.'

'And did you?'

'Yes. In the summer holidays.'

'You took the family?' There was irony in Elizabeth's voice.

'Of course not. My brother and I sometimes go off together for a few days on climbing trips. I . . . I'm not proud of this, but I said we were going to have a few days in the Alps. He covered for me. Sam. That's my brother.'

What else are brothers for?

'That's when we first became lovers. Mireille's father was away in Paris on business, so she told him she was going camping with a girlfriend. And we spent the week together. We were so happy. I didn't want to come back.'

'But you did?'

He looked down at the wedding band on his finger. 'I had to. I have a family. A career.'

Mireille handed him his coffee. He looked up at her and smiled. A slow blush went from her neck to her cheeks.

'So she decided to follow you back here?'

'When she finished school for the summer. Yes. She told her father she wanted to better her English. I heard that Jardin des Plantes took on French kids. She wrote to them and they gave her a job.'

'And all was going swimmingly until I turned up on the scene.'

'She panicked. We both panicked.'

'That's why she did her disappearing act? But the enquiries had nothing to do with the two of you.'

'We didn't know that. You kept asking questions at the restaurant. I told Mireille that all you were interested in was the Messel woman but she was worried that one thing would lead to another. That you would find out about us and tell my headmaster.'

'It wouldn't look good.' Elizabeth was forced to agree. 'So was she under age last summer when the affair started?

His silence said it all.

'And who does this house belong to?'

'My brother. He's working in York for a couple of months.' He saw the expression on her face and for the first time he seemed deeply affected. 'I know it all sounds sordid, but it's not like that. I love Mireille. I really care about her.'

'Do you?'

'You don't believe me, but it's the truth.'

Elizabeth turned her attention to Mireille. 'I need to ask you about Flora Messel. You returned a book to her, I believe?'

'Yes. It was the same colour as mine. I picked it up and put it in my bag by mistake.'

'And you took it to the theatre?'

'Yes. Madame Valéry said she was working there.'

'But why bother to take the book round to Lovett's Hotel,' Elizabeth asked, 'when you could simply have left it at the box office?'

A light shrug. 'She is — was — very famous in France. My father is mad about her. I thought I might ask her for her . . . what do you call it?'

'Autograph?'

'Autograph. *C'est* ça. For his birthday. *Un petit cadeau.*'

'And you saw her at the hotel?'

'Yes. They showed me up to her room.'

'What time was this?'

'About a quarter to twelve. Before I started work at the restaurant.'

'And did you get her autograph?'

'Yes. I bought a theatre programme and she signed it for me.'

'So how did she seem when you spoke to her?'

A Gallic shrug. 'As she was in the train.'

'Difficult?'

'A little. No, not really. She was like . . . ' Mireille struggled for the right words. 'She is like a lightbulb. She switches on and off. She was OK with me, but she was very mad with someone who called her on the phone.'

'In her room?'

'Yes. I thanked her for the autograph. She closed the door. I heard the phone ring and then I heard her shouting at someone.'

Elizabeth said, 'So what did she say exactly? Can you remember?'

'She said, 'Bloody hell! You again. If you don't stop pestering me, I'll call the police.' '

29

Elizabeth was on her knees in the spare bedroom planning a hanging made from the stray pieces of fabric she had found in the camel-backed trunk. In the centre would sit the degenerating crazy square — her fingers pushed it to its place on the stripped pine floor. Made of the finest silks, it glowed in the twilight, its vivacious Japanesy design wandering freely over the surface, picked out in stem stitch and feather stitch.

The crazy patches were almost always put together from remnants of clothing. Could there be anything more evocative? I wonder. Who wore all these silks? you want to ask. Well, in this case, we know. There's her name in blue thread on a strip of pink ribbon: 'Addie Foster. Age 59. 1888.'

Elizabeth shifted the pieces around on the floor. Next to the crazy square would go the small set of pieced hexagons in Turkey red nineteenth-century prints. And maybe the worn-out pink shantung. Or the appliquéd peony flower with several lines of quilting following the shape of it.

The peony, definitely. So bright and

blooming. Standing for healing in the nineteenth-century floral lexicon. Yes, and we could echo the peony shape in the border.

And for a central background colour? Some plain squares from the bolt of treasured fabric (pink and white print) she had acquired from an old farmer in Oregon on a vacation trip. He had sworn — and she had believed him — that it had been taken over the Oregon Trail to use for baby clothes and that his grandmother had been so desperate to have it from a pedlar and so short of cash that she had traded a pig to get the cloth.

Better go easy with it, then. Can't afford to waste even a snippet.

She eased herself up for a moment to stretch her knees. Climbed to her feet to fetch the bolt from the chest of drawers in the corner by the window. Her fingers brushed at the rough cotton. Over the years it had acquired a brownish hue common to fabrics of that time. The instability of colour caused by exposure to light and heat.

Elizabeth stood looking down at the vivid shapes with a satisfied smile. She could picture it all coming together.

Must get some more quilting thread, she thought abstractedly. I'm all out.

Must put some lamps on. It's getting dim in here.

But first something to eat. It was nine thirty and she still hadn't decided what to do about Mireille. Tell the police? I guess I'll have to sooner or later, for her father's sake. No question of it. Or else Mireille would have to do it.

Daniel Collins had begged her to give them time to concoct some story that would explain her absence to the Valérys without involving him or the school in the proceedings, and Elizabeth had arranged to call Mireille at the house the following morning.

Lax of me, she thought. I should have gathered her up and brought her home with me. She had even suggested it but Mireille had had a fit of the horrors at the very thought. Well, see it from her point of view. Bossy old grandmother figure chuntering away at her until her nerves jingled.

Kids that age don't have nerves. That comes later. Much later.

So she had promised to leave it, but had put the fear of God into them that if there were any more disappearing tricks she would go straight to Andy and tell him what she knew. Now, she told herself, you'd better go and make that omelette before you drop from lack of nourishment.

But before she could do so, Max turned up on her doorstep.

'Tea?' she said. 'Sure you wouldn't like something stronger?'

'Tea,' he said.

This was unprecedented. Elizabeth wondered whether she should ask him to say it again to make quite sure her ears were working. Max stood there in the comfortable, and at this stage of the evening tidy, sitting room looking at her with what could only be described as Slavic gloom.

'You all right, Max?'

'No, I'm not bloody all right,' he said.

'I'll put the kettle on. One lump or two?'

'Three.' He stared glumly at the dead television.

Elizabeth did a passable imitation of a cheerful and nonchalant hostess. 'OK. Hang on in there. Have you eaten?'

'Don't ask.'

'Er — right. Won't be a moment.' She would have liked a little time to gather her wits, also to shove a couple of cookies into her mouth, but no such luck. No sooner had she put the kettle on than he followed her into the kitchen.

'Make it coffee,' he said. 'I need the stimulus.'

'Any particular reason?' she enquired.

'I buggered it all up.'

'All?'

'Me and Ginger. It's dead and buried.'

'Oh, come on, now.'

'No. I mean it.'

'So what happened?'

He told her. She listened, patiently, a little fearfully until the whole painful episode had been plainly revealed. It didn't take long. Max went through it like an express train. When he had done, he stood there waiting for her reaction.

Elizabeth looked as though she were having a problem keeping her face straight.

Max said, 'Don't you dare laugh. It's not bloody funny.'

'I realise that,' she said precariously.

'What am I going to do, Betsey?'

'Apologise?'

'I did already.'

'And?'

'And she went up like a rocket.'

After a think, she said, 'Perhaps you should offer to apologise to her father.'

'You're joking? I can't face him again.'

'Might be the only way?'

'No. Knowing my luck, I'd just dig myself in even further.'

She didn't argue with that. 'Want me to talk to Ginger?'

'Would you?'

'I can but try.' All this toing and froing. Sometimes, thought Elizabeth, I feel I'm working for the Pony Express.

'Tell her I'll even apologise to sodding Oonagh as well.'

'Two for the price of one? I think you should concentrate on her father for now.'

'Maybe you're right.' He looked more wretched than she had ever seen him.

'Let's make that coffee,' she said, in an attempt at comfort.

'Changed my mind,' Max said. 'I'll have a large whisky.'

★ ★ ★

When he'd taken himself off at around ten fifteen, Elizabeth picked up her telephone book and found the number for Doome Down Barn. The ringing tone went on and on. The worst thing about offering commiserations to someone in Johnny Billington's situation was that words seemed absolutely useless. They came out as meaningless clichés, no matter how hard you tried to make them sound sincere.

'Johnny Billington.' The voice on the other end was unutterably heavy.

'Mr Billington, this is Elizabeth Blair. From

the Shepard Agency. I came to talk to your wife the other day regarding our investigation into her sister's death. I just want to say how desperately sorry I was to hear your sad news.'

'Yes. Thank you.' Very formal, very stiff upper lip.

'It seems dreadful to ask, but I heard that someone tampered with the brakes on her car. Is that true?'

'So the police say.'

'But who on earth would do such a thing?'

'I don't know. I can't imagine. It's quite beyond me.'

'Her car was OK until yesterday?'

'Running perfectly. It had just come through its MOT.'

'Look — this is a difficult question to ask and I don't do it lightly. Did your wife have any . . . well, enemies? Is there anyone you could think of who would wish her harm?'

'I've been asking myself that since it happened and the answer is . . . no one. She's very well known around here. Well respected.'

'I'm sure. Just one more thing, Mr Billington. Did your wife know Ginny Coote? Miss Messel's ex-housekeeper?'

'The girl who died at the cottage? No, I

don't think so. As you know, Daphne didn't get on with her sister. After Flora inherited the house, my wife wouldn't go near Nethershute. It hurt too much. She kept well away from the place.'

30

While Caroline dealt with a customer the following morning, Elizabeth stood looking out of the shop window and wishing she could grab hold of something that was floating vaguely around in the outermost reaches of her mind. It happened a lot, these days. Things got diverted. Sometimes permanently. Automatically she smiled as the customer left, but it was really bugging her that she couldn't place whatever it was and put it decently to rest.

The two Welsh quilts had now replaced the Cat's Cradle in the shop window. Red Paisley nudged companionably against the Crazy Patchwork, but Elizabeth couldn't seem to feel as much satisfaction in them as usual.

Her thoughts were still revolving around what Mireille had told her. Who had made a nuisance call to Flora Messel at Lovett's Hotel just an hour and a half before her sudden death? The same person overheard talking to her in the doorway of her room earlier that day? Not to mention the man or woman whose call had annoyed Flora on the train.

OK, so you heard her take that call. Was it someone she knew? I'd say so, both from the tone of her voice and that final put-down line. *Listen — the world moves on. It's time you did too.*

In that case, Elizabeth asked herself, who do we suspect?

One of her ex-lovers? How many had there been? God knows. Donahue seemed the best bet, but he had an alibi. He was supposed to have been in London the day Flora died. But Bath is only an hour and twenty minutes from Paddington station.

Who else? A fair old posse of jealous women. Rosemary Lovett? She certainly hated Flora's guts. But she had been on duty the day Flora died and the hotel was at its busiest with this Jane Austen convention, so she wouldn't have had time to lunch with Flora. And, anyway, I can't believe she would foul her nest. If she had intended to kill Flora, she would have done it well away from her own hotel.

Surely?

Daphne Billington, then? With what motive? She wanted Nethershute back. OK. That feels spot on. She's pestering Flora to have lunch with her so that she can shove peanuts in the sandwich. But in a public place with hundreds of hotel guests milling

302

around? Not so sure. Doesn't ring true. Anyway, poor old Daphne now seems to have been taken care of. Why, for heaven's sake? Did she know something? See something? I wish I knew.

Elizabeth's fingers stroked the red Paisley. And what do we make of Ginny Coote's death? Not a lot. Why did she suddenly make a return visit to the cottage? Because she read about what happened to Flora in the newspapers? And, if so, what did she hope to gain? I haven't a clue. This is making my head ache.

Caroline emerged from the kitchen with a pot of something in her hand. Elizabeth peered at it, trying to work out what it was.

'Redcurrant jelly,' the girl said, self-consciously producing a teaspoon with which to eat it. 'My latest craving. I hope you don't mind.'

'Feel free,' Elizabeth said. 'So how's Rupert coping?'

'Splendidly,' Caroline said.

'I must say, he didn't seem to have any sign of nerves.'

'He takes the dog for long walks,' Caroline said.

'Really?'

'At night.'

'Tell him to get his sleep now while he can,'

Elizabeth said darkly.

'He's bought lots of presents for it,' Caroline said.

'The baby or the dog?'

'The baby,' Caroline said. Then, realising suddenly that she had been somewhere in the proximity of a joke, turned pink and said, 'I'm going to miss you, Mrs Blair.'

Miss me? Elizabeth thought. I'm not going anywhere. Then it came to her what Caroline meant. 'You're not leaving?'

'I don't want to, but Rupe won't even consider letting me work after the baby's born. In fact, he wants me to hand my notice in this week.'

*　*　*

How will I ever manage without her? Elizabeth wondered, as she struggled to put up her deck-chair under the apple tree in her garden that evening. I mean, we all make fun of Caroline — no, we find her endlessly amusing. She's so upper-crust, so moneyed-Bath, so aristocratic and poshly helpful with her Hermés scarves and her appallingly plummy accent. You have to hear her to believe her. But she's been here since I opened up, since Day One at Martha Washington. She's part of the furniture, the ambience. Damn it, I like the girl. I rely on her. She creates order out of disorder. She calms the place down, calms me down.

What am I going to do?

Offer her more money? But money isn't the issue here. Rupert wants to coddle her. Gallant old Rupe with his Englishman's fair hair and his perfect profile and his vowels . . .

His-and-hers vowels. That's what they've got.

Perhaps if I slipped her a big fat cheque for the baby, she'd feel so guilty that I could entice her back later. Would that work? What a seedy thought. Elizabeth, I'm ashamed of you.

The thing is, I'm desperate.

The thing is, you'd have to spend one hell of a lot more hours in the shop without Caroline to cover for you.

'Want me to pop round and help with that?' Dottie's voice said from over the hedge. Elizabeth wondered briefly whether it would be a good idea to move house.

'No. No, I'll manage. I'll get it right in a minute.' The deck-chair slipped, made a clacking noise and collapsed itself flat.

'Blasted thing!'

'They're complicated,' Dottie said. 'My great-nephew once got his fingers trapped. Had to go to hospital.'

'It's worse than a bear trap.' Elizabeth hauled the thing to the upright position, eyed it for a moment, then upended it.

'But so comfortable,' Dottie said, 'to the old bottom. Sure you don't want me to help?'

'Positive.' Gritting her teeth, Elizabeth set about trying to fit the slats into the grooves. Surely now it would work? No.

Dottie pointed out that the grooves were upside down. 'You have to be brought up with these things,' she added sympathetically. 'That's the secret. Well, it's time I took my pill.'

Don't ask, Elizabeth thought, flinging the thing down on the grass.

Dottie said, 'For my bowels, dear. I've been bunged up for days. I was up at four this morning. Got myself a cup of tea and some toast and went back to bed. I got up again at six. Things were working by then, down below, so I made some porridge . . . '

I don't want to hear any more, Elizabeth thought. She muttered something about her oven being on and took herself back into the house. I should put up a high stone wall, she thought. Or grow *leylandii*. She threw a piece of bread into the toaster and warmed some baked beans. She was about to get the butter out when the telephone rang.

'Elizabeth?' It was Andy's voice. 'That list

you wanted me to get from Amelia. Got a pen? I'll read it out to you.'

* * *

'So can you make it?' asked Elizabeth, the following lunch-time, as she draped a Cherry Basket quilt over the rush chair by the shop door.

'Not sure,' Max told her. 'Got to see a man about a bimbo.'

'I beg your pardon?'

'A new case. This bloke wants us to find his fancy woman. No expense spared. Seems he started an affair because he couldn't say no to a quickie with a bimbo half his age. Left his wife to marry the bimbo, who's now walked out on him.'

'Retribution time. Sounds fine to me.' She sat there with the phone pressed to her ear. Middle-aged men, she thought, who were born half a century ago should stay at home with sensible women of their own age who are happy to do a bit of gardening. At least, it seems so to me.

Max said, 'Anyway, he wants us to track her down. Pronto.'

'But I really need you for back-up.'

'For what?'

'Well, I thought I might drive up to Dutton

Cary this afternoon.'

'What the hell for?'

'Remember that list of numbers Flora Messel gave her PA girl? Well, Andy came up trumps last night and I'm about to — '

'Betsey, until we find out if Lovett is paying for our time, we are no longer interested in Flora Messel.'

'I am. I'm very interested. In fact, I think I know who — '

'No,' Max said. 'Bloody leave it alone before I lose my temper.'

'You sound as if you've lost it already. So you won't come?'

'Can't.'

'OK,' she said. 'I guess I'll have to get by on my own.'

31

'You should go with her,' Ginger said, an hour and a half later.

'Too busy,' Max replied.

'I don't like the sound of it. You know what Elizabeth's like. Always got to prove herself right. Act first, think later. Where did she say she was going exactly?'

'Dutton Cary.'

'Then she's still chasing whoever murdered Flora Messel.'

'We don't know it was murder.'

'OK then. Whoever tried to murder Flora Messel's sister. I'm serious, Max. Elizabeth could be putting herself in danger.'

They were facing each other out across the filing cabinet. Very Freudian, Max thought. Keep the barriers up, you stay in your bit of space and I'll stay in mine. 'She'll be fine,' he said.

'You don't know that.'

'So what the hell could happen to her in a place like Dutton Cary?' Ginger was beginning to get to him. The sleeves of her shirt were rolled up to the elbows. Her arms were covered in freckles. Her hair in an unruly aureole, her whole physical presence, made him want to touch her. But he couldn't. She was still freezing him out. Only if he could get things brought into the open would they be able to resolve anything.

Fat chance.

Just then Caroline came tapping up the stairs. She pushed the door open as if it might bite her. She wore a white silk shirt with mother-of-pearl buttons and she smelt of lavender water.

'Caroline!' he said, with more bounce than he felt. 'How are you?'

'So-so,' she said. 'Would you remind Mrs Blair I have to go early? Doctor's appointment.'

'Does she know?'

'I told her this morning. She said she'd be back by three. It's not like her to break her word.'

Ginger shot Max a told-you-so look, which he ignored. 'I'll tell her. She won't be long. How's your better half?'

'Rupe? He's very well.'

'Looking forward to the impending arrival?'

'Absolutely.'

'Tell him if he ever needs emergency help changing nappies, give me a call. I've got seven nephews and nieces.'

'Seven?' Her face was a picture. 'My goodness!' She stood there thinking for a moment. Head tilted, pulling at one neatly cut strand of dark hair. At last she said, 'I don't think he'll be too bad. I mean, he's awfully good at upholstery.'

'Is that so?'

'Yes. He's done a wonderful job with the *chaise-longue* in the bedroom.' She smiled her polite little smile. 'It's quite splendid. He's done it in buff linen. Nothing glaring. If I tire of it, he says he'll have another go in *écru*.'

She tapped off down again. Behind the cabinet, Ginger was exhibiting severe signs of distress.

Max went back over to his desk and plonked himself in the chair. He swung it round so that Ginger could see only his profile. 'You don't really think I should go and check on Elizabeth?'

'It wouldn't hurt.'

'My car's having its MOT.'

'Take mine.'

'Nah. She'll be OK.'

Ginger by now seemed to have her face covered with her hand. She made a valiant effort to maintain her starchy air, but not entirely successfully. She buried her head in her desk drawer in an apparent attempt to locate her purse. Her shoulders were shaking, Max noticed, and she was either coughing or spluttering. After some moments, she emerged from the drawer, purse in hand.

'You all right?' asked Max.

'Fine.'

'Scratchy throat?'

'No. Just a frog.'

Max decided to take a closer look; her face was very red and her eyes streaming. 'What's wrong?'

'Nothing,' she said. 'Nothing at all.'

'Sure?'

'Quite sure,' she said, and spoiled it by bursting into a torrent of giggles.

'Caroline?' he asked.

'Caroline. Oh, God, Max — 'He's awfully good at upholstery. He's done a splendid job on the *chaise-longue*.''

'What's wrong with that?' Max asked innocently.

'You sod! You know what's wrong.' She was laughing helplessly, holding her sides and rocking to and fro in the chair. Every now and then she would try to recover herself, only for the little giggles and shrieks to erupt once more. Max, once he was sure that he was on a fairly safe wicket, finally gave in to it too.

Well, it was such a relief that the iceberg had finally melted.

When at last she had calmed down, he said, 'Does this mean I'm forgiven?'

'I suppose so.'

'Sure?'

'I said so, didn't I?'

'Look, I'll apologise to your dad if you want me to.'

'I'll think about it. Actually, I went over to see him last night. I finally plucked up courage to explain about the mistake. That you thought he was the other Steve.'

'And?'

'And he said he liked you.'

'He did?'

'He must want his head seeing to.' She started laughing again. Max wondered if she would ever stop. 'He wants me to bring you to tea.'

'You are joking?'

'No. He says he'd like to hear the rest of your very interesting life story . . . '

★   ★   ★

The village lay deserted. One pub, one church, no shop, no school, a dozen houses at the most. What do people do around here? Elizabeth asked herself. She thought she

313

knew the answer. There's a lot of secret sin.

The list of names Andy had given her was very short. Only five people had been given Flora Messel's new mobile number: James Lovett; Judy Dean, Flora's director at the Theatre Royal; her ex-husband in San Francisco; Thomas Bowman and Georgia Hutchinson.

Georgia Hutchinson . . . On hearing that last name, she had put down the receiver, but had not moved away from the phone. Instead she had stood gazing fixedly at the scraps of fabric spread out on the floor of her spare bedroom; at the crazy square and the red hexagons and the appliquéd peony flower.

Peonies for healing. That was what had been floating for days in the back reaches of her mind. Healing. Dr Hutchinson's wife; Flora's old and dear friend who had been so terribly agitated by her last visit.

Elizabeth climbed out of the car. It was a quarter to three. Traffic hummed on the motorway up on the ridge. Apart from that, the village seemed a little island of calm.

She had checked with four of the people on the list and none of them had called Flora on the train that day. Dean and Lovett in particular had had no need, because Flora had already called them. Elizabeth thought, I heard those conversations. The ex-husband had been on a film set in Los Angeles, so he could scarcely have made it to England for a lunch date. Old Tom Bowman? I don't think so. So . . .

Elizabeth crossed the road to Hay House. Inside the box and holly hedge, roses were blooming. Today there were no small bikes lying around. Just a red ball and a crumpled kite stuck on a branch in one of the trees. She pushed open the iron gate and walked up the front path.

A minute or so went by after she had rung the bell. She admired the brass knocker in the shape of a closed hand. Stood looking at two stained-glass panels traced with wisteria.

At last a figure appeared behind one of the panels. The door opened. The doctor's wife stood there, in a pair of skinny jeans and a green top.

'Mrs Hutchinson. Good afternoon. I wonder if we might have a word?'

'I'm sorry, this is a bad moment. I don't have time. I . . . I'm in the middle of something.'

'I rather think you are. Couldn't have put it better myself.'

'I . . . really don't know what you mean.'

'Oh, I think you do. When my partner called here to make a few enquiries, you told him you hadn't seen your friend, Flora, in several weeks.'

'That's right.'

'You denied calling her on her mobile the day before she died.'

'Yes.'

'Well, the thing is, I'm now in the position to call you a liar.'

'Who is it, Georgy?' A man's voice. Elizabeth, who had been fiddling around in her pocket for something, now pulled out a small piece of paper. 'Your husband?' she asked. 'He's not at the surgery?'

Georgia Hutchinson had gone very pale. Her fingers maintained a fierce grip on the door lintel. 'Not this afternoon.'

'Then perhaps we could all have a little talk?'

'No. No, please — ' She took a step backwards as if to slam the door in Elizabeth's face. But before she could do so, her husband appeared in the hallway behind her.

'What's going on?' he asked.

'My name is Elizabeth Blair, Dr Hutchinson. I'm from the Shepard Agency. I believe you already met my colleague, Max Shepard.'

'Yes. Georgy — what's this all about?'

'I . . . She . . . '

'It's OK.' He dropped one arm over his

wife's shoulders. 'Take it easy. Don't get yourself in a state.' Then, 'Mrs Blair,' he said. 'I'm afraid Georgy's not feeling too well today.'

It was true that the girl was now as white as a sheet. Her eyes had gone blank. She stood there swaying a little. Elizabeth thought she looked very thin and quite frail.

'So perhaps,' he said, 'you could come back another day?'

'I'm afraid that's not possible.'

'Oh, come on.' Dr Hutchinson frowned at her.

'The thing is,' Elizabeth said, 'would you rather your wife talked to me or the police?'

32

They sat in three chairs around the fireplace. The sitting room had a different feel today, not half so cosy. The air felt shut up and stale, and the desk in the corner held an untidy mess of papers.

Elizabeth explained about Flora's new mobile number and Foxy's list. Matt Hutchinson rather touchingly held on to his wife's hand. He looked tired, Elizabeth noticed for the first time. Deep lines under the intelligent brown eyes. He gazed across at Elizabeth with an air of great forbearance.

Finally, he said, 'The fact that my wife is the last person on your list doesn't necessarily mean anything. Flora may have given the number to someone else herself. She was very inconsistent.'

'That may be so,' said Elizabeth, 'but somehow I don't think so.'

'I can assure you that my wife isn't in the habit of telling lies.'

'Not in the usual run of things. But we're talking about exceptional circumstances.'

'What exceptional circumstances? I'm not with you.'

'I'm not absolutely sure at the moment. But I have to say that your wife seems incredibly stressed.'

'Not surprising when people like you keep turning up to hassle her.'

'I'm sorry about that. But I have very good reason to believe she knows more than she's letting on about Flora Messel's death.'

Why, she wondered, are we talking about her as if she's not here?

Dr Hutchinson said, 'What makes you say that?'

'Experience. Gut instinct.'

He almost laughed. 'Is that all?'

'Don't you sometimes follow your instincts, Dr Hutchinson, when making a diagnosis?'

'Occasionally. But for the most part I note symptoms and look for hard facts.'

'Hard facts play some part in my job too. But in the absence of them — ' Elizabeth turned suddenly to Georgia Hutchinson. 'Miss Messel was very rude to you when you called her that day. Did that make you angry?'

'Look, my wife's already told you, she didn't make any call that day.'

Elizabeth was getting tired of having him intervene, so she ignored what he had said and went on talking to Georgia. 'You accused Flora of being bolshy.'

'That's ridiculous.' The girl gestured weakly and refused to make eye contact.

'And then she said she didn't care to be dictated to. I heard her. I happened to be sitting right opposite.'

'You're mistaken. It wasn't me.'

'You wanted her to meet you for lunch,' Elizabeth pressed on. 'When? The following day?'

'It wasn't me, I tell you!'

'And just before she cut you off, she said, 'The world moves on. It's time you did too.' What did she mean by that, do you think?'

'Matt — '

'It's all right, sweetheart.'

'Had you had some sort of quarrel, Mrs Hutchinson? Couldn't she be bothered any more with an old friend? Flora was quite an expert at dumping people. That's one thing I've learned about her. She was quite ruthless, wouldn't you agree?'

Georgia flushed scarlet and threw a panicky, sidelong glance at her husband.

'Yes, the one thing I've learned about Flora was that she helped herself to what she wanted out of life without much regard to anyone else's feelings. Would you at least agree with me on that?'

'I've had enough of this.' Dr Hutchinson was on his feet. Elizabeth wondered if he was going to throw her out bodily.

'The thing is, now and again, one of her victims might have been tempted to hit back. And quite rightly, I'd say, wouldn't you?'

'If you don't get out of here, I'm going to call the police,' he said.

'I very much doubt it.' Elizabeth tried an old trick. Producing the scrap of paper she held screwed up in her hand, she said, 'Actually, I do have proof that your wife called Flora that day. And that she was at Lovett's Hotel the day Flora died.'

'No — '

There was no time to work out what the proof might be that was supposed to have been written on the paper. Before she even had time to unfold it, Georgia leaped forward and snatched it from her hand. Not too wise under the circumstances. But she was in no state to make reasoned judgements.

Elizabeth watched as the girl opened out the folds. Matt Hutchinson was trying not to look appalled. His wife gazed down at the blank sheet. Then up again but with no sign of panic. This was possibly because she couldn't speak. Her eyes were suddenly streaming with tears.

'Oh, God . . . Oh, God, will somebody please help me?'

'It's all right, Georgy.' Matt Hutchinson

went over and put his arms around her.

'It's not. It's not all right. I can't stand this. I can't take it any more.'

'Come and lie down.'

He attempted to lead her towards the door, but she broke free. Turned to say to Elizabeth, 'All right, I'll tell you.'

'Georgy — '

'I have to tell somebody.'

He said, 'Not right now you don't.'

'Yes, I do.' She was staring at him as though at a complete stranger. 'If I'd told somebody in the first place — '

'Darling, you're overwrought.'

'And is it any wonder?'

'Come on. Come upstairs and lie down.'

'I don't want to lie down. I want to get some of this — ' one hand went to her heart ' — off my chest.'

'Georgy — '

'Don't you Georgy me!' she said. 'I've had enough.'

Hutchinson still went on trying to smooth her down. 'What you need is strong, sweet tea.'

'What I need,' she whipped back, 'is a husband who doesn't have a zipper problem. That would make me feel one hell of a lot better.'

'Cool it!' he said, still holding on to her

arm. Elizabeth was interested to see that for the first time he was beginning to look rattled.

'Cool it? Why should I? What good has that ever done me? I kept quiet when you were having your sordid little affair with Flora and what happened? She just laughed at me. She didn't give a damn about my feelings or our family or anything except her own gratification.'

'You had an affair with Flora Messel?' Elizabeth asked Hutchinson.

'Of course not. My wife's ill. Out of her head. She's been under treatment — '

'You bastard!' Georgia wrenched her arm away from him, swung round to face Elizabeth. 'Yes, I killed Flora Messel. She was supposed to be my friend, but she was sleeping with my husband.'

Hutchinson was now trying to look seriously concerned about her. 'So when did that start?' asked Elizabeth.

'Last summer.'

That's why she finished with Donahue! Elizabeth was fitting it all together in her mind. Off with the old, on with the new. With possibly an interim period sleeping with the two of them.

'When I found out,' continued Georgy, 'I went to see her. I told her it had to stop. She just laughed. 'Or else?' she said. She knew I wouldn't leave because of the children. She also knew I couldn't tell anybody or he'd be in trouble with the BMA. She was his patient, you see. So I was caught between a rock and a hard place.'

'Did you ask your husband to end the affair?'

'Of course. And he told me he would, but it still went on. I was desperate. Yes, I called her on the train that day — '

'For God's sake, Georgy — '

'Shut up!' she told him. For the first time, the worm was turning. 'I wanted to plead with her to leave him — us — alone. But you heard how she reacted.'

'So you went to see her at the hotel the following day?'

'Yes. I knew she would be having her sandwich and where and what time. Flora had this ritual. When we were friends, I sometimes used to have lunch with her in the summerhouse. Anyway, the day she died, I went to her hotel and up to her room. She told me to get lost. She said she'd get me thrown out if I didn't leave.'

'But you stayed there? You followed her down to the summerhouse and doctored her sandwich?'

'It wasn't planned. Really it wasn't.'

At this stage, Hutchinson attempted once more to butt in. He was smiling, but there was a harder edge to his voice. 'You don't believe any of this?' he asked Elizabeth. 'She had post-natal depression, you know, after our last child was born. I'm afraid there are still ill-effects.'

'The only thing that depresses me,' Georgy said, 'is living with you.' She was obviously determined to tell the rest of her story. She was standing all this time with her back to the window. The words poured out as if some dam had burst.

'I almost left the hotel that day — I wish to God that I had — but I thought I'd give it one last try. I knew she would be in the summerhouse and that's where I found her. The garden was full of people eating and drinking, but the summerhouse was quite secluded. Not many people found their way in there.'

'So what happened?' Elizabeth asked.

'What do you think? She said, 'Get lost, Georgy, I really can't be bothered with you.' As if I didn't count at all. So damned arrogant. I felt such anger rising inside me. And just at that moment, she got called into the hotel to the phone.'

'Then whoever called her to the phone must have seen you?'

'No. James Lovett called out to her from the hotel dining room. 'Flora — phone!' And she said, 'I'm wanted. Be a good girl, Georgy, and bugger off before I get back.''

'So she went indoors? And that's when you put the peanuts in her sandwich?'

'It was a spur-of-the-moment thing. I stood there shaking with anger. And someone else must have been in the summerhouse before Flora got there, because there were two empty wine glasses and a half-eaten packet of peanuts on the bench at the side. So I picked up two or three and shoved them into her sandwich. I thought it would teach her a lesson.'

'You knew about her peanut allergy?'

'For years. She was quite ill once when she ate some while we were students.' Her voice shook a little as she said, 'I didn't mean to kill her. I just wanted to pay her back for what she was doing to me. I was so frightened when I heard she was dead. I went straight to Matt and told him what I'd done.'

'And what was your reaction, Dr Hutchinson?' Elizabeth looked over at him. He had moved a yard or two towards the door and was watching his wife with a heavy, concentrated expression.

'I was very shocked, of course.'

'But you didn't persuade her to go to the

police?' Elizabeth noted that he was looking at his watch.

'I didn't see how I could. All I could think of was how to protect my wife.'

'All you could think of,' Georgy said, 'was how to protect your own back if the scandal got out.'

'Sweetheart, you know that's not true.' He was all reason.

'It *is* true. And don't call me sweetheart!'

Hutchinson must have been a very controlling husband, Elizabeth thought, as Georgia flung him a look of utter disdain. Now that she begun to stand up for herself, she was beginning to enjoy the sensation.

So . . . how to phrase the sixty-four-thousand-dollar question? 'The thing I'd like to know,' Elizabeth said, 'is where Ginny Coote fits into the picture.'

Georgia flushed and glanced towards her husband.

'Not to mention poor Daphne Billington.'

Georgia said quickly, 'It wasn't me. I didn't have anything to do with that.'

'Then who did?' asked Elizabeth. But before anyone could tell her, she thought she knew the answer.

33

Elizabeth looked across the room at Dr Hutchinson. 'Your wife wouldn't have had the nerve to tamper with Daphne's brakes. It was you.'

He gazed back at her, eyes calm and clear and hard.

'You're quick,' he said.

'It's what they pay me for.'

'Perhaps a little too quick for your own good.' His voice was crisp and slightly menacing. He was watching her with almost a smile on his lips. Perfectly collected, perfectly sure of himself. She realised suddenly what a dangerous corner she had gotten herself into. 'You thought it was just poor little Georgy you were dealing with. How could you ever have imagined — ?'

'So why,' she enquired, 'did Daphne Billington have to die?'

'You do ask a lot of questions.' He was still watching her, intent, calculating. Elizabeth felt a surge of unease. 'You read the papers, don't you? There are some very creepy doctors about. What in hell's name were you thinking of, coming here on your own?'

'It's the best way I know to get answers. Did Daphne find out what really happened down at the hotel that day?'

'It's possible, I suppose.'

'And it's equally possible that she threatened to go to the police.'

'If you say so.' The supercilious sod was playing games with her. And enjoying it.

'On the other hand, I can't see how she could have found out. Unless she somehow bumped into your wife, who gave the game away — '

'I didn't tell her,' Georgia said. 'She didn't know — '

'She didn't know you killed her sister?'

Matt Hutchinson said, 'Shut it, Georgy, there's a good girl.'

Georgia did as she was told. Stood staring silently at her feet. Like a wax doll, Elizabeth thought. No wonder Flora Messel liked to stick pins in you. A silence fell over the room. Outside the long double-glazed windows, roses bloomed and a breeze shifted the chestnuts in the churchyard. That dot of silver on the far side of the box hedge was the top of her Citroën. If I made a dash for it, would I get out of here? No chance. He's young and strong. A rugby player by the look of him. You wouldn't even get to the front door.

'Then it must have been something

329

else . . . ' Elizabeth was thinking on her feet. What could Daphne Billington have found out that got her killed? Something connected with recent events? With Nethershute? With another mysterious accidental death? There was something ominous about the juxta-position of those two words. *Mysterious* and *accidental*. Hang on a minute . . . After what seemed like an age, she met Matt Hutchinson's eyes. 'You killed Ginny Coote as well . . . ' she said.

'I'm really sorry you had to figure that out,' he said softly.

'Well, now, seeing that I did, you may as well give me the reason.' Elizabeth's throat was by now so dry with fear that it seemed to be closing up.

He sighed. 'Why not? Ginny had been blackmailing me for months. Shortly before leaving Nethershute, she found out about my affair with Flora. She knew Flora was on my patients' list and she'd said she'd report me to the BMA unless I coughed up. I had no choice. And I would have gone on paying if she hadn't decided she wanted more,' he said. 'She read about Flora's death in the papers and decided that under the circumstances she could ask for a great deal more to help pay for her drug habit. She came back to the village and broke into the cottage where she used to live, and she rang me up to say that if I didn't pay whatever she asked, she would go to the newspapers with what she knew about me having an affair with one of my patients. 'Flora's hot news at the moment,' she said. 'They love a bit of juicy gossip.''

'So you decided you couldn't afford to pay her any more?'

'It's true. I really couldn't. The sum she was asking for was extortionate.'

'So you went to the cottage and killed her?'

'I decided that with her history of drink and drugs it was pretty safe. The cottage was secluded. She'd told me she was staying there for a few days ... She'd broken a back kitchen window to get in. So I said I'd meet her there one evening with the money. When I got there, she was already drinking. It was pretty easy. I kept her talking for a bit and then, when she was almost incoherent, I held her down and forced her to take the Nembutal.'

Elizabeth shuddered. 'I still don't see why Daphne had to go as well.'

'Daphne was clearing the bedroom at the cottage and she found a note Ginny had written to me. I thought I'd checked everywhere. I went through the bloody place with a fine toothcomb, but I must have missed it.'

'So what did the note say?'

'It was pretty explicit about my affair with Flora and how much I had to pay to keep quiet.'

'So Daphne was suspicious about the girl's death?'

'Yes, I'm afraid she was.'

'She came to you with the note?'

'Yes. She told me she was going to give it to you.' There was a hint of amusement in his voice. 'I thought I'd stopped her, but you got here anyway.'

'Poor old Daphne.'

'Poor old Daphne.' A mocking shrug.

A short silence. Then Elizabeth said, 'It was you, of course, who took Flora's mobile?'

'I realised that if there were any complications, it would lead the police to Georgy and then God knows what else would have come out. Yes, I slipped up there and took the mobile. Flora had given me a key. When she was at Nethershute, I used to let myself in at night.'

'Home visits! I didn't think the NHS ran to them any more.' It was out before Elizabeth could stop herself.

'Oh, we like to oblige when we can.'

'I bet. You're going to miss your little comforts.'

'Somewhat.' His voice was as dry as a

cracker. 'But it wouldn't have gone on much longer. It was coming to a natural end.'

'Flora being Flora?'

'And I was running a considerable risk.'

A cold, calculating young man under the surface charm.

'So what now?' Elizabeth asked.

'What now? Haven't quite decided.' He rubbed a hand over his eyes.

'You look tired.'

'Doctors are always tired.'

Elizabeth said, 'You know I have to go to the police?'

His voice was level and quite professional. 'And you know I can't let you?'

'So just how are you going to do that?' Her heart began to pound as she said it.

'Haven't had time to think.'

'You won't get away with another murder. You realise that?'

'She's right,' Georgia said from the fireplace. 'Matt — you can't kill anyone else!'

'And who started the killing, may one ask?' The look in his eyes was icy, his voice scathing. For the first time Elizabeth saw how he might have been affected by Flora's death. 'Keep your nose out of this, Georgy, unless you want to lose the children. I could do it, you know. Suggest that you have mental problems.'

Georgia closed her eyes for an instant. When she opened them again, they were full of tears. 'Don't say that. Please don't.'

He looked at her steadily over the top of the armchair. 'What time are the children due home?'

'The usual time.'

'Which is?'

For God's sake — didn't he know what time his kids got back from school?

It seemed that Georgia was thinking the very same question. 'You're never here,' she said. 'Not for them or for me.'

'Don't let's start on that again.'

'But it's true.'

'Look — this isn't the moment! Go upstairs and wash your face. Tidy yourself up and then collect the children.'

'But — '

'Take them into town,' he said.

'Until when?'

'Until I call you.' No doubt as to who was in charge now. The girl gave Elizabeth one last scared-rabbit glance and left the room.

'Sit down,' he said to Elizabeth. Then, 'Is that your car across the way?'

'Yes, it is.'

'Anyone else with you?'

'My partner, Max.' If only. 'He's . . . just popped over to see Tom Bowman. I told him to catch up with me here later.'

'Oh, come on! You can do better than that. Sit down,' he told her again. 'And sit very still, if you know what's good for you.'

Hutchinson sat down in the chair opposite. Time went on. The ten minutes that followed seemed to last an eternity. Elizabeth heard Georgia's footsteps above her head, heard several doors open and shut. And then Georgia finally came down the stairs. 'I'm off, then,' she called, through the half-open door. An uneasy, scared-sounding little communication.

'Right,' Hutchinson said. 'I'll call you. Don't come back until I do.'

More steps on the tiled hall floor. A slam of the front door. A car started up outside and eased away down the village street.

'So where do your children go to school?' Elizabeth asked.

'Great Dutton.' He was on his feet now and walking over to close the door and turn the key in the lock. Then he crossed the room to pick up something that stood next to the desk in the corner. A doctor's bag. Brown leather, brass clasps, a small padlock on one of them.

Elizabeth felt the fear go all the way down her backbone. Her stomach lurched. Her pulse was racing like an express train.

'You won't get away with it.' Her voice

came out so loud, it seemed to belong to someone else.

'We'll agree to differ on that.'

'OK, so Max isn't out there. I'll admit to that. But he knows where I am. If I'm not back at the office by five, he'll come looking.'

'Full marks for trying,' he said. Snap went the lock. The top of the bag popped open. He reached into it and took out a syringe.

'I warn you,' she said, 'I'll put up one hell of a fight.'

'That's OK.' He was doing something to the syringe. 'The neighbours are on holiday in Nantucket. I don't imagine they'll hear much from there.'

'I'm American. I can make one hell of a noise.'

'I doubt you'll have time.' He was across the room in an instant and standing behind her, syringe in hand. 'Morphine tends to work pretty quickly. And this amount will be lethal.'

But at that moment, the shrill of the doorbell shattered the stillness of the house. Two sudden, sharp rings . . .

In a moment, his hand was under Elizabeth's chin, the needle poised at the side of her neck. 'Quiet,' he said.

Two more rings, the second a prolonged one.

'Don't even think of shouting,' he whispered.

Footsteps scrunching on gravel. Glass being rapped. Then all at once, quite incongruously, a face appeared, pressed hard against the middle pane of the french windows.

More rapping, accompanied by a blessedly familiar voice.

'Betsey!' Max, peering in, one hand shading his eyes against the reflected sunlight. 'You in there? Just checking. Only you left your car unlocked.'

34

Max ducked as the champagne cork hit the shop ceiling, let the foaming fizz erupt into three glasses and carefully topped them up. He gave one each to Ginger and Elizabeth, took one himself and they took it in turns to clink glasses.

'Here's to us,' he said.

'Here's to us.' Ginger looked as if she'd been consuming bubbly all afternoon. Her face was flushed and she was wearing a pretty lunatic smile.

Elizabeth said, 'Thank God you turned up. I thought I was about to find myself in the after-life.'

'No worries,' Max told her. 'Buffy Adams would have had you back in no time.'

'I don't doubt it. But I mean it, Max, I've never been so pleased to see anyone in my life.'

'Thank Ginger,' Max said. 'She kept on nagging at me.'

How happy he looks, Elizabeth thought. Ginger too. She felt impelled to give them both a quick hug.

'Steady on,' Max said. 'What's that for?'

'Nothing.'

Ginger took a large handful of peanuts from the bowl on the counter without any apparent sense of distaste. 'So Hutchinson had to let you in?' she asked Max.

'What else could he do under the circumstances?'

'And as soon as the french windows were open, he took off?'

'Like a bat out of hell. He picked up his wife and children at the school and set off for the cottage they keep in France. The police intercepted and arrested him somewhere in Hampshire.'

'What will happen to Georgy?' Ginger asked.

'She's still being questioned about Flora Messel's death.'

'Those poor children. Who's looking after them?'

'The grandparents, I believe.'

'The thing is,' he said, 'will Lovett pay us for finding his murderer?'

'Us?' said Elizabeth, with an arch of the brow.

Max tossed a peanut into his mouth and grinned at her. 'OK. So that's settled. If a cheque rolls in, I'll hand it over. Just this once.'

'Any more of that champagne going?'

He refilled their glasses. Raised his own for another toast. 'Here's to the Reverend Stephen Dickinson.' He stood there gazing down at Ginger. 'Are you sure he said we could move in together?'

'Look, I didn't exactly have to ask his permission.'

'But he said he'd turn a blind eye?'

'It wasn't like that either. He said it was my life and I had to make my own choices.'

'As good as giving his blessing, then?'

Ginger said, 'It will work, won't it?'

'Of course it'll work.'

'I was just so scared.'

'No need. I promise you.'

They sat there in the shop in the early evening. The quilts reflected the golden light of the stone out in the mews. A cat walked by. That wild creature who escapes all domination.

Like Flora Messel.

'So, are we going to eat?' asked Max.

'You said you couldn't afford it,' Elizabeth reminded him.

'You said you'd treat us. Seeing that it was a special occasion.'

'Funny. I don't remember.'

'Old age,' said Max, 'plays havoc with the memory.'

As they left the shop, Ginger stood gazing

into the window of Martha Washington. 'The Cat's Cradle,' she said. 'I'll miss it.'

Elizabeth said, 'I'll make you one.'

'When?'

She remembered the old prayer. Dear God, make the day longer so that I can quilt a while.

'Oh, when I have a moment,' she said.

THE END

*Other titles in the
Ulverscroft Large Print Series:*

STRANGER IN THE PLACE

Anne Doughty

Elizabeth Stewart, a Belfast student and only daughter of hardline Protestant parents, sets out on a study visit to the remote west coast of Ireland. Delighted as she is by the beauty of her new surroundings and the small community which welcomes her, she soon discovers she has more to learn than the details of the old country way of life. She comes to reappraise so much that is slighted and dismissed by her family — not least in regard to herself. But it is her relationship with a much older, Catholic man, Patrick Delargy, which compels her to decide what kind of life she really wants.

PAINTED LADY

Delia Ellis

Miss Eleanor Needwood was about to be married to a most unsuitable suitor when Philip Markham came to her rescue. He arranged for Eleanor to be in London for the Season, a guest of his sister, who decided that everyone would benefit if Markham married Eleanor. And thus the rumour started. The surprised couple decided to play along with the mistaken impression until a scandal-free way to end the betrothal could be found. But when Eleanor agreed to pose for a daring artist, the result was far more scandalous than any broken engagement.